Owen peered through the open door for some glimpse of what lay beyond it, the inner working of the craft. He could see little more than the shadowy darkness, but something in that darkness drew him toward it. He reached up, grabbed for leverage, and hauled himself into the craft, while outside, the rancher and his sons waited for him at a safe distance.

When he reappeared before them a few minutes later, he knew that it was in his eyes, and that they saw it there, glimmering wildly, all the horror and wonder of what he'd seen inside.

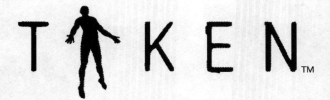

TAKEN™

A novelization by
Thomas H. Cook

Based on the series created by
Leslie Bohem

CONTENDER
BOOKS

Published in 2003 by Contender Books
Contender Books is a division of
The Contender Entertainment Group
48 Margaret Street
London W1W 8SE

This edition published 2003

1 3 5 7 9 10 8 6 4 2

TM & © 2002 DreamWorks LLC

ISBN 1 84357 082 3

By arrangement with the BBC
BBC logo © BBC 1996
The BBC logo is a trademark of the British Broadcasting
Corporation and is used under licence.

Printed in the UK by The Bath Press Ltd, Bath

First Published November 2002 in the United States of America by
Dell Publishing
Random House, Inc
1540 Broadway
New York, New York 10036

To Nick Taylor and Barbara Nevins Taylor,
friends to the end

Acknowledgments

I wish to thank Irwyn Applebaum and Kate Miciak for entrusting *Taken* to my care; Juliet Ulman for her gentle stewardship and extraordinary editorial guidance; and Kristy Cox and Corinne Antoniades from DreamWorks for their generosity and cheerful dispositions during the making of this work.

TAKEN

PART ONE

Beyond the Sky

Chapter One

Captain Russell Keys peered out into the expansive blue, his hands on the wheel of the B-17 that shook and rattled around him, bearing its heavy load of ordnance. To his left and right, he could see other planes, a squadron of Flying Fortresses in box formation, his own plane distinguished from the others only by the red devil painted on its nose, along with the words "Where Angels Fear to Tread."

"Navigator," Russell said crisply, "how's our time?"

"We've regained the two minutes, sir," the navigator answered.

"Good work." Russell glanced at his copilot, Lieutenant Lou Johnson. "Welcome to Germany, Johnson," he said.

Johnson patted the Rita Hayworth pinup he'd taped to the metal frame of the otherwise unadorned cockpit. "You hear that, honey?" he said with a broad smile. "We're in Germany."

Russell looked at the altimeter, then lowered the nose and began his descent to ten thousand feet. "There it is," he said after a moment, his gaze now fixed on a large factory thousands of feet below. "Pilot to bombardier, the plane is yours."

The bomb-bay doors opened and the bombardier began his count.

"Five."

"Four."

"Three."

"Two."

"One."

The plane grew eerily light as the heavy bombs filled the empty air beneath it, falling to the ground, where Russell could see them exploding in silent flashes far below.

Johnson let out a loud whoop, but Russell paid no attention. His focus was on the war-torn earth, swept with flame and smoke.

"Load delivered," he said quietly when the last of the bombs had fallen. "Let's go home."

He nosed the plane upward into what seemed a perfect, tranquil sky, so different from the ravaged earth, the wars of man. Up here it was calm and quiet and serene, and if you closed your eyes you could almost make yourself believe that the earth's ancient conflicts and rivalries might one day come to an end.

"Lights!"

Russell recognized the voice of his top gunner.

"What's that, Toland?" he asked.

"Lights, sir. Blue ones."

Russell looked at Johnson quizzically.

"They're following the plane," Toland said. "They just flew up and started tailing us."

Russell saw Johnson's face tighten. "Navigator," he said. "You see any lights?"

"No, sir," the navigator responded immediately.

Johnson released a quick sigh.

"Wait," the navigator burst in suddenly. "Now I see them. Three. Four. Right in front of us. Not in range yet, but . . ."

Russell felt a curious urge seize him. "Let's get a look at these lights."

He banked the plane slowly and the lights swam into view outside the cockpit window, blue globes about six feet in diameter that hovered without motion. They appeared both dense and airy, heavy and at the same time weightless, and in this physical contradiction, Russell sensed that nothing he'd ever known or read about could explain them.

Johnson's eyes widened in wonder. "What the hell are they?"

"I don't know," Russell answered. His voice filled with awe. "But they're beautiful."

For a brief moment, the crew peered at the hanging lights, unable to speak, or to turn their gaze away. A strange hypnotic glow filled the interior of the plane, and Russell felt his mind turn from war and peril as an inexplicable serenity settled over him.

Suddenly the radio operator's voice slashed through the prevailing silence.

"We got MEs at twelve o'clock. A whole mess of them, sir."

Russell's mind snapped into focus. "Roger, that," he said. "Gunners, give them short bursts when they're in range." He quickly checked his instruments, steadied himself, drew up the courage needed to steady his men as well. Beyond the cockpit, he glimpsed the glowing blue lights a final time, soft and oddly mesmerizing, but finally driven away, or so it seemed, by the frantic movement of the crew, the noise of the plane, the whole monstrous din of war.

A burst of machine-gun fire raked the side of the plane. The air filled with black puffs of flak. Russell's body tensed, all his attention given over to the battle ahead, the fight to survive and to make sure his men survived.

An explosion rocked the plane, filling its cramped interior with fire and smoke.

"We just took a direct hit, sir," the top gunner cried.

The nose of the plane sank, and Russell knew that it had finally happened, the moment he'd dreaded for so long. He and his crew were all going to die. Even so, he worked frantically to keep control of the plane while the cries of his men grew more desperate and the plane shook madly and the dull green eye of the earth came hurtling upward like a huge ball. In brief glimpses, he saw the MEs in their lethal dance, a swarm of angry bees that dove and climbed and circled, angry bursts of fire spitting from their guns.

Instantly a volley tore through the cockpit window, shattering it entirely and ripping into Russell's abdomen.

"Oh, Christ, Russ," Johnson cried.

Russell felt the steamy warmth of his blood as it poured out from the ripped flesh of his gut. "Copilot, take the plane," he said.

Johnson grabbed the controls. "Hang on, Russ."

Russell leaned back and drew in a quick desperate breath, his eyes now fixed on the empty sky beyond the shattered cockpit window, where, in the distance, the blue lights hung again, calm, soothing, a promise of peace. "Beautiful," he said. He knew that the dogfight still raged around him, MEs firing and being fired upon. He could see them diving helplessly toward the ground and hear the noise of the battle and the screams of his men, but it was as if all of this were happening in some distant, tortured world from which the blue lights had summoned him and now held him in their silent grasp.

"We've got to bail out now," Johnson cried.

Russell heard, but did not respond. He was not in the plane anymore. He was not crashing to earth. There was no fire and smoke, no fear or desperation. There were only the blue lights and they were coming toward him, their glow ever more intense as they drew in upon each other and finally melded into a single radiant light.

"Beautiful," Russell said again. The blue light expanded, filling the sky and engulfing him, embracing him. He smiled. "Trust me, Johnson. We won't die."

The light was now so intense Russell could see nothing else, feel nothing else. Time stopped. Movement ceased. Russell felt nothing but the warm, soothing light until, second by second, the light faded, and he felt the earth beneath him, heard the sound of wind rippling through a field of wheat.

He opened his eyes, and realized that he was lying in that very field. In the distance, four American soldiers warily approached him. He glanced about, trying to regain his ground. The wheat lay flattened all around him, and he could see the members of his crew slowly rising from the ground, staring at themselves and each other, astonished by the nakedness that greeted them. Russell glanced down and saw that he was naked too, and that the soft flesh of his abdomen was utterly unharmed.

BEMENT, ILLINOIS, JUNE 25, 1945

Nothing has changed much, Russell thought as the cab cruised down the streets of his hometown. The stores were the same, as well as the people, kids running along the sidewalks, old people in the park, the postman making his rounds. So why, he wondered, did he not feel at home here in Bement anymore? Why did he not feel a part of this small American town, one of its simple, ordinary citizens?

"The Bulldogs are last in their division," the cabby said. He laughed. "Some things never change."

But some things do, Russell said to himself, though he didn't know how he'd changed. He knew only that Bement, Illinois, was no longer the whole world to him. Once, he could not have imagined leaving it. Now he could not imagine returning to it. Once it had comprised his universe. Now it seemed so small he had to squint to see it.

The cab pulled over to the curb, and Russell reached for his wallet.

"This one's on me, Russell," the cabby said. He smiled admiringly. "We're all real proud of you."

The cab pulled away and Russell stared at the house he'd lived in all his life. It was a plain, wood-frame house with a broad porch and a well-tended lawn. A 1931 Model A Ford rested in the driveway, recently washed and polished, made ready for his return.

He walked over to the car and touched it softly, as if its metal frame were flesh.

A dog rushed toward him, wagging its long, bushy tail. He knelt down and drew it roughly into his arms. "Hello, Champ."

Then she was suddenly there, his mother, her gray hair shining in the bright sunlight. He saw that worry had done more than time to age her.

"Mom," he said, taking her into his arms.

"Russell," she said in a tone of wonder, as if still unable to convince herself that what she saw was true, that her son had actually returned to Bement safe and sound.

He glanced toward the porch where his father stood, peering down at him, still a big man, though he seemed smaller than before.

"You're still in one piece, I see," Mr. Keys said.

Russell stiffened slightly, like a boy called to attention. "Yes, sir, I am."

They stared at each other briefly. Russell could see a surge of feeling in his father's eyes, along with how very hard it was for him to control it.

"How do you like her?" his father said, nodding to the car as he came down the steps.

"She looks beautiful."

"Had to hide her from a couple of scrap drives," Mr. Keys added. "Kind of unpatriotic, I guess, but we did our bit in . . . other ways."

The "other way" was himself, Russell knew, and in that instant he grasped the terrible toll the war had taken on his parents, their long nights of worry, of not knowing where their son was, or even if he were still alive.

"Your father spent the last four days washing that old heap," his mother said.

Russell wanted to draw his father into his arms, wanted to hold him tight and sob like a little boy, release all the fear and dread that had accumulated within him during the war, simply let it flow out of him and pool at his feet and finally seep into the ground like a wash of black bile.

Instead he said, "Thanks, Pop."

"We did it like you asked, Russ," his mother told him. "We didn't say a word to Kate."

Kate.

Russell imagined her as he'd last seen her, a young woman with a bright, happy face, proof positive of love at first sight.

"Where is she?" he asked.

"At the bank," his mother answered. She seemed to see the longing in his eyes. "Go," she said, with a gentle push. "She can't wait to see you."

Kate was busy at her desk when Russell entered the bank, her back to him as she spoke into the phone.

"Miss," Russell began, making only a slight attempt to disguise his voice.

She wagged her finger for him to wait a moment.

"Miss," Russell repeated insistently. "Who do I see about getting one of those GI loans?"

She froze, and he knew that she'd recognized his voice. She whirled around and pulled him into her arms.

"Oh, Russell," she said. Her eyes glistened and her voice broke, and she squeezed him with such force that for a moment he thought he might lose his breath.

That night, as they sat together on the front porch, he gave her the ring he'd bought on the Champs-Elysées.

"It's beautiful," she said. "It's the most beautiful thing I've ever seen."

He knew that this was true, that the ring really was the most beautiful thing Kate had ever seen. He could still see the shine in her eyes later that night as he unpacked his duffel bag and made ready for bed. He peered around his old room, trying to reacquaint himself with the model cars he'd built as a boy, the Bulldogs pennant, all the things that had meant so much to him before he'd left for war, but which now, despite all his effort to reclaim them, seemed little more than artifacts of a vanished life.

He went to bed a few minutes later, still trying to snuggle into his old life, but the war returned to him in all its dreadful fury. He heard the roar of the planes, exploding bombs, the screams of the wounded, saw the earth torn and gashed, bleeding like a man. Each time he closed his eyes, some new vision returned to him, so that after a time he walked out of the house, down the porch steps and out into the yard. The night was clear and crisp, but it did not soothe him. He could feel nothing but the fever of war. He was like a piece of tangled steel, he thought, like a gutted plane—something torn away that could never be replaced.

The model A beckoned to him, reminding him of his days before the war, how proud he'd been of his small achievements, his victories on the ball field, feats that now seemed small, himself curiously incomplete, like a man who'd been given a mission he had not yet accomplished, a man waiting to be summoned, commanded . . . taken.

He walked to the car and got in. This had been his vehicle, he thought. He gripped the wheel and pressed his foot down on the accelerator. This had been his vehicle, but he no longer had the key to it, a way to make it go. He looked out into the night, the surrounding darkness, and felt utterly lost to his next move.

Then, without willing it, he screamed.

Chapter Two

Captain Owen Crawford stood in the vast gray hangar, his body dwarfed by the huge B-29 that loomed behind him. He was surrounded by various personnel, all of them young and eager. He knew with customary self-confidence that they hung on his every word, but there were two young officers who'd particularly caught his notice. Howard Bowen and Marty Erickson were clearly the most impressed with him. They were eager to please, and because of that they would be easy to mold. Perfect, Owen thought, sizing them up instantly, two young men who'd carry out his orders without a moment's hesitation.

"The war was not won by superior manpower," he began. "It wasn't won by strategy." He waited a beat, aware that this only heightened the anticipation of the people he addressed. "It was won by secrets." He lifted his head slightly, his chin thrust out boldly. "When the *Enola Gay* dropped its payload on Hiroshima, only one hundred and seven men in the entire world knew what that specific payload was." The assembled officers remained utterly silent. He'd focused them on the matter at hand instantly, and in doing that, he felt the power of his own voice and manner, the effortless way he gave off an authority and sense of command that was far beyond his actual rank. "That is the secret that won the war." He settled his gaze on the two young intelligence officers he'd already noticed. They were staring at him with rapt attention. "As members of the Army Intelligence Corps, your job is to keep secrets. Doing that job well is what determines the course of history." He let these last words sink in, then glanced at his watch and smiled. "And now, gentlemen, I must leave you. Dismissed."

An hour later, Owen sat down to lunch with Colonel Thomas Campbell and his nineteen-year-old daughter, Anne. She was a shy young woman, and Owen immediately understood that she'd lived all her life under the colonel's thumb. He also noticed the way she looked at him. Not exactly like the two intelligence officers had, but close enough. Long ago, Owen had decided that he did not seek love. What he wanted was someone he could mold to fit the life he planned, a cog in the wheel of his relentless forward movement. He had set himself to make a mark in the world, and only those who might serve that purpose drew his attention. Only fools were seduced by shapes and textures, hair of a certain length or color, a playfulness in the eyes. For Owen, every person had a context. And the context of Anne Campbell was her father.

"What do you make of the new recruits?" Colonel Campbell asked, breaking Owen's reverie.

"They seem eager enough, but I'm afraid that this new crop of officers won't have the same sense of mission now that the war's over. The last two years seem to have taken the wind out of them."

"I guess you'll just have to blow harder," the colonel said with a smirk.

Owen let a thin smile grace his lips. The colonel was no fool, that much was clear. His toast had been buttered by the best of them. There was no way flattery would impress him, nor patriotism, nor even high intelligence. Colonel Campbell was all crust, thick and dry and impenetrable. Colonel Campbell was a fossil.

"We had two more sightings today," the colonel said. "Dancing lights mostly. The bulk of them in the Pacific Northwest and three I think over the Great Lakes."

"People say they were from another planet," Anne said.

"We used to hear that a lot at Los Alamos," Owen told her.

"I forgot you were at Los Alamos," the colonel said, his voice now oddly distant.

"We got a new mare at the stables Tuesday," the colonel said, rapidly changing the subject. "I thought you might like to join me for a ride."

"I'd like that very much," Owen said. He turned his attention to Anne. "Will you be joining us?" he asked her.

"Well, actually . . ." she began.

"She doesn't ride," Colonel Campbell interrupted. "Too delicate."

Owen kept his eyes on Anne. She was shy, yes, but pretty, and he suspected that her father's grip was already loosening. Which was just fine since, in Owen's opinion, Colonel Campbell's days were numbered.

In the stables, Owen purposely delayed mounting his

horse, and instead walked briefly with Anne while Colonel Campbell saddled up a few yards away.

"Your father is a bit of a bully, isn't he," he told her.

"It's nothing personal," Anne said. "He's just like . . . that."

"If he doesn't let you ride, how does he feel about you going to the movies?"

Anne glanced back toward her father apprehensively. "I'd better meet you in town."

Owen seized the opportunity without hesitation "Eight o'clock," he said. "Tomorrow night?"

Anne smiled, then nodded toward the approaching stable hand.

Owen seized the reins from the stable hand and mounted. He knew he need do no more than offer Anne a final glance as he spurred the horse and galloped away. He could see that she'd taken in his broad shoulders, the cut of his jaw, the piercing look in his eyes.

The ride was brief, Colonel Campbell typically uncommunicative. Owen knew very well that he was not the old man's favorite, and certainly not his choice for son-in-law.

But Anne, she was a different story, Owen thought, a soft flower of a girl. He wasn't sure what he actually thought of her, nor even what use he might make of her, save the entertaining prospect of riling up her old man. He would know more after tomorrow night, he told himself, already imagining the two of them in the darkened movie theater.

She was standing dutifully under a marquee that proclaimed the night's feature as *Boomerang!* starring Dana

Andrews and Jane Wyatt, when Owen stepped out of his car a block away.

"Hey there, soldier," a woman said as she steered her car alongside the curb. "Looking for some fun?"

Her name was Sue, and Owen had been with her the night before, parked out in the desert beneath a full moon. They'd spent a passionate couple of hours together, but Owen had no time for her now. At least not with Anne Campbell waiting for him only a block away.

"Not right now," he said. "I'm on duty."

She looked at him pointedly. "You look ready for action, but you don't look like you're on duty."

"I'm meeting the colonel to go over something," Owen explained.

Sue glanced toward the theater, her gaze fixed on Anne. "Sure you are."

Owen tried to smile, but the chill in his eyes argued against it. "I'll call you later," he assured her.

Sue's eyes flashed with anger. "I won't be there," she snapped.

Owen stood in place as she screeched away. What was he losing, he asked himself. Nothing. A roll in the hay. There were plenty where she came from. He slapped his hands together, as if ridding himself of some barely noticeable dust, then turned sharply and made his way to the theater, where, to his delight, Anne greeted him with an adoring smile.

On the desert highway, Sue was not smiling. She glared out the window at the desert waste and fumed at the way Owen Crawford had dismissed her. Like she was nothing, that's how he treated her. Like she was just some small-time slut he could use and throw away.

She stomped the accelerator violently, then gave a quick twist to the radio's volume control. Louis Jordan was singing "There Ain't Nobody Here But Us Chickens." A dumb song, Sue thought, perfect for some dumb girl who gets herself tangled up with a bastard like Owen Crawford

Suddenly the radio turned to static. Just my luck, Sue thought, not even a stupid song to cheer things up. She reached for the dial, spun it, but still got nothing but static.

Okay, she thought, just go home. Have a drink. Sleep it off. She pressed down on the accelerator, but the car refused to pick up speed. Then suddenly the engine died and the car drifted to a halt on the isolated road.

Sue sucked in a fierce, angry breath and pounded the steering wheel. She lowered her head, exhausted by her own fruitless fury, then looked up again at the night sky where, to her amazement, an array of blue lights was moving weirdly, darting about, then moving together, in unison, assuming a formation.

Sue got out of the car and stood watching, mesmerized as two of the lights merged into one that grew larger and larger, assuming a vaguely circular shape as it sliced across the desert sky in full and sharp descent until it disappeared behind a jagged spine of hills.

The explosion that followed was muffled by the distance, but the light that rose from it threw the mountain range into dark silhouette.

Sue stood frozen as the light faded, the air around her eerily still, and nothing in the dark bowl of the sky but the usual scattering of harmless and unmoving stars.

FOSTER RANCH, NEW MEXICO, JULY 5, 1947

In his office, Owen listened to a story he knew Colonel Campbell and the other dinosaurs would find utterly ridiculous despite the fact that it was coming from two middle-aged nuns who looked entirely incapable of lying.

"We believe that what we saw was God's angels dancing," the first nun said.

"That or some new airplane from White Sands gone out of control," her companion added.

Owen drew a pencil from a cup that bristled with them and rolled it between his fingers. "You mentioned that you saw a crash."

"Clear as day," the second nun said. "If that was God's angels, then right now they're camped out about a mile and a half above Pine Lodge."

Intrigued, Owen was about to question them further when Howard suddenly opened the door. "Excuse me for interrupting, sir," he said. "But there's a rancher with something I think you ought to take a look at."

Owen nodded at Howard, then turned back to the nuns. "We'll send some people out to this crash site you mentioned," he told them. He rose and escorted the women from his office and out into the waiting room where, to his surprise, Sue sat stiffly, holding a paper bag.

"I really need to see you," she said as she quickly got to her feet.

She looked tense and drawn and Owen knew he had to do something. An irate woman could make quite a scene, and this was one who needed to be defused immediately. He tried for a bright smile. "And I really need to see you," he said in a faintly suggestive tone. "I'll call you later." He turned and followed Howard out the door without giving her time to answer or argue.

On the way to the ranch, Howard filled him in on what a rancher named Mac Brazel had found scattered across a rugged area of his land. "It looks like some kind of debris," Howard said. "Like pieces of tinfoil scattered all around."

At the site, Owen picked up a piece of the debris. It did indeed look like tinfoil, but it didn't have the feel of any material he'd ever handled. When bent or twisted, it returned to its original shape. The site was strewn with a second material as well, a kind of dark balsa wood, very soft to the touch. Whatever it was that had crashed on Mac Brazel's land, Owen thought, it was not the remains of a fallen angel.

He was pondering exactly what the debris might be when Colonel Campbell roared up in his jeep. The colonel quickly leaped from the jeep, walked briskly past Marty and Howard, oblivious to their smart salutes, and strode over to Owen.

"I want every bit of debris out of this pasture and back to the base," he commanded. "All of your men are confined to the base, pending debriefing." He turned to Marty and Howard. "That means the two of you."

Owen noted the colonel's odd behavior, his frantic arrival and brusque commands. It struck him that something had happened in this field that was far more important than he'd previously suspected. The colonel was obviously unnerved by something, and since old war horses weren't easily rattled, the "something" that was bothering the colonel had to be important. He looked at the debris scattered across the desert floor, then up into the empty sky. All his life he'd heard fantastic tales of

flying saucers, but never until that moment had he enter-
tained the notion that those who told such stories were
anything but kooks.

By now the colonel had turned his attention to Mac
Brazel. "We'd appreciate if you didn't speak to anyone
about this," he told him. "It's a matter of national
security."

"It's from outer space, isn't it?" Brazel asked.

Outer space.

Owen considered the words, their life-transforming
import. What if it were true, he wondered. What if this
debris actually were from a craft from outer space? It
would be the single greatest threat the world had ever
faced. It would hold up the horrific specter of an alien in-
vasion. It would change the life of man forever. If they
were out there, then the whole world would have to pre-
pare to defend itself against them. The man who could
prove that they were out there, watching us, probing us,
testing our defenses, that man would be the savior of the
world.

Owen was still considering the grandeur of such a
prospect later that day as he stood in Colonel Campbell's
office, watching silently while an Air Force major examined a large blueprint along with pieces of the debris.

"This is a design for a constant level balloon train,"
Colonel Campbell said. He indicated the pieces of debris
that resembled bits of tinfoil. "The balloon's radar reflec-
tors are made of this material," he added. He picked up a
piece of the foil, bent it, then returned it to the desk
where it instantly regained its original shape. "Amazing
stuff, isn't it?" He looked at Owen. "If the Russians have
figured out how to make the bomb, we need to know it.
These sensors can pick up a bomb test, a ballistic missile

launch." He laughed edgily. "If they sneeze, we'll hear it."
He smiled, but his eyes remained curiously somber.
"This monitoring project is called 'Mogul,' and it has a
security classification of A-1."

Owen nodded. "A-1." The military's highest security
classification, and he'd just been let in on it.

Or had he?

The problem with the "Mogul" story was that the material didn't really look like anything that could be found
on earth.

Outer space, Owen thought again, the idea building
steadily in his head, a spacecraft that had crashed to
earth, or perhaps merely jettisoned its cosmic trash, used
the earth as its own private dumping ground. What if it
were true, he asked himself again. What if it were true
that an alien craft had actually penetrated the earth's atmosphere, and the colonel along with the rest of the
old guard knew it, but were determined to keep it to
themselves.

"We'll need to give reporters something on this, of
course," Owen said, cautiously playing along, testing the
waters, bent now on finding out if the colonel and his
men were covering up a momentous event.

"Somebody already has," the major said. He flipped
the wire recorder to a local radio station. Mac Brazel was
blithely talking his head off, telling the world about the
crash, how the debris was like nothing he'd ever seen before, like something from "another world."

"People eat this stuff up," the major said contemptuously. "I figure we should go along with it. As long as
people are thinking about flying saucers, they're not
thinking about 'Mogul.' "

"But they may be thinking something worse," Owen said. "That we don't control the skies."

The major paid no attention. "So what'll it be," he asked Colonel Campbell, "Flying disc or flying saucer?"

Owen felt his whole body stiffen. He was being ignored and he didn't like it. Still there was nothing he could do but play the ever-obedient soldier.

Twenty-four hours later a newspaper was already carrying the major's story. Owen smiled as he read the headline in the local paper, "RAAF CAPTURES FLYING SAUCER ON RANCH IN ROSWELL AREA."

"Is that for real, Captain?" Marty asked. He glanced at Howard, then back at Owen. "That stuff was from a spaceship?"

Owen folded the paper. "Can I trust you?"

"Yes, sir," Marty said.

"Absolutely, sir," Howard said.

"All right, here it is," Owen said. "It was a spy balloon. Super classified. A-1. It hit something and fell back to earth." He felt a shiver run through his bones at the realization that he may well have found his mission. The question was, what did the balloon hit, and why didn't this "other craft" crash too?

Chapter Three

BEMENT, ILLINOIS, JULY 6, 1947

Russell Keys tossed the burger and listened to it sizzle on the grill. The day was bright, and very warm. He felt a trickle of sweat run down the side of his face. Across the yard, various friends and neighbors huddled in small groups. Kate stood among them, their son Jesse in the grass at her feet. Everything appeared entirely normal, but nothing felt that way. At least not to him. He didn't know why. He knew only that all the things that should have brought him joy left him feeling curiously bereft instead, left him moody and withdrawn like a man held by some distant grief, mourning a loss he could not name or find a way to get beyond. Lately he'd turned to alcohol to dull that pain. He knew his drinking had cost him one job, then another, that his life was spiraling downward, as if he were trapped in a crashing plane.

"You've got a good-looking boy there," Bill Walker said as he approached the grill.

"Takes after his mom," Russell told him. He placed a

few buns on the patties. "Kate tells me you're with the police."

"Yeah," Bill answered. "It's an easy job for the most part. Nothing much to do in a little town like this."

"You should find a girl, get a family started."

Bill glanced toward Kate. "You already took the best girl in town."

Russell's gaze moved toward the children on the lawn. They were chasing each other and scuffling happily in the grass. So why in the midst of such a scene, did he feel this odd and inexpressible dread, as if he could see their young lives unfold before him, darken in time, and come to their dreary ends?

"And not only the best girl in Bement," Bill went on. "But a great kid."

Russell held his gaze on the children. "Yeah, I got it all," he said softly, though he felt that he had nothing, or that what he had was not really his—it all seemed vague and insubstantial, part of a world he had only one foot in, the rest of him . . . somewhere else.

"You should be the happiest man in the world," Bill added.

But he wasn't, and he knew it. He sensed his unease sinking deeper and deeper as he watched one kid go down, tackled, then tickled good-naturedly by the others as they held him down. He felt the tangle of arms and legs around him, the feeling of being held down against one's own will. It was all he could do to hold back a scream.

Bill looked at him pointedly. "You okay, Russell?"

"Yeah," Russell answered quickly, his eyes still on the pile of children.

The kid beneath the others was fighting to free himself, and Russell felt his dread spike into desperation, as if he were like that kid, strapped down, unable to move, fighting to be free. "Stop it!" he blurted suddenly. "Let him go!" He bolted forward, as if blown by a violent gust of wind, rushed to the pile of children and began pulling them off with such desperate violence that when he'd pulled the last one from the heap, he realized that he'd scared them all, and that their parents were now watching him with troubled faces and cruelly questioning eyes.

ROSWELL ARMY AIRFIELD, JULY 7, 1947

Sue was sitting outside Owen's office, holding the same paper bag she'd tried to show him earlier.

She rose as he came toward her, a strained look in her eyes. Whatever was bothering her, it wasn't something Owen wanted to hear about, not something he cared about. He was relieved when a large man suddenly blocked his way.

"Are you the people we talk to about flying saucers?" the man asked. "Because me and my boys have some information."

Information about flying saucers, Owen thought, eager to check out anything now, no matter how crazy it seemed, because it would all have to seem crazy . . . until it was proven true.

And so, within minutes, he was following Edward Watkins and his sons up a ridge.

At the top of the ridge there was a large gorge lined with pine trees, some of which had been uprooted and now lay on their sides like fallen soldiers. At the center of their fall, Owen made out a huge disc, as large as a B-29, but without wings, the sides smooth and gray, a craft of some sort, he guessed, but not like any he'd ever seen. It might well be a hoax, he knew, something Watkins and his boys had cooked up to rib the military brass. But what if it weren't a hoax? What if this disc really were from outer space? That was the way he had to look at such things now, he told himself, not in order to dismiss them, but in order to investigate them fully.

The descent into the gorge was treacherous, but within a few minutes Owen stood beside the disc. Now he could see things from a better perspective. Trees that had looked liked saplings from the rim of the gorge were in fact full-grown pines, scores of them, torn out of the earth and heaved away from the craft. If this were a hoax, he thought, then it was a huge one that had taken days and days of work to pull off.

And it wasn't just the trees, as Owen saw on closer inspection. The disc too was much larger than he'd guessed, its "nose" embedded deep within the earth while the "tail" rose upward at an angle, like half a drawbridge, casting a deep shadow beneath its upraised bulk.

Cautiously, Owen stepped under the lifted craft and gazed at its undercarriage. As he studied the shiny base of the craft, the air grew oddly cold, and something dense pressed in upon him like thousands of invisible weights. Overhead, the belly of the craft was marked with strange pits and circles, the writings, perhaps, of another world.

For a moment, Owen hesitated, then he lifted his hand and touched the bottom with his outstretched fingers while Watkins and his boys stood and watched in awe.

Something sounded, a rustling, metal scraping metal.

He whirled around and saw a panel open, something coming from it, in the shape of an arm, but not a human arm, thinner and more elongated, with a four-fingered hand, each finger with an extra joint. He glanced at the rancher and his sons, all of them stepping back, mouths agape, eyes staring.

Owen turned back to the dangling arm, then moved around it slowly, methodically, peering through the open door for some glimpse of what lay beyond it, the inner working of the craft. He could see little more than the shadowy darkness, but something in that darkness drew him toward it. He reached up, grabbed for leverage, and hauled himself into the craft, while outside, the rancher and his sons waited for him at a safe distance.

When he reappeared before them a few minutes later, he knew that it was in his eyes, and that they saw it there, glimmering wildly, all the horror and wonder of what he'd seen inside.

BEMENT, ILLINOIS, JULY 7, 1947

Russell looked at the clock on the nightstand. Three forty-two. The windows were open, a soft summer breeze filtering through the curtains, lifting them slowly, as if by invisible strings, then letting them fall again. What could look more normal than the play of wind on fabric, he wondered. And yet the movement looked strange and oddly frightening, like long shrouded arms beckoning to him.

He turned from the window, to where Kate slept beside him, soft and tender. He really was the luckiest man in the world, he thought for a moment. He had a loving wife and a perfect son.

He touched her hair, his gaze very tender, then smiled and turned back toward the window.

And they were there.

Standing beside the bed.

Five German soldiers.

He heard the scream break from him, then Kate's frantic effort to calm him.

"Russell," she was saying. "It's only a dream."

But it wasn't a dream, and he couldn't accept that it was a dream no matter what she told him. He buried himself in Kate's arms, sobbing now like a little boy. She held him gently, lovingly, and after a time he pulled himself away, calm now, but helplessly glancing about, searching the room for the vanished soldiers.

"You're all right, honey," Kate said. "You're with me."

He believed her suddenly, believed that it was only a dream. He relaxed and took a deep breath, trying to fight back even the slightest notion that the soldiers had been real. He looked at the room and nothing had changed. The summer wind blew softly, raising and lowering the curtains. He looked at Kate, and she was the same, her beauty undiminished. He glanced at the clock. Five-thirty. He felt a terrible shiver pass through him. Two hours had vanished. Where had he been for two hours? He drew his eyes downward, toward his body, moving along the fingers and the upper arm to where his gaze suddenly froze on a series of small punctures that were as real as the wind and the curtains and Kate beside him, and where he knew instantly and with utter certainty, the needles had gone in.

PINE LODGE, NEW MEXICO, JULY 9, 1947

The colonel looked up sharply as Owen burst into the room.

"There's something you have to see right now," Owen said.

The colonel stared at him irritably. "You have an important reason for interrupting me? One that's going to stop me from stripping you back to sergeant?"

Owen smiled. "That super-secret spy balloon of yours?"

" 'Mogul.' What about it?"

"Want to see what it crashed into?"

At the crash site, the colonel's eyes widened in disbelief. "Could it be Russian?"

Just then, Owen emerged from inside the ship, carrying a body in his arms. "Russian?" he echoed.

Owen's eyes rested on the alien figure briefly before they returned to Colonel Campbell. "I don't think so."

Within minutes, a vast array of soldiers and technicians had arrived, all at the colonel's command. A large truck, fitted with a cable pulley and a stanchion, stood ready to retrieve the ship. Four bodies lay on a tarp near an ambulance.

Owen and the colonel stood together, staring at the bodies.

"You going to let them give this to the press, too?" Owen asked.

The colonel shook his head. "It was one thing when it was a lie. We could control that. Now that it's real, there's no way we can let it get out." He paused. "Who found this?"

"A father and his sons out hiking," Owen said.

"Can you clean up?"

Owen nodded to the right, where, in the distance, Watkins and his sons stood, surrounded by soldiers. "I already have."

"I appreciate you coming right to me with this," the colonel said. "When the time comes, you won't be forgotten." He remained silent for a moment, considering the situation. "We'll have a press conference. We'll say this debris is from a weather balloon. That there are hundreds in the air at any given moment." He smiled. "That it was made in Cleveland, not in outer space."

Owen glanced at the alien bodies before them.

"When I went inside the craft, there were five seats," Owen said. He looked at the swirl of activity around him, soldiers everywhere, tents, lights. "But there are only four bodies, Colonel."

Colonel Campbell nodded. "I'll have my best men put on it."

Owen paused before continuing. "I was wondering, sir, what you're going to do now."

"Do? About what?"

"And as far as the craft is concerned, and the bodies, I could . . ."

Colonel Campbell looked at him sharply. "What craft?"

"Sir?"

Colonel Campbell peered at Owen sternly. "What bodies?"

"But I . . ."

"You, Captain, are not involved in this . . . situation."

"Yes, sir."

Campbell nodded toward the craft. "A weather balloon crashed, Captain. That's all anyone needs to know."

Owen nodded crisply. "Yes, sir."

"Including you, Captain."

"Of course, sir," he said stiffly. Like hell, he thought, like hell you're going to freeze me out.

BEMENT, ILLINOIS, JULY 10, 1947

Russell placed the board across the closed front door and nailed it into place while Kate stood by, watching him worriedly.

"How are we going to get out?" she asked cautiously.

"It doesn't matter as long as they can't get in," Russell answered. He turned quickly and rushed into the den. He had to protect himself, he knew, and he had to protect Kate and Jesse. They had come for him, and they would come again. He had something they wanted and they wouldn't stop until they got it. He could feel them around him. Their eyes hung invisibly in the air and their fingers reached for him from the clear, crisp breeze. In the whispering leaves, he heard the falling tumblers of their ever-calculating minds.

"Russell, look at me," Kate pleaded.

Russell ignored her and drew a pistol from the drawer of his desk and began to load it.

"Russell, no!" Kate cried. She reached for the pistol and the cartridges spilled onto the floor. Was it Kate? Or had they slapped his hand? He dropped to his knees and frantically began gathering up the scattered cartridges.

Kate stared at him brokenly. "What's happening to you?"

Russell peered at his wife. He could see the terrible worry in her face, the dread. He knew what she thought.

That he was crazy. But he wasn't crazy, and he knew it. They had come for him. They had pierced his skin. He knew they had done these things, and that they would come again . . . for him. But how could he expect Kate to know what he knew? She hadn't seen them. No one had seen them. He was as alone as if he were floating high above the earth, drifting in the empty darkness, unreachable, burdened with a terrible knowledge he couldn't share, and which no one else could understand.

A voice called to him from some distant chamber of his memory, *Lights!*

He recalled the blue lights he'd first seen in the skies over Germany, the men who'd been with him that day. "My crew," he whispered.

"What?" Kate asked.

"My men," Russell said. "I have to find out what happened to my men." He sat down at his desk, retrieved the old crew list he'd brought back from the war and frantically began going through it.

"What are you doing?" Kate asked.

"I have to know," Russell said.

"Russell, please."

Russell looked up at her through the haze of his own exhaustion. "I'm no good to you, Kate. No good as a husband or a father." His eyes returned to the list. "I have to find out what's going on."

He was not sure when Kate left the room, only that she'd eased herself out cautiously, as if to let his madness run its course. Perhaps she'd listened as he'd dialed the first number, tracked down the first of his crew. Dead. Then the second. Dead. And the third . . . until.

When he looked back at the door, she was there again, watching him.

"They're all dead," he told her. "Except Johnson, my copilot. He's at Fort Bliss." He could hardly believe his own words. "He's the only one who's still alive."

WRIGHT-PATTERSON AIR FORCE BASE, POWER PLANT LABORATORY, JULY 11,1947

As Colonel Campbell led the team of scientists down the corridor, he recalled the way Owen's body had gone taut as he realized just how thoroughly he'd been cut out of the loop. Not that he'd had a choice in the matter. The job ahead required people the colonel could trust, and Owen was not such a man. True, Owen was observant. He'd noticed the five seats in the craft. But that did not make him trustworthy. Especially in regard to the extremely sensitive matter the colonel now faced.

"The craft has the material-evaluation lab baffled," the lead scientist, Dr. Goldin told him. "And as for the bodies, we've dissected the one that was dismembered and we can't find anything that would be analogous to our own internal system."

"What about the other three?" Colonel Campbell asked.

"We'll start on the second one, to see if we missed something," Dr. Goldin answered. "It's a shame really."

"What's a shame?" the colonel asked.

"To have to ask the dead instead of the living," Goldin replied, and stepped forward to open the door of the dissecting room where, atop a cold steel table, the alien sat alone, turning slowly to stare at them with knowing eyes.

Chapter Four

Sally Clarke briefly eyed the man at the end of the counter, then returned to the story she was reading in *Famous Fantastic Mysteries*. The story was called "We Are Not Alone," and it was about aliens. It wasn't all that great a story, Sally decided, as she glanced over the top of the magazine again, her gaze settling on the man at the end of the counter. He'd been sitting there for a long time, and she'd filled his coffee cup at least twice. He hadn't said much to her, but there was something about him, a sadness and loneliness that was, she thought, sort of like her own, the kind that got you up in the middle of the night and drove you out into the yard and lifted your eyes toward the heavens, where you hoped to find something waiting, perhaps the answer to a question you still couldn't frame.

But so what, Sally thought, the world was full of melancholy drifters. No point talking to a guy like that. He was a vagabond and always would be, his trouble buried so deep inside nothing less than a miracle could set him free. She was about to go back to her magazine when he suddenly glanced up and caught her four-square looking at him.

"Sorry to disturb you," he said. "I'd like more coffee."

Sally flashed him her best jolly-waitress smile. "You're not disturbing me," she told him. "It's my job."

"Good story?" he asked after she'd filled his cup. "The one you're reading."

"It passes the time."

"I don't read much myself," the man said. He took a sip from the cup, and suddenly seemed in a hurry. "How much do I owe you?"

"Thirty-five cents."

The man placed a fifty-cent piece on the counter. "Thanks," he said, then turned and headed for the door.

Something odd about this guy, Sally thought, something desperate. The kind of guy you stayed away from if you knew what was good for you. And yet, the kind she was always drawn to, so that it didn't surprise her when she was still thinking about him a few hours later when she finished her shift and headed home.

Her two kids, Tom and Becky, were in the living room when she arrived. She took a few minutes to watch Tom practice his magic tricks, while Becky teased him, as always.

Her husband Fred was in the upstairs bedroom, packing for the road.

"Shoehorn," he said dully as she came into the room. "Have you seen it?"

Sally opened the dresser drawer, dug through her husband's socks and came out with the shoehorn. "You have to leave tonight?" she asked as she handed it to him.

Fred nodded sullenly.

"Did the kids eat?"

Fred's eyes flashed toward her. "You're the waitress. You feed them." He turned away, closed the suitcase. "I'll see you in three weeks," he said as he swept out of the room.

Lonely . . . Sally decided, the guy in the diner suddenly on her mind again. She heard her husband say a quick good-bye to Tom and Becky, then the slap of the screen door as he left the house. Lonely, she thought with a shrug, like me.

509TH BOMBER GROUP, ROSWELL, NEW MEXICO, JULY 12, 1947

Owen's shadow cut a jagged swath across the tarmac as he strode toward the looming hangar. He'd made a decision. No one was going to cut him out of the loop. Not some goofy scientist. Not Colonel Campbell. Not God, Himself.

The door of the hangar opened and a tall officer in pilot's gear stepped into the bright light of the field.

"Bishop, right?" Owen asked. "You flew Colonel Campbell out of Fort Worth the other night?"

"Right," the pilot said.

"Destination?"

The pilot looked at Owen warily. "That's a 'need to know.' "

Owen took out his ID. "Army Intelligence. I need to know."

The pilot glanced at the ID. "Captain Crawford. The

colonel told me you might show up." He shook his head. "Sorry, Captain," he said as he stepped away.

Owen remained in place as the pilot walked briskly across the tarmac. All right, he thought, the colonel had anticipated his move. But it was only his first move, he told himself, already making his second.

A few minutes later, Anne opened the door. She seemed surprised to see him, and Owen took that as a good sign. It was always good to catch a woman off guard.

"Can you go for a ride?" he asked her.

She smiled delightedly. "I'll get my car coat."

"I said a ride, not a drive."

Within minutes they were alone in the desert, dusk settling over the rocky hills as they rode their horses together slowly, like two lovers strolling down a familiar street.

"You're doing great," Owen told her.

"Can we go faster?" Anne asked excitedly.

"Just loosen up on the reins a little," Owen said. He took her hand and showed her just how much to relax the reins.

Anne's horse began to trot, Owen careful to keep pace beside her, noting how easily her timidity slipped away.

"Are you all right?" he asked after a moment.

"I'm wonderful."

He slapped his horse and the trot became a canter, the two horses in stride with each other, Anne's hair blowing loosely in the wind. Her smile was as radiant as a child's, and Owen was quick to realize that in a way, a child is what she remained, utterly under her father's command, a woman already trained to obey.

He brought his horse to a halt at the edge of a rocky precipice, then waited as Anne drew up to him.

"I was afraid you wouldn't come out with me," Owen told her.

"Why wouldn't I?"

"Your father. He's dead set against you seeing me."

"I'm not my father," Anne said determinedly.

"I know that," Owen said.

He knew the moment had come, leaned forward and kissed her. "You're the sun and the moon to me, Anne," he said. He could feel her surrender to him, and in her surrender, the greater victory he sought.

WRIGHT-PATTERSON AIR FORCE BASE, POWER PLANT LABORATORY, JULY 14, 1947

Colonel Campbell studied the projected slide, a cross-section of cell tissue. All around him scientists and military officers peered at the same slide. For the last few minutes, the experts had argued about the nature of the tissue. It had certain characteristics that seemed essentially animal, and others that resembled a fungus. Still others were convinced that the cell tissue actually changed from animal to vegetable, that it could be . . . anything.

Suddenly the door opened and Dr. Helms walked in. "I think you need to see this," he said urgently.

Colonel Campbell and the others followed Helms down the corridor to an observation room.

On the other side of the glass Dr. Goldin stood facing the alien. The alien was silent and gave no hint of movement. It was Dr. Goldin who was doing all the talking, his body swaying forward and backward repetitively as he spoke.

"What's he saying? Is it German?" Colonel Campbell asked.

"Goldin would never speak German," Helms replied. "It's Hebrew. He's reciting from the Haphtorah."

Colonel Campbell peered at the alien, and for a moment seemed to lose himself in the unfathomable depth of its eyes. Then he shifted his attention back to Dr. Goldin. A small trickle of blood had suddenly emerged from the scientist's nose.

"My God," the colonel whispered as the trickle became a red torrent and Goldin slid to the floor. "Get him out of there!"

Guards rushed into the room, picked Goldin from the floor and brought him hurriedly into the observation room.

"How long was he in there?" the colonel demanded.

"Ten minutes," Helms answered. "Maybe less."

Dr. Goldin lay on a table a few feet away. He looked pale, exhausted. "I was there," he whispered.

Colonel Campbell leaned closer to Goldin. "Where?"

"At my bar mitzvah in Dresden," Goldin answered. "If I could have stayed a little longer, I could have spoken to my father." He grabbed the colonel's lapel. "My father," he cried desperately. "I could have spoken to my father." His eyes shifted to the observation window, where the alien stood, staring silently. "I want to see my father," Goldin pleaded.

The colonel trained his gaze on the alien. For an instant their eyes locked. Then the alien turned and faced the wall, entirely motionless, save for the rippling undulation of its back.

ROSWELL AIR FORCE BASE, JULY 15, 1947

Owen knew that something had happened, something . . . important. All morning scientists and military people had gone in and out of the colonel's office. During that time, only Dr. Helms had remained with the colonel. The reasonable assumption was that whatever the colonel knew, Helms knew it too. The question was how to get Helms to talk. Owen considered various plans, chose the most direct one, then put it into operation.

A few hours later, he signaled as he saw Dr. Helms' car approach, and obedient to Owen's earlier instructions, the policemen hit the light and the siren. Just as he knew it would, Dr. Helms' car pulled over. Owen got out, walked to the driver's window and pulled out his ID. "Captain Crawford, Army Intelligence. This a routine debriefing, Dr. Helms. Nothing to be alarmed about."

"Routine?" Helms asked. "Why couldn't you just . . ."

"There's a leak in the project, Doctor," Owen said authoritatively. "We don't suspect you of leaking anything but . . ."

Helms looked at Owen nervously. "Does this have anything to do with what happened to Dr. Goldin yesterday?"

"In part," Owen answered, though he had no idea that anything had "happened" to Dr. Goldin.

"I don't see how Dr. Goldin's death could have anything to do with a leak . . ."

"Why don't you tell me what you think happened," Owen said.

There'd been an "incident," Helms said. Dr. Goldin had had a strange encounter with "the one that was alive." Goldin had gone into some kind of trance, Helms went on, and during the trance he'd spoken Hebrew and believed himself to be thirteen again, reciting in the synagogue while his long-dead father looked on.

"This first encounter nearly killed Dr. Goldin," Helms said.

"First encounter?"

"Last night he went back into the room," Helms said. "I guess he wanted to see his father again. So he went back into the room. Of the . . . visitor."

"And the experience killed him," Owen said, careful not to phrase it as a question.

"It killed them both," Dr. Helms said.

Owen felt a jolt of excitement. "You've been a lot of help," he said. "And, Doctor, I'm sure you can appreciate how important it is that you mention our discussion to no one."

LUBBOCK, TEXAS, JULY 16, 1947

Sally Clarke sat in her living room, reading the paper while Tom and Becky slept upstairs. According to the lead story, a trucker had been murdered on the state highway, and as she read the details of the killing, Sally once again felt how cruel life on earth actually was. Here was a working guy who'd probably picked up the wrong hitchhiker and ended up dead. The simplest thing could turn on you, an act of kindness flip around and bite you like a snake.

She didn't like to think too long about the darker aspects of life, and so she folded the paper and picked up the magazine she'd been reading at the diner and read the last of its fantastic mystery stories. The story was a little creepy, but Sally liked that. She liked to feel the tingle of something strange, something unexplainable. So much of life was predictable. You got up each morning and the world looked the same, the air smelled the same. You went to the same job and did the same things once you got there. But in these fantastic stories nothing was predictable. Weird things were commonplace, and the world was always turning a blind corner or displaying some strange new design.

She heard a heavy thud. The shed door, she thought. It was always coming unlatched and banging in the wind. If she let it go it would wake the children.

She retrieved a flashlight from the kitchen and walked out into the night, the yellow beam nosing along the green lawn, casting the distant shed in a hazy light. The door was flapping against the side of the building in hard, rhythmic thuds, and suddenly Sally felt a tingle of dread pass over her, as if the world had abruptly changed, become not the predictable thing it had been moments before, but instead that other world she'd read about, dark and mysterious, where nothing was as it seemed.

She drew in a long breath, steadying herself. Don't be ridiculous, she thought. There's nothing in the shed. Nothing lurking there, crouched in a dark corner . . . waiting.

She moved forward boldly now, persuaded by her own argument, secure in the knowledge that the world was as it had always been.

At the door, she paused and shined the flashlight into the shed's dark interior. She heard a rustling, and knew that it was not the wind in the trees, but something inside the shed. A mouse, perhaps. She aimed the light at the ground, then moved it slowly to the right, the beam crawling along the edge of the wall until it came to a figure lying on the ground. Not some weird creature from outer space, Sally saw instantly. But a man who looked injured somehow, despite his sad smile, and the way his eyes seemed to peer into her soul.

"You're hurt," she said.

The man nodded slowly.

"You need a doctor," Sally said urgently.

The man smiled softly. "I'll be all right. I just need to rest."

"What's your name?"

"John."

She felt his gaze almost physically, like the delicate play of window curtains across her face.

"I need to rest," John said.

It seemed to Sally that he needed more than rest. He needed comfort, security, safety, and the urge to provide these things abruptly overwhelmed her.

She rushed to where he lay, drew him tenderly from the ground, holding him firmly, but gently, as if he were made of some infinitely fragile material.

Inside the house, she rushed to Tom's room, and woke him up while the man stood, leaning in the doorway.

"Who's that?" Tom asked.

"We'll talk about it in the morning," Sally answered hurriedly. "Get some pillows and an extra blanket from my bed. You're going to sleep on the sofa tonight."

Tom did as he was told, then Sally carefully lowered the man onto the bed.

"I'll be fine," he assured her, "just as soon as I collect my thoughts."

It struck her as an odd choice of words, since he didn't

seem in the least confused or disoriented. "Do you need any . . . help with your clothes?" she asked.

"No, I'm fine," John answered. "Thank you for taking me in."

Sally stepped to the door, turned off the light and headed back down stairs.

Tom was making his bed on the couch. Becky stood beside him,

"Who is that guy?" Tom asked.

Sally knew she had no real answer. Who was he? She didn't know. She only knew that she felt inexplicably connected to him. "You two should be in bed," she said.

"Who is that man?" Tom repeated insistently.

"He's a stranger, Tom," Sally said. "And he's hurt."

"How long is he going to stay in my room?"

"I don't know, honey," Sally answered. "Until he's better." She glanced toward Becky, whose face was suddenly drawn with worry.

"Mommy, did he hit you?"

"What?" Sally asked with a quick laugh.

"Your nose," Becky said.

"My nose?" Sally asked.

Becky stared at her worriedly. "It's bleeding."

ROSWELL AIR FORCE BASE, JULY 17, 1947

Owen looked up from his desk as Howard and Marty entered his office.

"Anything on the fifth . . . occupant of the craft?" he asked.

"Nothing so far, sir," Howard answered.

"Well it turns out there was another live one," Owen told them.

Howard and Marty glanced at each other astonished.

"It lived long enough to demonstrate certain . . . abilities," Owen said somberly.

"What kind of abilities?" Howard asked.

Owen smiled. He could see the spark he'd lit. "In good time," he said. He sat back in his chair. "Colonel Campbell is a small and petty man. He confiscated the bodies and initiated a high-level cover-up." He noticed the shock in his aides' faces, along with the pride they took in his confiding in them. "He froze me out the way he froze you out in the field that day. But he's not going to get away with it." Owen's tone grew menacing. "I'm going to take this project away from him. And I'll take down anyone who gets in my way." They were with him now, heart and soul. He could see it in their eyes, the glint of conspiracy. "So if you get any leads about the missing visitor, I expect you to share them with me rather than the good colonel."

"Yes, sir," Howard said.

"Absolutely, sir," said Marty.

"Good," Owen said. "But keep the abilities I mentioned in mind, and don't confine your search to little gray men. Look for someone . . . some thing . . . a little more human."

LUBBOCK, TEXAS, JULY 17, 1947

Sally entered the room quietly, determined not to wake John if he were still asleep. But he stirred as she entered, and she felt the odd sensation that he'd sensed her presence, saw her without using his eyes.

"How are you feeling?" she asked.

John turned to face her. "I'm much better."

She handed him the tray she'd brought for him. "Breakfast."

He hardly looked at the food. "Maybe in a few minutes."

"I put some towels out," Sally told him. "And a shirt and some pants. My husband's." She smiled. "Before he put on weight."

"That's very kind," John said. He seemed to study her a moment. "Your husband doesn't appreciate your kindness. He doesn't see your sadness either, but you've stopped wanting him to. I think you're right. There are some things you don't share with an uncaring person."

Sally felt as if some part of her had been peeled away and now lay exposed before him. It was as if John had somehow pierced all the protective layers of her life and touched its tender core.

"What happened to you?" she asked.

"I was in an accident," John said.

"What kind of accident?"

"Farming."

"You have a farm around here?"

"No, I . . . someone gave me a ride."

A sudden pain streaked across Sally's brow. She winced.

"What's wrong?" John asked.

"Just a headache."

Again, she sensed that the man was studying her in a way she could not grasp. It wasn't the way some of her customers looked at her, and it didn't make her feel uncomfortable or on display. Instead, it was a kind of inner probing, and she felt it like millions of tiny invisible wires, each simultaneously penetrating her skin and making infinitely small connections.

"You were telling me about your accident," Sally said.

She could tell that he didn't want to talk about it.

"I'm sorry, would you mind letting me rest for a while?" he said.

"Of course," Sally said. "I'll leave the tray in case you wake up hungry." She started to leave, then felt herself drawn back to him. "You were right, you know. He doesn't appreciate . . ." She stopped, astonished that such words had broken from her. "I mean . . ." She laughed nervously. "Anyway, get some rest."

She rushed from the room, the pain in her head now almost more than she could bear, a hard, steady pounding. For a moment, she leaned against the door, then pulled herself up again and went to the bathroom. The medicine cabinet was already open, though she didn't remember leaving it that way, the bottle of aspirin clearly visible, as if waiting for her. She opened the bottle, took out two aspirin and quickly swallowed them. It was only then that she saw the trickle of blood that oozed from her nose.

FORT BLISS, EL PASO, TEXAS, JULY 17, 1947

Russell made his way between two lines of empty beds. Distantly, he could see the one bed that was still occupied. The figure who lay in it did not move as he drew near.

"I brought you something," he said.

Johnson's eyes drifted over to him.

Russell showed him the photograph of Rita Hayworth, then propped it against the water jug on the table beside Johnson's bed.

"What do they say is wrong with you?" Russell asked.

"No one knows," Johnson answered weakly. "They say it's in my head. A psychological thing. From the war maybe."

"All the others are dead," Russell said bleakly.

"Except you," Johnson said. He smiled quietly. "And me . . . for now."

"Do you remember what happened?" Russell asked him.

A strange terror gripped Johnson's face.

Russell bent forward. "Tell me. Because except for these dreams I've been having, I don't remember a thing."

Johnson hesitated, his eyes now searching the room, as if for a way out. "Whatever they did to us, they did it for a long time," he said.

"What did they do?"

"I don't know." Johnson's face trembled slightly. "But whatever it was, they did it to you, too."

"How do you know?"

"Because you were on the cot next to mine."

And instantly, Russell was there, on his back, tossing in pain, his anguished gaze boring into the German soldiers who stood idly within the tent. He felt himself roll out of the cot and onto the floor, knocking over oxygen tanks and hospital trays, rolling desperately until he found himself behind the ball turret gun of the B-17, his hand reaching for the trigger, firing and firing, spraying doctors and nurses and the idling soldiers with a hail of bullets, filling the tent with acrid blue smoke until the gun finally went silent and he lay in the quiet, with no sense of who he was or where he was, but only that the gun had stopped and that everyone was dead, and suddenly he and his men were all in a French field.

"You and I both know it wasn't Germans you killed that day. It wasn't Germans at all," Johnson said. "What did they do to us, Captain?" he pleaded. "What did they do?" He looked at Russell, drew in a labored breath, then suddenly began to twitch, his eyes rolling upward as his body went slack.

"Johnson," Russell called. "Johnson."

But he was dead.

Chapter Five

Sally pulled into the driveway, retrieved the grocery bags from the backseat, and headed into the house.

"Tom," she called. "Becky."

Odd, she thought, when they didn't come dashing out of their rooms to greet her. She glanced across the empty living room to the door of Tom's room. It was closed, but she could hear laughter coming from behind it.

She walked to the door, opened it and saw Becky floating three feet in the air, John standing beside her, passing his arms around her at all angles to demonstrate that there were no strings attached.

"How do you feel?" John asked her.

"Like I'm floating," Becky answered.

"No headaches?"

"No."

"That's good," John said, then caught Sally in his eye, and with a wave of his arm softly returned Becky to the floor.

"That was amazing," Becky cried.

Tom shrugged. "Levitation's easy," he said sullenly.

Becky glared at him. "I've never seen *you* do it."

At dinner, Sally couldn't get the sight of Becky floating in the air out of her mind. It had not looked like a magician's trick, but something else, a . . . power. She looked at the stranger who sat across from her, hardly touching his food.

"You're not hungry?" she asked.

"Breakfast lasted me all day," John answered.

"You didn't eat any of it," Tom said accusingly. "I saw your plate."

John kept his eyes on Sally. "Your headache?" he asked.

"It's gone."

John smiled. He looked curiously relieved. "That's good," he said.

For the next few minutes, Sally cautiously asked a few questions. She found out that John was from Des Moines, that he'd been working here and there at whatever job he could find. His answers were carefully thought out, and she sensed that he was checking some invisible notebook before each answer, making sure that it was right, and only then giving it: a process done at lightning speed, and yet, a process.

All the while Tom stared at John suspiciously, and with a hint of hostility.

"They're looking for someone," Tom said.

John's eyes swept over to him.

"Some Army men came to the school today," Tom continued. "They said to be on the lookout for a deserter, that he'd killed a truck driver a few days ago."

John gazed into Tom's eyes for a moment, then shifted

to the window. "It's beautiful country," he said to Sally. "Would you like to take a walk?"

She nodded softly, and everything Tom had just said, all the alarm it should have caused in her, abruptly vanished. "Yes," she said. "A walk would be nice."

They left the children at the table, Tom still staring accusingly at John, daring him to reveal himself.

They mounted a nearby slope in the cool air. Sally felt strangely light, as if she were floating just above the earth, the bottoms of her feet lightly brushing the upturned grass.

"You're a very special woman," John said. "You need to believe me when I tell you that." He stopped and looked at her pointedly. "I've done some things," he admitted. "Hurt people."

She saw how troubled he was, how desperately he sought peace. She felt herself give way to him, took his hand. "Come with me," she said.

In the shed, clothed in darkness, she made love to him as she had never made love to anyone, softly and sweetly, yet with a strange abandon, possessing even as she was possessed, gaining ground as she gave it up, like a soldier who senses victory in surrender.

Tom stood at his bedroom window, peering down at the shed, his sister beside him, watching him silently.

"Let's find his clothes," Tom said darkly.

"But he's supposed to be dangerous," Becky told him fearfully.

Tom seemed not to hear her. He threw himself on the floor and peered under the bed. Nothing.

"Look at this," Becky said.

Tom got to his feet. "What?"

Becky handed him the magazine. "It's a weird magazine."

Tom looked at the magazine. It was called *Famous Fantastic Mysteries*. He turned the page. The first story was called "The Visitor," and the illustration showed a strong, handsome man with a young woman in his arms.

"It's him," Tom said.

"It's who?"

Tom whirled around to see the man in the doorway.

"It's who?" John repeated.

Tom drew back and made for the door, but John caught him and lifted him, their faces almost touching.

"Listen to me," John said. "You think you know something, but you don't."

Tom squirmed violently in John's arms. "Let me go," he cried. "Let me go."

Becky bolted forward and began kicking John's shins, but he seemed not to feel the hard point of her shoes, and kept his eyes riveted to Tom. "My business here is almost done," he said.

Tom's nose started to bleed.

"I'm sorry," John said. He slowly returned Tom to the ground. "I didn't mean to hurt . . ."

Tom wiped his nose and stared, horrified at the blood.

"Tom, I . . ."

Tom whirled around and bolted from the room, Becky rushing out just behind him, just as Sally came into it.

"What's with them?" Sally said lightly as they rushed past her.

John shrugged.

Something in John's face changed, a sudden shadow

passing over it, and Sally sensed that a dark thought had crossed his mind.

"Tyler, my boss at the restaurant," she said. "He called to tell me that soldiers are looking for a deserter from an Army base in New Mexico."

John said nothing, but only picked up the magazine Tom had dropped at his feet.

"I know that you came from someplace farther away than that," Sally said. "They'll be coming for you soon, won't they?"

John nodded silently, glancing away for a moment before returning his gaze to her.

Sally plucked a lone star earring from her ear. "These were my grandmother's. Will you take one with you?" She stepped over and took his hand and saw that it had changed. Now it had only four fingers and each finger had an extra joint. She knew that she should be horrified, that horror would be the normal reaction. But she felt no horror, only that he'd revealed something to her, deepened their intimacy. In doing so, he had taken her into his world, and she believed that some part of her would always live there.

"I'd better go," John said. "I don't think I can keep from hurting you if you're with me."

She walked him out to the porch, watched as he stepped into the yard, noted that he did not look back. She lifted her hand, but did not say good-bye.

Then she walked back into the house, and in an instant she knew that he was gone. She returned to the porch, glancing up at the sky where she saw two large blue orbs flying in formation across the heavens. She sat down in a chair, and she was still there, sitting quietly, when Tom and Becky came home. She could tell from their faces that they'd also seen the strange lights in the night sky.

Later, just as dinner was on the table, she answered a knock at the door.

"I'm Owen Crawford," the soldier said. "Army Intelligence."

Sally nodded.

"He's gone, hasn't he?" Owen said.

"He has," Sally answered.

She could tell that the soldier knew who the stranger was, that he was not a deserter from an Army base, but something else entirely. Something that defied understanding and had bestowed on her a wisdom and sweetness that was deeper than anything on earth.

"Home?" he asked.

"Yes, home."

The soldier nodded. "Then I guess I'm too late," he said, and with those words, tipped his hat and walked away.

She watched him drive off, then tucked Tom and Becky into bed. She knew that her children probably thought her crazy.

But she knew differently.

She'd seen the four-fingered hand, seen his powers, and even now felt him stir inside her, something left behind, so small she could barely feel its pressure inside her, so small . . . but growing.

EL PASO, TEXAS, JULY 18, 1947

Russell lay in bed, tossing fitfully. Johnson was screaming, and he was rolling out of the bed and onto the floor, reaching for the trigger, firing, firing, firing, until suddenly, he was bathed in light, and he saw that the light came from the creatures in the tent, the Germans who were no longer Germans, he saw now, but something . . . other . . . small, with large pear-shaped heads, huge almond-shaped eyes, and long fingers that hung from spindly hands.

He bolted up in bed, wide awake, eyes staring into the darkness. Sweat cascaded down his back with the cool curious touch of bony fingers. *Not Germans,* he thought desperately, *not Germans at all.*

ROSWELL ARMY AIR BASE, JULY 18, 1947

Owen headed down the corridor, then stopped. She was there again. That woman. Sue. He pivoted quickly, bent upon a hasty escape, but found himself face to face with Howard.

"I thought I told you to keep that woman away from me," he snapped.

"She's very persistent," Howard said. He glanced over Owen's shoulder. "Too late, sir."

Owen turned to face Sue and flashed his best smile. "Sue, so glad to see you. Corporal Bowen, this is Sue . . ." He stopped, at a loss.

"You don't even know my last name," Sue said. "But don't worry, Owen. This isn't about . . . us." She lifted the paper bag she held in her right hand. "It's about this."

Owen took the bag and looked inside, his expression now very grave. "Where did you get this?" he asked.

"Up at Pine Lodge."

Owen closed the bag. "Come into my office."

Once inside the office, Owen reached into the bag and drew out a metal artifact, its inner surface covered with odd markings, curves and geometric shapes.

"The night you ditched me, I went for a drive," Sue told him. "I saw something crash. I couldn't see what it was, but when I walked over to where it had gone down, I found this."

"And brought it to me," Owen said sweetly. He touched her arm seductively. "You never let me explain about that night. I was supposed to meet Colonel Campbell. His daughter came to tell me he was ill."

"Sure she did."

"You completely misread the situation."

"Sure I did." But she smiled as she said it.

He could feel her falling beneath his spell. "You're the sun and the moon to me, Sue."

He was in her trailer later that night, all his thoughts on the object she'd found, how important it was, and how necessary that he should have sole possession of it. Now he had something the colonel had never seen. Something no one had ever seen . . . but Sue.

And so it's come to this, he thought, a witness the project can't afford. He touched Sue's face, but not to awaken her, only to suggest that it was too bad what he had to do, too bad that the most valuable artifact in the history of the world had to be protected from even one more set of human eyes.

The air was dark outside, but he had found just what he needed, something very heavy. She was sleeping soundly when he lifted it above her, and never woke again when he brought it down.

ROSWELL, NEW MEXICO, SEPTEMBER 16, 1947

Owen stood among the throng of well-wishers, their glasses lifted in a wedding toast as Howard brought his remarks to a close. "Anne, you're not just marrying Owen," he said, "you're getting me and Marty, too."

Owen laughed, then glanced toward the bar where Colonel Campbell stood off to himself. Now was the moment, he thought, time to go in for the kill.

He inched his way out of the crowd and walked over to the colonel.

"Could we have a talk?" he asked. "In your study."

Colonel Campbell shrugged. "Okay," he said.

In the study, Owen took in the luxurious room, the high walls of books.

"If it wouldn't break my daughter's heart, I'd kill you where you stand," Colonel Campbell said.

Owen smiled confidently. "But it really would break her heart." He lifted his chin arrogantly. "You know what I'd like as a wedding present? I'd like to be a major."

Colonel Campbell laughed.

"A major," Owen repeated firmly. "Anything less and you couldn't put me in charge of that little project of yours at Wright-Patterson."

Colonel Campbell's face was motionless. "That project is mine. You will never see inside that laboratory."

"I disagree," Owen said haughtily. He took the small piece of metal Sue had given him. "It's an alloy unknown on this planet. The markings are also unknown. It was found at Pine Lodge." He pocketed the metal. "And either you give me exactly what I want or I'll go public. That should bring your flying saucer crashing down on your head."

The colonel drew in a shaky breath. "Enjoy your promotion," he said.

Owen nodded, turned to leave, then stopped and faced the colonel once again. "And don't worry about Anne. She's the sun and the moon to me."

PART TWO

Jacob and Jesse

Chapter One

Kate Keys continued the story of Artemis, a huge squirrel who lived in a gigantic oak tree in the middle of the forest. Jesse listened attentively, his face nearly motionless save for his large, expressive eyes. He was seven years old now, but in bed he still looked like an infant, perfectly formed and innocent, a storybook child.

She finished the story, closed the book, gave Jesse a good-night kiss, then rose and headed for the door.

"Mom . . ."

"Go to sleep, Jesse."

He looked troubled, and Kate knew what the trouble was. His question didn't surprise her.

"Mom, do you think Daddy ever thinks about us?"

Russell had been gone for five years, and Kate had no idea where he was. But she felt that she still knew Russell, knew his decency, and the love he'd had for his son. Wherever he was, whatever he might be doing, she was certain that he thought of Jesse all the time, dreamed one day of seeing him again, that from the depths of this madness that tormented him and had finally driven him away, he still reached for Jesse . . . and for her.

"Of course he does, honey," she said. She wished she had more consoling words, something that would explain Russell to his son, explain the torturous look she'd seen in his eyes as he'd frantically searched for his old crew, then the sense of mission that had overwhelmed him, his determination to find Johnson. He'd gone in search of his copilot, she knew that much. She also knew that he'd found him, and that the man had all but died in Russell's arms. She'd learned that much in her own efforts to find him. She could only imagine the pain of that moment, the baffled, animal fear that must have settled over Russell, the futility and the hopelessness. It didn't surprise her that he'd vanished after that, willed himself to stay away from his family despite how much he loved them. She'd seen the way he felt about himself, the sense that he carried some dark seed within him, some dreadful trait or quality that imperiled those he loved, so that his only choice, bitter and painful though it was, had been to separate himself, simply go off, like a dying animal. She wanted to explain all this to Jesse, but couldn't find the words. He was only seven, after all.

"Go to sleep, now, Jesse," she told him gently as she closed the door.

Bill was at the kitchen table, thumbing through the evening paper when she came into the room.

"Jesse asleep?" Bill asked.

Kate walked to the window and peered out. "He's asking about his father again."

Bill put down the paper. "How about you, do you still miss him?"

Kate walked over to Bill and knelt beside him, her face very near his. "He ran out on us, Bill. And he never came back." She touched his face. "But you were there, and you didn't go anywhere." She leaned forward and kissed him softly. "Don't you think I know that?"

He nodded silently, accepting her assurance that she would never leave him, but she saw it in his eyes, the insecurity, his fear that Russell would turn up again one day and take her and Jesse away from him She knew that would never happen, but she also knew that in the dead of night, when the house creaked and the wind rattled the windowpanes, Jesse probably dreamed of just such a return, dreamed of sleeping in the warm protection of his father's arms, of mending the broken circle that had once made his life whole, and that despite herself, despite the wonderful husband and father Bill had become, she sometimes dreamed it too.

Jesse heard the scratching first, soft but insistent, like fingers on a windowpane. He shifted beneath the covers, tried to press the noise from his mind, then rolled over and opened his eyes.

And he was there.

Artemis, the squirrel.

Jesse propped himself up in bed and stared into the gray, furry face. The squirrel didn't move, but he felt drawn to it, summoned to follow it. He slid out of his bed, walked to the window and opened it.

Artemis drifted away from the window and hung in midair, smiling softly and with an eerie sense of beckoning, as if to say, *Come with me.*

Jesse climbed out of the window, and stood on the

second-floor ledge, his cowboy pajamas billowing out in the chill autumn breeze. At the edge of the roof, he stood stiffly, arms plastered to his sides, a little cylinder of flesh high above the green lawn to which Artemis had now descended, a huge gray doll in the rippling grass.

For a moment their eyes locked. Then Artemis blinked slowly, and Jesse heard his silent command, *Jump*.

He jumped and Artemis swept forward and up into the air and caught him as he fell, the two of them spinning wildly in the warm summer darkness. He felt the furry arms around him, holding him protectively. Then he was on the ground, surrounded by a vast green lawn, Artemis leading him away, across miles and miles of green, time flowing in all directions, like a river overflowing its banks, the world a moving carpet beneath his bare feet, drawing him deeper and deeper into the entangling forest.

A giant oak stood out from the rest of the trees, and Jesse knew that this was Artemis' home. A black mouth gaped at the center of the tree, the door to Artemis' world.

"Can I?" Jesse asked.

He felt Artemis' soft furry arms embrace him and lift him to the doorway, then through and inside it, where he waited until Artemis leaped in, the door closing behind him, sealing them inside.

At first it was dark, then shade by shade the black air brightened and brightened until it shimmered all around, a light that came from everywhere, as if everything gave off its own radiant glow.

He felt the tree lift, like the slow rise of a rocket as it pushed against the heavy gravity of earth, then rising faster and faster, streaking across the nightbound sky. The next thing he knew, he was standing on the blue road, two beams of light closing in upon him like the shining eyes of a ravenous animal until the brakes shrieked loudly and the tires squealed to a halt and he stood in the truck's blinding beams, a little boy, alone, Artemis hidden somewhere behind the stars, no more than the memory of a warmth he'd once known.

LAS VEGAS, NEVADA, DECEMBER 14, 1958

Owen Crawford stood on a ladder, hanging Christmas decorations outside his house while Anne and his two sons, Eric and Sam, scurried about the yard, shooting at each other with toy ray guns.

"Hey, watch it," Owen snapped when Sam crashed into Anne, knocking her against the ladder.

"Sorry," Anne said meekly.

"Just be careful," Owen told her sternly.

He returned to his work, though he took no joy in it. For what was Christmas, after all, but an enforced holiday, trivial and meaningless, perfect only for people who had nothing better to do than hang these ridiculous lights.

From the top of the ladder, he saw the staff car move down the tree-lined street and pull up to his curb. Thank God, Owen thought, I can get out of here.

"I have to go," he said brusquely as he hurried toward the car, leaving Anne alone to watch the boys chase each other wildly across the neatly trimmed lawn.

They reached Groom Lake a few minutes later. As the car moved smoothly across the tarmac, Owen glanced at

the latest military advance, a black bomber with swept-
back wings, a plane no radar could detect.

In the staff room, he took his seat at the end of a long
conference table where various scientists and military
personnel sat around, chewing pencils and flipping
through reports as they waited for him to speak. Dr.
Kreutz sat in a chair at the back of the room, idly fasten-
ing and unfastening a Velcro strap, one of the "advances"
that had been discovered in the craft, the only piece of
information from which they'd been able to benefit after
years of study.

"We took this craft apart more than ten years ago,"
Owen said. "More than ten years and we still have no
idea how it ran. No clue what its power source was or
what the aerodynamics involved were." He nodded
toward Dr. Kreutz. "This is Dr. Kreutz," he said. "He has
agreed to come over to our program for an indefinite pe-
riod of time." He cast a merciless eye over the assembly.
"As of now," he said, "the rest of you are reassigned to
other duties." He smiled coldly. "In Iceland."

The men around the table glanced at each other in
shock and disbelief.

Dull and unimaginative, Owen thought contemptuously, mere slugs, men who lacked the passion of pursuit, who did one thing until they were told to do
another, men who lacked the mettle of a true commit-
ment. Not one of them deserved any further explanation.

And so he gave none, but simply rose and escorted Dr.
Kreutz out of the room.

"There's something you should know, Doctor," Owen
said as the two men headed toward a distant hangar. "I
report directly to President Eisenhower, and he is not a
patient man. I've let him believe a few of your technolog-

ical advances were derived from our research. I hope when you meet the President, you won't disabuse him of his impression."

Dr. Kreutz chuckled. "And wind up reassigned to Iceland a week before Christmas? Certainly not."

They stopped at the doors of the hangar.

"Let me see your little bird," Dr. Kreutz said.

Owen swung open the doors and it stood in the shadowy light, the craft Owen had retrieved from the desert years before.

"The interior wasn't damaged," Owen told Dr. Kreutz. "It's exactly as it was when we found it."

They had now reached a small stepladder that rose to the open door of the craft. Kreutz mounted the stairs, followed by Owen.

For a time, Kreutz moved about the interior of the craft, noting its sleek design, the seats with their finger-pad controls, everything smoothed and buffed to a shimmering perfection.

"None of those white coats could figure anything out," Owen said with a smirk. "For years they've scuttled around in here, but they never came up with anything." He laughed. "For all their degrees, they couldn't even find out how the damn thing was powered."

Kreutz shrugged. "It is easy to see what baffled your researchers," he said. "No instrument panel. No monitoring devices."

"You'll notice some kind of energy field," Owen said. "In about six minutes your head will begin to ache. Twenty minutes later, you'll have a cerebral hemorrhage."

Kreutz nodded as if not at all surprised, then pressed

his hand against the smooth interior wall. "You will never get this craft off the ground without an engine."

"But there is no engine."

Dr. Kreutz smiled as he nodded to the five empty seats. "Actually, there were five of them," he said.

"The crew?" Owen asked incredulously. "The crew supplied the . . ."

"Power, yes," Dr. Kreutz said. "The power of the mind. That's the energy source you're looking for."

"We had one alive," Owen said. "He had powers." He told him the story of Dr. Goldin's vision, then his death and the visitor's, how alien and human blood had briefly swirled together on the laboratory floor.

Kreutz looked at Owen pointedly. "We have to find someone else with unimaginable power of mind."

LUBBOCK, TEXAS, DECEMBER 19, 1958

Jacob Clarke held a *Lone Ranger* lunch box to his ear, as if listening for the sounds inside, its tiniest vibration. A group of fifth graders watched silently,

"Oreos and a peanut butter and jelly sandwich," Jacob said quietly.

Travis grinned mockingly. "Wrong," he said. "My mom promised me a steak sandwich and a slice of pie."

Jacob opened the box and there it was, exactly as he'd predicted, neatly wrapped and placed side by side, a packet of Oreos and a peanut butter and jelly sandwich.

Travis' eyes widened in angry disbelief. "How'd you do that?"

Jacob looked at Travis pointedly. "Your parents had a fight last night about your father being drunk. She used the steak on her eye, and besides, she didn't feel much like making anything fancy this morning."

Travis' features turned stony. "You're dead, brainiac," he snarled.

Later that afternoon Travis and a few of his friends skidded their bikes to a halt, blocking Jacob's way home.

"Tell me where you were, you little creep," Travis demanded menacingly. "In the bushes outside my house?"

Jacob watched silently as Travis' friends surrounded him.

"You're gonna die," Travis said.

Jacob backed away, tripping over the curb, and in an instant Travis was upon him, his knee pressing down on Jacob's chest.

"Travis," Jacob said quietly. "Look at me."

Travis stared into Jacob's eyes, his expression hard and threatening until suddenly it changed, and a look of sheer terror swept into his face. Jacob knew that Travis was seeing his own leg blown off on a hill near Da Nang, his screams now so loud and wretched his friends backed away in terror.

Jacob got to his feet, watching expressionlessly as Travis trembled before him, pale and stricken. He knew he could do more to this boy, but each time he used the power, some measure of strength drained from him, like a light slowly fading with each use. And so Jacob merely turned and made his way down the road, unblocked now, toward home, where he knew he'd find his mother doing the usual things, cooking, cleaning, different from other mothers only in the odd way she gazed at the sky at night, searching the stars with a curious urgency, like someone looking for a face in the crowd.

BURNHAM TRAIN YARD, DENVER, COLORADO,
DECEMBER 19, 1958

Russell Keys huddled inside the boxcar with four
other hobos, half listening as one of them declared that
rock and roll had died when Elvis went into the Army.
Russell's eyes were sunken, and he was rail-thin, the
mere shadow of the man he'd once been. Life on the road
was never kind, but it seemed to him that the ten years of
his sojourn had taken a heavier toll upon him than it had
upon the other men on the train. It was what he knew
that withered him, a knowledge no one else could comprehend, but which locked him in a terrible solitude,
made him the silent scarecrow he had become.

"The captain there's not one for conversation," one of
the hobos said.

Russell drew his old duffle bag more tightly into his
arms.

The hobo laughed mockingly. "You'd think that was a
sack of gold, the way you hold on to it."

Russell said nothing, but only continued to clutch
the bag.

"Leave him alone, Dave," another hobo said.

Dave shrugged. "I'm just trying to make a little
friendly conversation." His cracked lips curled down
scornfully. "Man thinks he's the only one with a past."

That wasn't true, Russell knew, though he said nothing. It was only that his past—as well as his present—
was unlike any other man's.

Dave stared at the bag. "So, what you got in there anyway?" He leaned forward and reached for the bag.
"Lemme see."

"Don't touch it," Russell warned.

Dave glared at Russell, his eyes red with rage. "Gimme that bag, Captain." He drew a length of pipe from his pocket, and before Russell could move, brought it down hard on the side of his head.

Russell crumpled to the floor, blood dripping from his head.

Dave grabbed the bag and reached into it. "Nothing but a bunch of medals," he said with a laugh. He looked at Russell. "You some kind of hero, way back when, Captain?" He lifted the pipe again. "Well, you ain't much of one now."

Suddenly a burst of light swept over Dave, freezing him in its brilliance. "Railroad guards," he said. "Let's get out of here." He raced to the door and pulled it back, started to leap then stopped, the other hobos now behind him, staring down at the earth a hundred feet below, speechless and amazed, as the railroad car rocketed upward into the night.

The hobos stared at each other stunned, then rushed back from the open door as the light grew brighter and brighter.

From his place on the floor, Russell saw two creatures step out of the blinding radiance. They were coming into the railroad car, and he knew they were coming to get him. He heard his own scream slice the air, but they came on anyway, took his hand and drew him from the floor. He could feel their wiry fingers, the extra knotted joints, the terrible power they possessed, and against which he could do nothing but go with them into the excruciating light where, in a tiny glimpse of shadow, he saw a teenage boy hanging upside down above a table, like a lamb at slaughter, his eyes filled with terror, eyes that were incontestably familiar, and that seemed to recognize Russell, understand that he was a human being, helpless and alone, beyond the aid, or even the understanding, of his fellow men.

AMARILLO, TEXAS, SPACECRAFT CONVENTION, DECEMBER 19, 1958

The speaker's name was Quarrington, and from her seat in the convention hall, Sally listened closely as he claimed to have been in a flying saucer and thus could assure the world that creatures from outer space meant no harm.

Sally knew that this was true. The man she'd found in the shed had had plenty of chances to hurt her and her children, but he'd shown nothing but an overwhelming tenderness that still lingered in her memory.

"I've met them, too," she said to Quarrington a few minutes later as he autographed his book, *My Life Inside the Flying Saucers.*

"Do you think they'll be coming back?" Sally asked expectantly. "I mean, at some time in the future?"

Quarrington handed her the book with a dismissive shrug. "Our time and their time are not the same."

Sally stepped away, aware that Quarrington had not taken her seriously. But then, why should he? She was just a waitress from a dusty little Texas town. He probably thought she was yet another lonely housewife who'd concocted a flying saucer story to get attention. Such women were out there, Sally knew. But she also knew that she was not one of them. She remembered the stranger, John, felt the gentleness of his caress. No, she told herself, she was not like other women at all. John had made sure of that. The burden of her life was that she knew absolutely that he'd been real. A man from another world had come to her, touched her, loved her . . . and left her with a son. The impossible and the fantastic had joined to create the single searing experience of her life. But it was an experience about which she could speak only to the likes of Quarrington, and these other people whose stories she sometimes believed and sometimes didn't, and who sometimes believed her story, and sometimes didn't, all of them brought together and at the same time separated by the sheer fantastical nature of their experience.

On the way out she looked at the other people in the line, all of them clutching Quarrington's book to their chests as if it were a lost child they'd miraculously found. There was weariness in their eyes, a terrible isolation. Some of them were probably crazy, she thought, but which ones? It didn't matter really, she decided. All of them bore the mark of the outcast, the scorned and the ridiculed. She bore that mark, too, and she knew that Jacob was doomed to bear it as well.

He was waiting motionlessly in the truck when Sally returned to the parking lot.

"You look tired," she said. "You can sleep on the way home."

He looked at her wearily, a little boy older than his years, burdened with a secret dread he couldn't describe or even understand. She thought of the night of his conception, felt herself once again within John's alien arms, and suddenly realized that Jacob was held in that same embrace, the two of them touched by the same presence, she to live on in memory and longing, endlessly in hope of John's return, her son to live on in search of something else. She recalled a scene in *Alice in Wonderland*. In the scene, a lock rushes ceaselessly about, searching everywhere for what it calls "the key to me."

For a moment she held Jacob in her gaze, longing now for the key to her son, so that she could give it to him, and by that gift, make him safe. But she knew that only John could do that, and that all she could do was try to find him, speak to him, beg him to come back just one more time, be, however briefly and in what blinding light, a father to his son.

Russell opened his eyes and winced at the hard white light that fell over him in a brilliant slant. He felt the wooden floor of the railway car beneath him, smelled the hotdogs a hobo named Hank was cooking over a home-made fire a few feet away.

"Breakfast. Compliments of Irish Dave and the others," Hank said with a grin.

Russell struggled to his feet and staggered over to the fire, his head still aching from the beating Irish Dave had given him.

Hank reached into his pocket and took out a piece of fabric hung with medals. "Dave wanted you to have these back. Said to say he was sorry, and if he ever saw you again, which he hoped he didn't, please forgive him."

Russell took the medals, then glanced about, looking for the duffel bag. "I had a map," he said.

"In the bag," Hank told him.

Russell quickly rifled through the bag, found the map and brought it out into the light.

"Seems like you care more about that old map than you do your medals," Hank said. He eyed the map Russell clutched tightly. "What is it, secret treasure?"

Russell shook his head. "It's just a topographical map."

"So what makes it so special?"

Russell didn't know how to answer. He knew that if he told Hank what made the map special, he would be dismissed as just another hobo lunatic. And yet something rose in him despite the fear of once again being thought crazy. A need to tell, or perhaps only a need to communicate the desperate nature of his search to at least one other human being.

"I was a pilot in the war," he began softly, like a broken man trying to explain himself, trace the dark and downward trajectory of his life, reveal the meaning of his rags. "Twenty-three missions. All with the same crew."

Hank nodded toward the medals. "Guess you earned those the hard way."

"Nine men," Russell added. "All dead." He stared at the medals. "Something like what happened last night. We were taken."

He glanced up toward the sky. "Whatever they did to us, it killed my men. I know that for a fact. What I don't know . . . what I can't understand . . . why am I alive?"

Hank considered what he'd been told, took it seriously and turned it over in his mind. "Maybe the fact that you didn't die, maybe that's why they keep . . . taking you. Maybe they want to know what makes you special."

Special, Russell thought, and felt some distant piece of an even more distant puzzle fall softly into place. In what way was he special, he wondered. He considered his life, but found nothing particularly special about it.

He had grown up a small-town American boy, then gone off to war, fought . . . survived. The word caught in his mind. Hank was right. Out of all his crew, he alone had survived . . . being taken. If that were what made him special, then it was something in his makeup, he reasoned, sheer physical stamina, perhaps, or an unexpected form of immunity, some characteristic he'd inherited from his parents and which he might have passed on to . . .

A chill passed over him.

To Jesse.

BEMENT, ILLINOIS, DECEMBER 24, 1958

Russell saw the carolers through a concealing veil of snow, and the strangeness of the scene, himself hidden behind the great oak on Kate's front lawn on Christmas Eve while carolers moved freely down the wintry street, once again reminded him of the terrible journey of his life, the loneliness which now enclosed him and set him apart and made him a creature of the shadows.

He waited for the carolers to leave, then made his way to the front door, knocked softly and waited.

The boy who opened the door was thirteen, and he saw himself in the boy's large eyes, the angle of his jaw, the width of his shoulder.

"Jesse," he said.

Suddenly Bill appeared at the door.

"Hello, Russell," he said evenly. He placed his hands on Jesse's shoulder and turned him back toward the inside of the house. "Your mother needs you in the living room, son."

Jesse obeyed instantly, and the two men faced each other alone.

"You're not welcome here, Russell," Bill told him.

"I have something to tell Jesse," Russell said urgently.

"You lost that right a long time ago," Bill said. He looked at Russell's worn-out clothes and scraggly beard and seemed to see the vagrant life he'd lived, a bum among bums, homeless and bedraggled. "You can stay at the station," he said. "I'll call ahead so . . ."

"Jesse is in danger," Russell interrupted. "I need to talk to him."

Bill stepped back from the door and steadied himself, as if he expected Russell to charge him. "That's not going to happen," he said, then abruptly closed the door.

For a moment, Russell stood, facing the closed door, unable to leave, yet knowing that he had to leave. He had tried to act openly and honestly to save his son. Now that way was closed to him, and Jesse was still in danger, and he alone knew the real nature of that danger, that the ones who'd taken him had also come to take his son. He had to be protected from them, hidden from them, taken somewhere from which he could not be . . . taken.

Russell stepped away from the door and made his way through a lightly falling snow, his mind already searching for a plan.

Chapter Two

Russell peered at his son, and remembered the look in Jesse's eyes when he'd stepped into his path a few hours before. His son had been in the woods near his house, gathering sticks for a snowman. Watching him, Russell had known that this was his only chance to save him. The odd thing was that Jesse had seemed to sense why his father had come for him, and gone with him immediately and without question.

Now they were father and son again, both on the run, hobos together, huddled in a boxcar.

"What are you looking at?" Jesse asked.

"You look like your mother."

"Everyone says I look more like you."

Russell reached into his pocket and drew out the medals. "I want you to have these."

Jesse took them from his hand and stared at them in amazement. "Your war medals."

Russell indicated the silver star. "I got that after my last mission."

"The one where you got shot down and captured and saved your whole crew?"

"Yes," Russell said softly. He could see that something in his tone, the overarching sadness, had registered with his son.

"Mom said it was the war that made you go away," Jesse said.

"But you know it wasn't that, don't you?"

Jesse nodded very slowly. He seemed to be thinking about all the things Russell had told him during the last few hours. His eyes roamed the interior of the railroad car. "Is this what you've been doing all this time? Is this where you live?"

"I live where I can," Russell answered. "What was happening to me . . . I didn't want to bring it home to you and your mother."

Again, Jesse seemed to go deep inside himself. "Who are they?" he asked finally.

"I don't know, son."

"Can you keep them from coming back for me again?"

"I don't know that either," Russell answered, drawing his son into his arms. "I'm sure as hell going to try."

LUBBOCK, TEXAS, DECEMBER 25, 1958

Jacob parted the curtains and looked out the window as a brand-new Buick Special pulled into the driveway, Tom at the wheel, Becky on the passenger side.

He waited for them to come inside, his eyes utterly

still, like two small stones at the bottom of an impossibly deep lake.

"Hey, little brother," Tom said happily as he came through the door.

Jacob nodded silently.

Becky leaned over and kissed him.

"Where's Mom?" she asked.

"She's in the shed," Jacob answered.

"What's she doing in the shed?" Tom asked.

"She's working on something."

"On Christmas Day?" Becky asked. She glanced at Tom, then the two of them walked out of the house and made their way toward the shed.

Sally saw them coming across the lawn as she stepped out of the shed. "You're early. I thought you weren't going to be here till evening," she said as they rushed up to kiss her.

"Mom, it's almost five o'clock," Tom said.

Sally shrugged. "How did that happen?"

Tom looked at her suspiciously. "What were you doing in the shed?" he asked.

"Oh, nothing," Sally answered dismissively. "Come, let's get to the house."

In the house, Tom and Jacob headed for the living room while Sally and Becky prepared dinner in the kitchen.

"You know, with all the money Tom's made," Becky said. "We could put Jacob in a school where he . . ."

"Jacob's fine here with me," Sally interrupted.

But Becky continued, undeterred. "There's one in Montana. For children who are . . . different."

"Jacob is fine," Sally repeated.

Becky looked at her pointedly. "When's the last time Jacob smiled, Mom? Or laughed? Or cried?"

"He is just not that kind of kid, that's all."

"But Mom . . ."

Sally squared her shoulders and faced Becky determinedly. "There is nothing wrong with Jacob, and he is fine here with me," she said, turning to pull the turkey TV dinners out of the oven, and thus ending the conversation.

GROOM LAKE FACILITY, DECEMBER 25, 1958

"There it is," Dr. Kreutz said.

Owen watched the bus as it made its way across the tarmac. He knew who was inside, Mavis and Gladys Erenberg, twin sisters he'd tested again and again and each time found that indeed they did have "powers." Now it was time to test those powers.

The bus drew to a halt and Marty stepped out, turned and lifted his hand first to Mavis, then to Gladys Erenberg.

They looked ordinary to Owen, just a couple of middle-aged women dressed in cheap clothes. And yet they'd been able to read each other's mind, one able to draw a picture of whatever the other one was looking at, even though separated by thick concrete walls. Still, in the end, they were only . . . specimens.

Now they were moving toward the real purpose of Owen's study. He knew that the first sight of the spacecraft might alarm them, and he noticed that Mavis hesitated slightly as she approached, but Marty stepped over quickly, assured her that everything was fine, that it was all perfectly safe, just another test.

The sisters disappeared into the interior of the craft. Owen looked at his watch. Within seconds they'd be strapped into seats only aliens had occupied before. He waited, glanced at his watch again as Marty took his position beside him.

Seven-thirty. Within minutes he would have a finding.

And so he waited, sweat accumulating on his brow, while Dr. Kreutz stood beside him, his gaze fixed on the craft.

Twenty minutes passed, and Marty glanced fretfully at Dr. Kreutz.

"Give it another five minutes," the doctor told him.

Marty looked helplessly at Owen. "Sir, that will kill them."

Owen's voice was as hard as the man he had become. "They were dead the second they set foot on this base."

Eight o'clock, and nothing, no sense that the Erenberg sisters had demonstrated any capacity to power the craft. It stood as it always stood, silent and motionless, as if waiting for the code Owen could not yet supply, or some secret order he could not give.

Owen looked at Dr. Kreutz and as if in obedience to a silent command, the doctor stepped up beside him and the two men made their way toward the craft. The door opened as they approached it and they went inside. Nothing they saw surprised them.

The Erenberg sisters rested faceup in the alien seats into which they had been strapped. Their eyes were closed and their bodies remained motionless. They might have been sleeping calmly, save for the blood that had drained from their noses and mouths and accumulated on the identical gray coat dresses they'd selected for the occasion.

"Have this mess cleaned up and the ship put away," Owen ordered. He turned and saw Howard rushing toward him, a field telephone in his hand.

"It's the White House," Howard said.

Owen took the phone, and flashed the bright smile that had served him long and well, but which now bore a faint, demonic crook. "Colonel Crawford here," he said. "And a Merry Christmas to you, Mr. President."

LAS VEGAS, NEVADA, DECEMBER 25, 1958

The house was dark as Owen entered it. He could smell the lingering aroma of the Christmas dinner he'd failed to attend. In the living room, the last embers of a Yule log glowed faintly in the hearth. Christmas paper, torn from Sam and Eric's presents littered the room. His boots crushed it as he made his way across the room.

"We waited a long time, Owen."

Anne stood in the doorway, dressed in a nightgown, though clearly she had not gone to bed.

"I'm sorry," Owen told her. "Something came up."

Anne took a deep breath. "You gave them both the Lionel train set. You gave Sam the *Space Patrol* board game and the *Leave it to Beaver* lunch box. Eric got the *Leave it to Beaver* board game and the *Space Patrol* lunch box."

"What did I give you?" Owen said with a cold smile.

"A lot more than I bargained for," Anne answered sharply as she turned and left the room.

Owen walked to his office and stared out into the night. A light snow was falling, but its beauty did nothing to lift his mood. The Erenberg sisters had died for nothing, but that was not the point. The real problem was that for all the power they had demonstrated, it had been nothing compared to the power that had destroyed them, literally within minutes, as they sat inside the craft. That was a power beyond anything human, Owen thought, and until he found something within the human world to match that power, the craft would sit motionless inside the darkness of the hangar, as heavy and unliftable as his dream of making a mark in the world.

He walked to the safe, dialed the combination and took out the artifact Sue had given him years before. This was the only proof he had that he could call his own. He stared at the markings, but they remained indecipherable. Somewhere in the stars, there were creatures who could read it, but for all he knew, they would never return to earth unless they were lured back, or unless he found a power as great as theirs, and with that power force them to return. In the end it all came down to that one thing, he thought, his fingers moving delicately over the artifact. It all came down to Power.

LUBBOCK, TEXAS, DECEMBER 25, 1958

"A little more to the right," Tom said.

"This is kind of mean, Tom," Becky said

Tom retrieved his mother's copy of *My Life Inside the Flying Saucers* from the ground at his feet. "Mom believes this kind of crap. She takes Jacob to these conventions. If we can show her how easy it is to fake . . ." He dropped the book, took the Brownie camera from his pocket and lifted it to his eye. "Okay, swing."

Becky swung a fishing rod to the right and the hubcap that dangled from the end of the fishing line took wobbly flight. "But Tom," she interjected. "You were with me. We saw those lights in the sky."

"There was an article on them in *Popular Science*. Do you know what they were?" Tom asked. "The reflection of streetlamps on the breasts of a flock of plover birds." He shook his head. "Becky, we were little kids. We saw what we wanted to see." He snapped the picture, then pocketed the camera, clearly pleased with the plan he'd just implemented.

"So we show Mom her hero is a fraud," Becky said. "Then what . . . we leave her with nothing?"

Tom glanced over to the front porch. Jacob stood there, his face expressionless.

"Hey, Jacob," Tom said, taken aback by his brother's sudden appearance.

"I don't want to go away to school," Jacob said. "If I go, who will take care of Mom?"

Becky walked over to Jacob and knelt beside him. "Jacob, you've got to try to understand . . . you've got a gift, an insight into . . ."

"I got it from my father," Jacob said stiffly, his voice in the usual monotone, despite the odd thing he'd said.

"Jacob, you need to be in a place where people understand you . . ." She stopped and glanced across the lawn to where Sally waved to her from the entrance of the shed.

"Hey, kids," Sally called. "It's finished."

Tom and Becky glanced at each other apprehensively, then walked to the shed where Sally swung open the door with a cheerful sense of accomplishment.

"I call it a contactor," she asked. "What do you think?"

Tom stared at what appeared to be some kind of Buck Rogers contraption made of tinfoil and bristling with antennae.

"It's like a radio," Sally announced. "I can send messages into space."

"Why do you want to send a message into space?" Becky asked.

"I miss Jacob's father," Sally answered. "I want to tell him that we're all right and ask him to come get us." She glanced into the night sky. For years she had kept it all to herself, the strange man she'd found in the shed, his odd power to see into her soul, the sympathy and generosity he had offered her, and the love she had given him in return. "I want him to know that we're ready to go with him."

"Go where?" Tom asked.

Sally continued to search the star-spattered sky. "Home," she said.

The light awakened him, and startled by its blinding radiance, he knew that they had come for him . . . or Jesse.

"Jesse!" Russell cried as he bolted up from his place on the floor of the boxcar. "Jesse!"

A figure stepped into the light, blocking his path.

"Hold it right there, Russell."

He could see Bill's stern face, rock-hard and determined. "Where's Jesse?" Bill demanded. "What the hell have you done with Jesse?"

Over Bill's shoulder, Russell saw the line of police cars, their lights beaming brightly in the darkness that surrounded the boxcar. Scores of police officers had

taken up positions among the cars, all of them poised to
fire, a hundred guns aimed at him.

"Where's Jesse!" Bill cried.

Russell glanced about the empty boxcar searching.
"He's . . . gone."

Bill glared at him. "You're going to jail, Russell," he
said. "And you're going to stay there until you tell me
what you did to Jesse."

But Russell knew he couldn't tell him, and later, as he
sat in a holding cell, his mind searched for some explanation of what had happened to his son. If they had
taken him, they had done it differently, taken him without the shocking light and the numbing noise and the
paralyzing terror.

"Russell."

He looked over to where Kate stood outside his cell.

He got to his feet. "Kate, you have to believe me. I
came back to save Jesse, not to . . ."

"Save him? What are you talking about?"

"They're done with me, Kate," Russell told her. "I was
too weak and so when they first took me . . ."

"I don't want to hear this," Kate snapped. "What did
you do with Jesse?" She glared at him for a moment, then
her face softened and she began to cry.

"They took him," Russell told her gently. "I think they
want to know if he's . . . ready."

"Ready for what?" Kate asked.

In his mind, Russell suddenly saw Jesse hanging upside down, his body paled by the harsh lights of the craft,
a single tear coursing down his cheek. And he knew that
this had actually happened, that Jesse had already been
taken. He shook his head brokenly. "That's something I
still don't know," he said.

LUBBOCK, TEXAS, DECEMBER 30, 1958

Sally loaded her contactor into the back of her truck while Becky and Tom looked on disapprovingly. A cold wind blew over the flat Texas landscape, but her mind was on the stars.

"Mom," Becky began cautiously, "we don't think Jacob should go with you to this . . . what . . . this New Year's Eve party you're . . ."

Sally continued loading. "You don't think he should be exposed to all these crazy people."

"That's right," Tom said without hesitation.

Sally continued to load the truck. "You're not going to sneak Jacob off while I'm gone, are you Tom?"

"Of course not," Tom answered exasperatedly. "We're going to just stay here and do card tricks, I promise."

Sally laughed. "The poor kid. He'd be better off with the loonies who think they're going to Venus." She stopped loading and looked Tom dead in the eyes. "Okay," she said. "He can stay."

Tom smiled with relief. "I'll go tell him."

Sally glanced to where Jacob stood on the front porch. She could see it in his eyes. "I'm sure he already knows," she said.

GROOM LAKE FACILITY, DECEMBER 30, 1958

Owen sat at his desk, reviewing the data while Marty and Howard waited.

"So, there were about two hundred sightings in central Illinois on Christmas Day," Owen said as he glanced up from the folder. "But it's all nutty. A guy sees six hundred yellow discs hovering over Duluth. A woman believes television broadcasts are from outer space." He closed the folder. "You're not helping me."

"We have the surveillance photos in from the Quarrington lecture in Amarillo," Marty said with a slight laugh. "The guy'll say anything we tell him to say. Trips to Venus. 'Space brothers.' "

Howard turned on the slide projector. The first picture showed the audience at the Amarillo convention. "These people call themselves 'contactees.' A bunch of them have built machines to talk to their 'space brothers.' They're getting together on New Year's Eve."

Howard continued moving through the slides, faces of old people, middle-aged people, even children. Most were dressed casually. Some looked certifiably insane, while others could not have appeared more normal. Owen studied the slides, concentrating on the faces as Marty and Howard continued with their jokes.

"Maybe we could borrow one of their machines and call a spaceman," Marty said with a chuckle. "Ask him to come fly the ship for Ike."

Suddenly, one of the pictures drew Owen's attention. "Maybe we don't need to call anyone," he said. "Go back one."

Marty instantly obeyed.

Owen leaned forward and peered at the slide of a woman whose face he recognized. A young boy was sitting next to her. *Ah, Sally,* he thought, *looking for your lost love.*

Chapter Three

A hush moved over the crowd the moment Quarrington stepped onto the stage. All movement stopped, and even the newspaper reporters, only seconds before so boisterous, fell silent.

For a moment, Quarrington's gaze moved over the assembly. He seemed to see each face in turn, judge it according to some unfathomable system of measure, pick one face from the multitude of faces, then speak to all as if he spoke only to that one.

"Those of you who have contactor devices," he said, "turn them on."

The people in the audience sprang into action, pulling levers and turning dials and adjusting antennae, their movements the only sound the area seemed capable of holding.

Some of the machines appeared enormously complex, bristling with tubes and spidery coils, but as he approached, Owen noticed that Sally's contactor had only a single toggle switch and a set of rabbit ears.

"That's a sophisticated-looking device," he said when he reached her.

She turned toward him and he saw that she didn't recognize him, but that didn't surprise him. The civilian clothes were part of the ruse, after all, a necessary element of the story he'd concocted as he'd made the long drive to this absurd gathering of kooks.

He gave her his winning smile. "How does it work?"

"I built it from a plan in *Fate* magazine," Sally answered. "The antennae are supposed to broadcast my brain waves out into space."

"How do they do that?"

"You had a choice. You could either buy this thing that looked like a salad bowl or you could use a metal bucket." She smiled, then noted the man's serious expression. "I'm kidding." She nodded toward the contactor. "There's a radio transmitter built into the machine, and a microphone." She shrugged. "I just talk and hope for the best."

Owen's smile remained in place, as if pasted to his lips.

"You don't remember me, do you?"

Sally shook her head.

Owen let the smile dim. "Your machine, it's to send a message to that . . . friend you found in your shed."

Sally's eyes sparked suddenly. "You were . . ."

"With the Army," Owen said. "I came to see you once. I lost my job because of your friend. I filed a report that said he was a 'visitor' who'd returned to his planet. I was only telling the truth, but it cost me my job . . . and my marriage." The smile returned, softer now, beguiling. "I was never a believer. Until I saw the lights." His eyes caught on the lone star earring that hung from Sally's neck. "I like your pendant."

Sally's hand reached up to the pendant. She touched it softly. "It's an earring actually. My grandmother's."

Owen continued to peer at the earring. "Where's the other one?" he asked.

"I gave it away," Sally answered.

Owen's eyes lifted toward her tenderly. "So now it really is a lone star," he said. He glanced around the area, watching the contactors as they struggled with their machines. "If your machine worked, what would you say to him?"

For a moment she hesitated, but he saw that she was the type of woman who told the truth, no matter what the cost.

"That I miss him," Sally said. "And that there's something he should know about." She reached into her wallet and pulled out three photographs. "This is Tom and this is Becky. They're mine by my late and not at all lamented husband." She turned to the next photograph. "And this is Jacob."

Owen looked at her pointedly, making certain that she could see that he knew who Jacob's father was. "I'd like to meet Jacob." He offered his hand and noticed that she took it very gently. "By the way," he added, "my name is Owen."

They talked on for a few minutes, and with each passing second Owen felt the hook sink deeper into Sally. She was a lonely woman who'd lived a lonely life, a woman who'd fallen in love with an alien, borne his child, and now sought this vanished father in the sky.

An hour later, he stood at the door of her motel room. Her gaze had changed by then, and he knew that there was an element of desire in it, and a need for love, to be touched in a way she had not been touched in years.

"It was nice running into you again after all these years," Owen told her.

"Maybe we'll . . . see each other again at one of these get-togethers."

"I hope so."

Sally laughed lightly. "Although to tell you the truth, I'm getting a little tired of the great Dr. Quarrington and his many trips to Venus."

"With Renuthia?" Owen added with a smile.

They both laughed softly, then Owen said, "You heading home in the morning?"

Sally nodded.

"I hope we do," Owen said, his eyes upon her softly.

"Do what?"

"See each other again."

"I'd like that," Sally said, then reached for her key.

Owen turned away, but her voice drew him back.

"Owen?"

He faced her again.

"You said that filing that report cost you your marriage," Sally said. "I think your wife must have been a very foolish woman to let you go."

Owen smiled as she closed the door gently behind her, then walked to Sally's truck and removed the distributor cap. He knew that in the morning, she'd be unable to start the truck, and would come to him for help. Then he would generously suggest that he drive her back to Lubbock.

The plan worked as Owen knew it would, and they arrived in Lubbock the next day. As they pulled into the yard, Owen saw a woman hanging sheets on a clothesline while a man tossed a football to a boy who looked over at him suddenly, his eyes wary and curiously afraid.

The dread was still in Jacob's eyes a few hours later when they gathered around the dinner table. Sally talked about her work, how someone named Tyler was thinking of selling the diner where she worked. Tom and Becky asked a few questions, but none Owen couldn't easily answer. But Jacob said nothing, and noting his silence, Owen knew absolutely that this boy knew why he'd come and what he intended to do.

Still it was important to keep to the plan, and so, after the others had gone to bed, he lingered with Sally until the hour grew late and he finally rose to leave.

"I'd better get into town," he said. "I need to find a motel room."

He stopped, as if a thought had just occurred to him, then said, "This Mr. Tyler. Think he'd sell his restaurant to me? I'm looking for an . . . opportunity."

Sally laughed. "Well, if he does sell it to you, change the chicken recipe. Tyler makes the worst fried chicken in west Texas." The laughter trailed off and Owen saw the long years of her loneliness reflected in her eyes. "You don't need to go into town," she told him.

Owen moved toward her, but she gently pushed him away. "I'll change the bedding in the spare room," she said, then disappeared up the stairs.

He could hear her above him, leaned back and drew in a long breath, proud of what he'd accomplished. He closed his eyes for a moment, then opened them to find Jacob standing a few feet away.

"I'm never gonna fly your saucer," Jacob said.

Owen gave no indication that he had the slightest idea

what Jacob was talking about. Instead he only smiled quietly. *Oh yes you are,* he thought.

LAS VEGAS, NEVADA, JANUARY 1, 1959

Anne sat stiffly in the living room while Sam and Eric frolicked around her, punching at each other and tumbling to the floor. She didn't bother to stop them. Her mind was on something much larger than her children's play. Owen was gone. He had been gone for days. This had happened before, but this time the absence had gone without a call either from Owen himself or Marty or Howard or anyone who might know where her husband was or what he was doing.

She reached for the phone, then drew back. You're an Army wife, she told herself, and an Army brat, and you should hold firm and keep silent, and never, never, ask questions.

Sam and Eric scurried into the room, then back out of it, but Anne paid no attention. There were questions she had to ask now, she realized, things she had to know.

She picked up the phone and made the call.

"Marty, Anne Crawford," she said. "There's been a terrible accident. Sam fell off the roof. He broke his neck . . . I have to get in touch with Owen. I know he's not in Washington. Where is he, Marty?"

She could sense Marty's hesitation. It lasted three seconds, then he spoke.

"Lubbock," he said. "Lubbock, Texas."

LUBBOCK, TEXAS, JANUARY 1, 1958

They came over a rise, and it lay before them, a bare patch of earth, almost perfectly round, with nothing touched at the rim of the circle, not so much as a singed blade of grass.

"I found this two days after he left," Sally told Owen. "Nothing's grown here since." She shook her head. "My heart's sort of like the ground here." She looked at him tenderly. "You need to know that if you stay."

Owen lifted his gaze from the bare ground and settled it on Sally. "I come from a long line of farmers. We can grow corn in a field where grass won't grow." He smiled and drew her into his arms. "I'm not going anywhere, Sally," he told her. "You're the sun and the moon to me."

They kissed, and Owen felt her surrender to him briefly, then return to herself, her features clearly troubled.

"Jacob," she said.

"He doesn't like me, does he?" Owen asked.

"No."

Owen kissed her again, then said, "Maybe I should take him fishing on the lake. Just the two of us. We could get to know each other."

"I don't think he'll want to do that," Sally said.

"Maybe I can persuade him," Owen said.

When they returned to the house a few minutes later, Sally decided to take down the Christmas lights. Jacob held the ladder as she unstrung the last of the lights.

"Hold tight to the ladder, son," Owen said softly, suddenly behind him.

Jacob looked at him silently.

"Accidents come out of nowhere," Owen added significantly. "There's always a tragedy around the corner."

"Mr. Crawford and I were talking about the two of you getting to know each other," Sally said as she came down the ladder, her hands filled with a string of lights. "He's offered to take you fishing."

Jacob looked at Owen warily.

"There's nothing like a day on a lake for getting acquainted," Owen said. "And I'm sure your mother will be fine here without us." He smiled, but he knew his threat had hit home.

They left later that same afternoon. The sun was bright as they made their way toward the lake.

Owen peered out at the open road while Jacob sat beside him, silent, but full of dark apprehension, like a kid waiting in an open field as the twisting cloud draws near.

LUBBOCK, TEXAS, JANUARY 3, 1959

Sally flipped a piece of breaded steak into a pan of hot oil, the sizzle so loud she barely heard the knock at the front door.

She wiped her hands on her apron and walked to the door. A woman stood before her, well dressed, but curiously desolate. "I'm Anne Crawford," the woman said. "I'm looking for Owen."

"Owen?" Sally asked.

"Owen Crawford," Anne said coolly. "He's in Army Intelligence. I'm his wife."

"Wife?" Sally asked, her fear spiking now.

"Yes," Anne replied stiffly. "Where is he?"

Sally felt all her hope turn to dread. "With my son," she whispered.

On the way to the lake, Owen decided to end all pretense with this kid. He knew everything anyway, so what was the point.

He turned to him sharply. "It'll go easier for your mom if you help me out."

Jacob stared straight ahead, his hands in his lap. "Are you going to dissect me when it's over?"

So he really does know everything, Owen thought, knows specifically his use. "That depends on how much you tell us without being cut open."

Jacob's face remained expressionless. "It doesn't end with me," he said. His eyes remained fixed on the road ahead. "I'm not the only one."

BEMENT, ILLINOIS, JANUARY 3, 1959

Kate lay awake in her bed, thinking of Jesse. She could feel him around her, all but hear his breathing in his adjoining bedroom. She knew he wasn't there, and yet his presence hung in the air around her, palpable as his slender arms.

She pulled herself from the bed and walked down the corridor to her son's room. His things lay in piles, just as he'd left them the day his father took him. But where had he been taken? What had Russell done? She imagined the most dreadful possibilities, and with each one, sank deeper into her loss, a misery that was almost suffocating.

She sat down on Jesse's bed, half-expecting to feel the rustle of his body as he snuggled closer. She looked at his closet, his desk, the bookshelf, and finally at the book she'd read to him when he was younger, *The Adventures of Artemis P. Fonswick*.

She smiled at the cover, Artemis standing at the doorway of his tree house.

Something broke the silence, a faint scratching at the window. She rose, walked to the window and looked out into the night. She could feel something calling to her, beckoning her out of the house and into the yard. She headed down the stairs and out into the ebony air of the backyard. The great tree at the end of it appeared to motion for her, urging her forward.

She stepped around the dark trunk and he looked up, his eyes widening in wild relief.

Jesse!

BEMENT, ILLINOIS, JAIL, JANUARY 3, 1959

Bill unlocked the door and entered the cell.

"They told me Jesse was home," Russell said as he got to his feet. "Is he all right?"

"No thanks to you," Bill said dryly.

Russell grabbed Bill's arm. "Did he say what happened?"

Bill drew his arm from Russell's grasp. "Just that you fell asleep and he wandered off into the woods." He looked at Russell sternly. "I wanted to hold you for kidnapping, but Kate wants me to let you go."

"As long as Jesse's all right," Russell said softly.

The blow came from out of nowhere, and he felt his stomach cave in around Bill's clenched fist.

"Don't come back here," Bill warned. "Ever."

Owen kept his eyes on Jacob as he dropped the coins into the diner's only pay phone. He was sitting alone in the booth, staring out at the desert, his eyes curiously lightless, his body as motionless as if he were already dead.

"Marty, we should be there by tonight," he said.

Marty's voice was strained. "Your wife called," he said. "She told me Sam had gotten hurt and she needed to know where you were."

"And you told her?"

"I thought she needed to . . ."

"Listen to me," Owen snarled. "Get over to my house and see if the kids are okay. If they are, start shopping for a very warm jacket."

He slammed the phone into its cradle and strode back to the booth.

Jacob was still staring out the diner window, the hamburger and fries untouched on his plate.

"You should eat something," Owen told him. "You're going to need your strength."

Jacob slowly turned his eyes on Owen. "Mr. Crawford," he said. "Look at me."

Seconds later, Jacob could still hear the man screaming as he left the diner and began to make his way back home. He knew the man in the diner would never look for him again, never want to look in his eyes, see what he had seen there. One thing was certain, he was safe from Owen Crawford, and he always would be.

And so he walked determinedly along the side of the road until, later that afternoon, he saw his brother's car slow as it approached him, then Becky's welcoming smile.

"Oh, Jacob," she said and she rushed toward him. "We were so worried."

It was night before they reached Lubbock. Sally rushed out of the house and gathered Jacob into her arms, kissed him over and over, holding him tightly all the while. Then released him and told him to go inside.

He did as he was told, but even from inside the house he could hear his mother's frantic whisper.

"Jacob can't stay here," she told Tom desperately. "I want him to go to that school."

Tom nodded. "All right," he said.

She walked back into the house, took Jacob by the hand and led him back out to where Tom and Becky waited by the car.

"You have to go, Jacob," she said. She opened the door of Tom's car and ushered him inside.

"I want you to have this," she told him. She placed the lone star pendant around his neck. "Keep this safe for me, will you?" She touched his hair. "Will you think about me once in a while?"

He saw how much she loved him, and with what cost she was giving him up. Very slowly, a smile broke over his face. "Every day and twice on Sundays," he said.

ILLINOIS HIGHWAY, JANUARY 3, 1959

The driver pulled over and Russell gathered up his duffel bag.

"You sure you want to be dumped off like this?" the driver asked. "All you can see out here is the stars."

"That's the idea," Russell said as he opened the door and stepped out into the night.

He walked away from the truck without looking back,
turned off the road and headed out into an open field. He
lowered the duffel bag, opened it and drew out a sextant
and his topographical map. Then he spread the map out
across the ground, plotting a course, then another and
another, his rage building with each failed attempt until
there was nothing left but rage, and he stood up and
faced the sky, his head raised defiantly. "Take me," he
cried. "Take me, but leave my son alone."

PART THREE

High Hopes

Chapter One

THE GREENSPAN SCHOOL, WALLACE, MONTANA, OCTOBER 8, 1962

As he made his way to home plate, Jacob Clarke knew what the other kids were thinking, that he was an easy strikeout.

He picked up the bat. It felt tremendously heavy in his hands, as if it were made of steel. He placed the bat on his shoulder and looked at the pitcher. For a moment he felt too weak to swing, his pale fingers barely able to hold the bat in place.

"You all right?" the coach asked.

Jacob nodded.

The pitcher wound up and threw a fastball. Jacob watched the ball whiz past him. He didn't move.

Strike.

A second ball cut past him in a straight line across his chest.

Strike two.

Jacob noted the cocky smile on the catcher's face. He

squinted slightly, focusing his concentration, stared the pitcher right in the eye, and for an instant, the pitcher seemed captured in his gaze.

The ball came hurtling toward home plate and Jacob felt a terrible strength gather in his arms. He swung hard and fast, the bat cracking loudly as it connected to the ball.

Kids were yelling at him madly now, but their voices were distant, and he stood in place, unable to move as the ball lifted in a wide arc over the field, soaring higher and higher, the earth tilting oddly as it rose . . . or so it seemed to Jacob as his knees buckled and he collapsed to the ground. The next thing he knew, he was in the school infirmary, lying on a hospital bed, light streaming through the window, bright and engulfing, but a different light than the one before, mere ordinary sunlight rather than . . . some other kind.

"Jacob, do you know who I am?"

Jacob opened his eyes to see a man standing before him. He was dressed like a doctor, but his eyes were black pools, intense and unlighted.

"You have certain capabilities, Jacob," the man said. "But you shouldn't use them again. They're making you weak."

"I'm sorry," Jacob whispered.

"We'll find another way," the man told him.

As if on command, Jacob closed his eyes

"Jack! Jack!"

Jacob opened his eyes, and everything had changed. Time had gone by. Perhaps an hour. Perhaps an age. Now a different doctor was at his side, with different eyes, soft and full of care.

"I'm Dr. Benson. I'm sorry it took so long to get to

you." He smiled warmly. "Now, let's take a look at you," he said.

BEMENT, ILLINOIS, OCTOBER 8, 1962

Jesse Keys felt the wind in his hair. He was moving fast, pedaling rapidly, the bike speeding along. He felt his teenage legs pumping hard, but the bike seemed to float beneath him, surging ahead under its own power, as if it were alive.

He wheeled into the alley, braking slightly at the sight of an old truck. The truck was pulled over to the side, and as Jesse went around it, he noticed its painted sign, TRAVELING ATTRACTIONS.

A carnival van, Jesse thought. He pumped the pedals and glided past the cab of the truck, where a man sat behind the wheel. The carny turned to Jesse, nodded briefly, and offered a dark smile.

Jesse pumped again, harder this time, and the bike lurched ahead. From behind, he heard the engine of the truck, glanced back and saw that it was following him.

He slammed down on the pedals, his legs pumping fiercely now, but the truck continued to bear down upon him, the roar of its engine growing louder and louder as it closed in.

He wheeled around, and gasped as two orbs of light swept toward him from the far end of the alley. He glanced back, and the truck was gone, replaced by a third light. Frantically he whirled around, then back again, all the lights closing in. He could feel them like arrows, coming at him faster and faster, the light building to a blinding radiance that suddenly engulfed him and lifted him, the world falling away as his bike rolled down the alley, staggered and finally collapsed, riderless and abandoned, its front wheel spinning in the fading light.

WRIGHT-PATTERSON AFB, RESEARCH CENTER, OCTOBER 10, 1962

Owen sat at his desk. Marty and Howard stood in front of him, waiting to hear the results of President Kennedy's visit.

"He doesn't think our visitors are a threat," Owen sneered. "We have one month to prove to him that they are. If we don't, he'll shut us down and give our money to the space program." He sat back for a moment and considered the years of effort that were about to go up in smoke, the two sons he barely knew, the wife who'd become a drunk and a pill-popper he dreaded seeing at the end of the day.

"There's this couple," Marty began cautiously.

Owen looked at him. "Go on."

"Named Betty and Barney Hill," Marty said. "Encounters in 1961. On their way back from Niagara Falls. He's a postal clerk. She's a child welfare worker. Very solid people, both of them."

"Very solid people who claim they were taken aboard a craft," Howard added.

"Taken?" Owen asked. His eyes brightened. "What else?"

"They're being treated by hypnosis," Marty said. "Like they use on amnesia victims."

Owen nodded. "This could be what we're look-ing for."

Marty handed Owen a picture of the couple.

Owen's face soured. "No Negroes," he said as he handed it back. "That clouds the issue." He glanced from one man to the other. "Keep trying. There must be some-body else."

MASON, ILLINOIS, OCTOBER 16, 1962

Russell Keys pulled himself out from under the '56 Buick Special. His boss, Mr. Kennelworth, was already headed home for lunch. Over the past five years, he'd gotten the man's trust, proven that he wasn't a bum or a criminal, just a middle-aged guy who needed steady work, and was willing to stick to it.

He walked to the workbench, where he'd left a can of soda before climbing back under the Buick. He took a sip, and suddenly felt a searing blade of pain across his brow. He placed the can against his head, hoping the cold would help, and closed his eyes.

When he opened them again Jesse stood before him, tall and slender, as handsome at sixteen as Russell had been at the same age.

Russell felt his eyes grow moist. "Hey, Jesse," he said. "How did you know I was here?"

"I heard Mom talking to Bill. She said you'd gotten a job as close to us as you were legally allowed."

Russell looked at Jesse, a sad smile on his face. "You grew up."

Jesse was quiet for a moment, then seemed to remem-ber his purpose. "I've been reading these books where the government knows about flying saucers and they're afraid if they tell us there will be a panic." He drew the book from his pocket and handed it to Russell.

Russell glanced at the book. On the cover, two shadowy men faced an illustrator's version of a flying saucer. The title was equally melodramatic: CONSPIRACY— WHAT THE GOVERNMENT DOESN'T WANT YOU TO KNOW ABOUT UFOS.

Russell glanced up from the book and saw it in Jesse's eyes, an unbearable dread. "They started taking you again," he said.

"Yes."

Russell drew his son quickly into his arms.

For a time, Jesse remained in his father's embrace. Then, like one returned to his purpose, he pulled himself out of it. "It says it's mostly the Air Force that knows about this sort of thing," he said. "I was thinking. You were a pilot, so why don't we go talk to them?"

It was a naïve idea, Russell knew, the desperate hope of a frightened young boy who'd suddenly found his world dissolving around him. It was born of a need to find the truth, and Russell suddenly felt in league with his son, no less desperate to try anything, even the most far-fetched connection. "Yes, why don't we," he said with a quiet smile. "We can start with the son of my old bombardier. He's in the Air Force. We can go talk to him."

They'd done just that a few days later at Hill Air Force Base in Ogden, Utah, and with the result Russell could have easily predicted. Lieutenant Wylie had been nice enough, polite and open until the first talk of flying saucers. He'd tried to be indulgent after that, but Russell had seen the dreadful conclusion in his eyes, falling like a hammer: Wylie's certainty that Russell and Jesse Keyes were a father-and-son nutcase. Still, Wylie had kept listening, and even offered to make a report. But there would be no report, Russell knew. Nor should he have expected Wylie to react any differently than he had. The problem was that there were moments when your own loneliness and desperation made you briefly hope that something might change, that someone, somewhere would believe you. Jesse had roused that hope in him. But Wylie's response had returned him to reality, the sheer fact that only those who had truly been taken knew the truth, and that it was this anguished certainty that kept them in permanent isolation from their fellow man.

"He didn't believe us," Russell said now as he and Jesse sat in a local diner. "No one ever believes us."

"Then what can we do?" Jesse asked.

Russell started to answer, but the searing pain in his head abruptly returned, silencing him. It was like a fire moving through his brain, a blade of boiling steel. "I . . . I . . ." He felt the room close in and then expand, the walls tip and slide. The last thing he saw was Jesse reaching for him as he fell.

It was night when he awoke again. Jesse stood beside his bed, along with a tall man in a white coat. He could see the worry in his son's face.

"Tell me," he said to the doctor.

"You have a brain tumor," the doctor said. "In the frontal lobe."

"Can you take it out?"

The doctor shook his head. "I've never seen one quite like it," he said.

Jesse's face tightened, and Russell realized just how

deeply and permanently his son's world had changed. Fear was the ever-rising water Jesse swam in now, fear and bafflement and the overwhelming sense that the visible world was little more than a whirling montage, film on film, the flickering windows of a passing train.

"What is it, Jesse?" he asked. "What are you thinking?"

"That if you have a tumor, I may have one too," he said. He looked at the doctor. "Can you give me the same tests you just gave my dad?"

The doctor seemed to see Jesse's fear and desperation. "All right," he said.

The tests were conducted the same afternoon, the results displayed in stark black and white a short time later: two brains, each with identical spots at the front.

"Exactly the same size," the doctor said. He seemed hardly able to believe his own eyes. "And in exactly the same place."

GROOM LAKE, NEVADA, OCTOBER 19, 1962

Howard and Marty strolled alongside the vast gray hangar.

"One month," Howard said. "One month to find Owen something he can give to Kennedy."

Marty peered about glumly. "What are we going to do?"

"Do you remember Jacob Clarke?" Howard asked.

Marty stopped and looked at him, puzzled. "Sure. The only person I've ever seen that scared the colonel."

"The day after the . . . incident, the kid's brother drove to Montana," Howard said. "He had no business dealings there, no known friends. I did a little research.

Jacob Clarke disappeared right after Owen tried to nab him. The thing is, his mother still lives in Texas."

"So where's the kid?" Marty asked.

Howard smiled. "Turns out there's a school in Wallace, Montana, for 'special' kids. Run by a Dr. Ellen Greenspan."

Marty grinned back. "Let's find out what it is that scares the colonel so badly," he said

Owen listened carefully as Dr. Kreutz concluded his report.

"Seventy-six encounters with our little gray friends," the doctor said. "The nature of the encounters seems to be changing. We have stories of missing time. In a few cases, hypnotherapy has filled in those hours, and they appear to be abductions."

"Missing time," Owen said thoughtfully. "They're exposed during this time?"

"Probably."

"But in the past, exposure to more than ten minutes was fatal."

"So they've learned from their mistakes," Kreutz said. "Something has changed in their agenda. Or, if not in their overall view, certainly in their methodology. They are 'upping the ante' as I believe you say."

"Why now?" Owen asked.

"Why not?" Kreutz replied.

"Can we prove this?"

Kreutz shrugged.

"I need the most credible of these people," Owen said, almost to himself. "I need evidence that I can drop in Kennedy's lap before he pulls the plug."

GREENSPAN SCHOOL, WALLACE, MONTANA,
OCTOBER 21, 1962

Dr. Ellen Greenspan stepped into the corridor and
faced the two men who'd accompanied her to the classroom. "I don't know what else I can tell you," she said.
"He's gone."

Howard and Marty exchanged glances, then Howard
turned back to Dr. Greenspan. "Do you generally just let
your students go off like that without checking on them?"

"Of course not," Dr. Greenspan replied. "Two federal
officers came here. Their credentials looked every bit as
genuine as yours . . . shall I notify the police?"

Marty shook his head. "We'll take care of that."

"Maybe I'd better," Dr. Greenspan said. She looked at
Marty pointedly. "Do you generally just let two sets of
government agents do the same job without checking on
them?"

Marty bristled. "Dr. Greenspan, we are from the
United States Air Force. This is a matter of the utmost security. We need your cooperation."

Dr. Greenspan shrugged. "I'm doing my best."

The two officers stared at her silently for a moment,
then turned and headed down the corridor.

Dr. Greenspan waited until they were safely outside
the building, then walked quickly to her car, got in, then
turned to the backseat.

"Jacob?" she said softly.

The small body rustled under the blanket. "Yes."

"You're going to have to stay under there a little while
longer. I'm not sure I convinced our friends that you
were already gone."

She turned to the wheel, hit the ignition and pulled

away from the curb. In the rearview mirror, she saw an old brown Ford draw in behind her.

"Dr. Greenspan?" Jacob said.

"Yes, dear."

"Those men are following us."

"What do you want me to do?"

"Go a little bit farther. Don't worry. I won't let them hurt you."

Dr. Greenspan continued until she reached Highway 12, then headed west, the air darkening around her as night fell.

From behind the wheel of the old Ford, Marty watched Dr. Greenspan turn west on Highway 12 while Howard studied the map spread out on his lap.

"If she hits eighty-seven and turns north, she's heading for Canada," Howard said.

"I hate driving in the dark like this," Marty told him. "It makes me nervous."

Howard continued to study the map. "If she goes south, she could be heading for Billings."

"What if I hit a deer?" Marty said worriedly.

Howard looked at him sharply, then reached under his jacket and pulled out his pistol. "Pull up alongside," he said. "I'll shoot her before she gets going too fast. The kid won't get hurt."

Marty glanced at the pistol, then pressed down on the accelerator.

"Here they come," Dr. Greenspan said, her eyes fixed on the rearview mirror.

Jacob pulled free of the blanket. "On three, stop the car and then lie down flat on your seat. It'll be all right." He drew in a long breath. "One . . . two . . . three."

Dr. Greenspan slammed on the brakes and dove down against the front seat.

Jacob waited, listening as the men brought their car to a halt behind Dr. Greenspan's car, got out and came forward. He could hear the crunch of their feet as they approached. When he knew they were at his window, he turned his gaze upon them. "Look at me," he said.

HILL AIR FORCE BASE, OGDEN, UTAH, OCTOBER 22, 1962

Jesse knew the moment he entered Wylie's office that the man didn't want to see him, thought he was a nut, a chip off the old blockhead.

"I want you to put me in touch with whoever runs the UFO program," he said.

"There is no UFO program run by the US Air Force or any other branch of the government."

"I don't believe that," Jesse said. "My father's in a hospital," he continued. "He has a tumor in his brain."

"I'm sorry," Wylie said.

"The doctors found an identical tumor in my own head," Jesse said. "I believe the tumors were put there by . . ."

"Jesse, listen . . ."

"Put there," Jesse continued emphatically, "by whoever comes in those UFOs the Air Force knows nothing about."

Wylie got to his feet. "Jesse, you can't . . ."

"Our fathers fought together," Jesse said. "That ought to count for something. I don't expect you to believe me. I just expect you to help me."

Wylie stared at him for a moment, then released a long breath. "Okay, but if you ever say that you got this name from me, I'll deny it." He wrote the name on a piece of paper and handed it to Jesse.

"Thanks," Jesse said as he took it from his hand.

Outside he looked at the name, *Owen Crawford*.

Wylie had not actually said the name, but Jesse had noticed the dark veil that had fallen across his features as he'd handed him the card. Because of that, he'd expected to see a far more sinister figure than the one he observed from his hiding place in the bushes outside Crawford's house. From that limited perspective, Jesse could see only an ordinary man who had two sons and a wife who seemed at times unsteady on her feet.

He waited until Crawford left the house, then stepped before him, blocking his way to the car.

"My name is Jesse Keys," he said. "My father's name is Russell Keys. He was a pilot over Germany in the Second World War. He and I have both had encounters with UFOs. We have both been inside them." He waited for a response, but the man merely waited silently for him to go on.

"They have come for us," Jesse told him. "And they have taken us and they are going to come for us again."

The man nodded and Jesse could see that, unlike Wylie, he was seriously considering what he'd just been told. He smiled softly. "Take me to your father," he said.

On the way to the hospital, Jesse gave the man more details, so that by the time they stood at his father's bed, he was fully informed.

"Whatever they did to me killed all the members of my crew," Russell said. "I don't know why it didn't kill me. I tried to run from it. Then they started chasing Jesse. They seem more interested in him now, than in me."

Crawford nodded. "You're talking about the tumors?"

"They're not tumors," Russell answered. "They're something they put in our heads. In a place where the doctors say it can't be taken out."

Jesse shook his head disconsolately. "If someone put it in, then someone ought to be able to take it out."

"They can take it out," Crawford said with certainty. "But it would kill you." He smiled at Russell. "You have a very brave son, to be willing to go head-on at danger. To 'fly blind.' " He turned back to Jesse. "I'm impressed. Especially by your initiative. In finding me, I mean."

Jesse glanced at Russell and saw it in his father's eyes, the first hint of a dark suspicion.

"The fact is, I'm in command of a very secret group," Crawford said. "There are several of us. We pose as regular officers, but our real mission is to gather stories of people who have been . . . taken."

"So Lieutenant Wylie works for you?" Jesse blurted.

Crawford smiled. "Wylie, yes, he's one of ours."

Jesse looked at Russell and saw the silent command in his father's eyes, *Say nothing.*

"Jesse here did the right thing in coming to me," Owen told Russell. "You're right, they are after him. Because it's been passed down to him, whatever kept you from dying like the others. It's a trait that probably runs in your family. But you're not alone." He glanced back toward Jesse. "There must be others, too."

Russell saw a sinister flash in Crawford's eyes. "Jesse," he said. "I need to talk to Colonel Crawford in private."

Jesse looked at Russell apprehensively.

"Just for a moment," Russell added.

Jesse nodded, then reluctantly left the room.

Russell leveled his eyes on Crawford.

"You've seen them, haven't you?" he asked.

Crawford nodded.

"Don't hurt my son," Russell said.

Owen released a dismissive chuckle. "Hurt your son?"

"I know you want the . . . tumors," Russell said coolly. "The things they put in our heads. You can have mine, but not his. I want your word that you'll never do anything to my son."

"I would never hurt Jesse," Owen assured him.

"We have a deal then." Russell asked. "I'll give you the tumor."

Owen smiled. "Thank you for volunteering again to help your country."

TWO-LANE HIGHWAY, CANADA,
OCTOBER 24, 1962

Dr. Greenspan pulled over at the crossroads, got out and leaned against the side of the car. The plain seemed to stretch endlessly in all directions. The road was deserted, and for a moment, she enjoyed the stillness. In the backseat, Jacob slept soundlessly, a little boy, exhausted.

She glanced to the left, and saw a truck approach from the distance. She watched silently as it drew in upon her, then hurtled by, followed by a car that drew over to the side of the road and pulled up behind her.

"Jacob's in the backseat," she said, as Tom and Becky got out. "We were followed, but Jacob stopped them."

"Is he all right?" Becky asked.

"He's in a lot better shape than the men who followed us," Dr. Greenspan answered.

Tom glanced into the backseat of the car. "Thank you, Dr. Greenspan," he said. "From my family."

"He's a very special boy," Dr. Greenspan said. "Take care of him."

"There's a family he can live with," Tom told her. "An older couple. He'll be safe there until he's ready to go out on his own."

In the backseat, Jacob rustled slightly, then opened his eyes.

"Hey, Jake," Tom said.

HILL AIR FORCE BASE, OCTOBER 24, 1962

Owen and the wing commander stood at the end of the corridor as Jesse Keys was led toward the cell where, only a few hours earlier, Lieutenant Wylie had been taken.

"That's the boy," Owen said to the wing commander as the two MPs stopped before the cell door, each holding firmly to one of Jesse's arms. "I saw Lieutenant Wylie giving him specific figures. Numbers and types of planes, payloads." He shook his head as if appalled by such treachery. "At the time, I didn't realize what they were doing, but when the Defcon order came through . . ."

"You tricked me, you bastard," Jesse cried. He tried to break free of the MPs, but they held him in place. "You were supposed to help us and you tricked me."

Owen smiled coldly. "Kind of young for a spy."

"A spy!" Jesse shrieked. "What the hell are you talking about? What about the UFOs? What about the flying saucers?"

Owen shook his head, as if in astonishment at such lunacy. "He must be hopped up on something to give him the nerve to do what he did," he told the MPs. "I just pray to God he didn't manage to deliver his information."

The wing commander nodded. "I'll notify the Pentagon, let them know we have a breach."

"Where's my father?" Jesse demanded as the two MPs pushed him into the cell. "I want to see my father!"

Owen stared briefly into Jesse's desperate face. Then he turned, walked out of the brig and headed toward his car. Jesse Keys was now well in hand, he thought, absolutely secure. And as to Russell Keys, what did it matter? He was worth no more than the tumor that was about to be taken from him, no more than whatever it was the visitors had sunk into his brain.

Chapter Two

Russell rode silently in the backseat of the car, listening absently to the drone of the conversation, two soldiers discussing various trading commodities, cottonseed oil, poultry, their minds focused on ways to make a killing. Their world was ordinary, Russell thought, just a couple of guys trying to figure out some way to get ahead. He yearned to feel as they did, live an ordinary life, plan ahead in a world where the future was predictable, and nothing watched you from behind the overhanging stars.

"Here we are," the driver said as he brought the car to a halt in front of Utah Bob's Used Cars.

Russell pressed his face closer to the window. Utah Bob's was a run-of-the-mill auto lot presided over by a small trailer. There was nothing to distinguish it from a hundred others he'd seen.

"Okay, let's go," one of the soldiers said as he opened the door.

Russell got out of the car and, escorted by the two soldiers, walked to the trailer, opened the door and stepped into a state-of-the-art medical theater, all stainless steel and spotless tile and gleaming light. Two medical technicians stood waiting by an operating table. Along the walls, variously colored lights blinked efficiently from softly purring banks of dials and screens.

A doctor stepped forward from the group. "Good evening, Mr. Keys," he said. "I'm Dr. Kreutz and I want to thank you for letting us take a closer look at that tumor of yours."

Russell glanced about. "Where's Crawford?"

"Colonel Crawford has left this phase of his operation to me."

Russell's voice hardened. "I don't do anything until I talk to Crawford."

Dr. Kreutz's warm bedside manner chilled. "It doesn't appear to me that you're in any position to make demands, Mr. Keys."

Two armed soldiers suddenly appeared.

"Prep him," Dr. Kreutz said.

Russell summoned the last reserves of his strength, wheeled around and kicked one of the technicians just as the other swept forward and sank the needle into his side.

"Stay away from my boy," he cried, the words coming from him like something screamed from the stage as the curtain falls.

"All right, let's begin," Dr. Kreutz said.

The two soldiers lifted Russell onto the table while the surgeon waited.

"Good," Kreutz said. He looked at the surgeon. "Be very, very careful."

The surgeon nodded, then made an incision in Russell's forehead, peeled back the skin, and with a surgical saw, took off a large section of the skull. Then he took a probe from a metal tray and gently inserted it into Russell's brain. "There it is," he said after a moment.

Kreutz smiled as he watched the surgeon draw out a small, darkly glistening mass. "At last," he whispered. "Physical proof of . . ."

Suddenly the table rattled as Russell's body heaved and began to thrash about.

"Seizure," the surgeon cried. "Get me the retractor!" He glanced at the technician who stood beside him and saw that he was in some kind of trance. "What the hell's the matter with you?" he shouted.

The technician dropped to his knees and in a quick, slashing motion cut his own wrists, red torrents gushing from the severed veins.

Kreutz stared about, his face frozen in shock and terror. They were all moving like robots now, soldiers and technicians, responding to nothing but the inaudible commands inside their own heads. In stricken horror, he watched one soldier step up behind the surgeon and cut his throat. The other soldiers suddenly raised their rifles and fired in all directions, shooting mindlessly, filling the room with fiery sparks and thick smoke, until a bullet hit the oxygen tanks and a blast rocked the building and the trailer exploded in a single ball of flame.

HILL AIR FORCE BASE, OCTOBER 27, 1962

Jesse startled as an MP entered the cell.

"Come with us," one of them commanded.

"What's going on?" Jessie asked fearfully.

"We got orders to move you. That's all I know."

Jesse followed them down the corridor, then out of the building. He could see military personnel scattering in all directions, a frenzy of activity.

"What happened?" he asked.

"Russians shot down one of our U2s," the MP said as he ushered Jesse into another building. "You're being taken to a bomb shelter."

Inside, the room was pitch black, save for a single naked bulb.

The MP stared at Jesse threateningly, then stepped out of the room,

Jesse slumped down on the bare floor. He could hear the two MPs talking beyond the door.

"You hear what happened to Henderson and Slide? They were transporting some guy for a secret surgery, and the building blows up."

Jesse got to his feet, rushed to the door and pressed his ear against it.

"Killed the guy."

Jesse felt the world empty, all brightness dim. "Dad," he whispered as he slumped to the floor.

"Did you hear what happened?" Owen asked as Marty and Howard took their places before his desk.

"Happened, sir?" Howard asked tentatively.

"To Russell Keys."

Howard and Marty exchanged glances.

"Where the hell have you two been, anyway?" Owen demanded.

"Montana," Howard answered shakily.

"You told us to bring you a smoking gun, sir," Howard said. "We were following a lead and . . ."

"And?" Owen asked.

"Dead end," Howard answered.

Owen eyed Howard suspiciously.

"All right," Owen said. "You can go."

Howard and Marty headed for the door.

"Oh, Howard," Owen said suddenly. "Can you stay for just a minute, I need your help with something at home. Personal."

"Yes, sir," Howard said, then stepped over to Owen's desk as Marty left the room, closing the door behind him.

"Something going on with Marty?"

"How do you mean?"

"He feels to me like someone who's about to try an end run," Owen said. He looked at Howard sternly. "Keep an eye on him. I rely on you completely. You're my eyes and ears out there, Howard."

Howard came to attention. "Yes, sir."

LAS VEGAS, NEVADA, OCTOBER 28, 1962

Anne took the photo that showed her husband standing on the tarmac at Roswell and hurled it against the wall. Drunkenly, she tottered to Owen's desk. "Come out, come out, wherever you are," she sang blearily.

Outside the room, Eric and Sam huddled by the door, listening as their mother ransacked their father's office.

"I'm calling Dad," Eric said urgently.

"He'd just make things worse," Sam replied. "Let me try to talk to her first."

"Talk to her if you want to," Eric said dismissively. "But I'm calling Dad."

He rushed down the hallway as Sam opened the door to Owen's office and stepped inside.

"What are you looking for?" he asked his mother.

"Evidence," Anne said. Her head tilted slightly, like a vase about to topple.

"What do you mean?" Sam asked. "Evidence of what?"

Anne studied Sam's face briefly, then said, "You're your father's favorite. Do you know that? You always have been." She paused. "I hope that doesn't ruin your life." Something flashed in her eyes and she walked to the wall safe. "That's it. Your birthday," she said. "Seven twenty-eight fifty-one." She dialed the numbers.

The door opened, and she peered inside. The interior of the safe was bare save for a small piece of metal. She turned the metal in her hand, her gaze fixed on the odd markings that had been carved into it.

"What is it?" Sam asked.

"Part of your inheritance," Owen replied.

Sam turned to see his father standing massively in the doorway.

"Your mother and I need to talk," Owen said.

Sam obeyed immediately, though Anne hardly seemed to notice. She was peering at the metal. "My father told me about this. It came from a spaceship."

"Anne, your father had a drinking problem," Owen told her. "He imagined things." He took a small step toward her. "I'm an intelligence officer. If there were a spaceship, I would have heard about it. That piece of metal is from an experimental plane the Air Force is working on. I thought I'd get it mounted for Sam."

Anne's gaze remained riveted on the metal.

"Anne," Owen said, taking another small step toward her. "Do you remember the first time I took you riding?"

Anne gave no indication that she heard him. Her gaze remained fixed on the metal.

"I want it to be like that again for us," Owen said. He gently eased the artifact from her fingers and set it down on the desk, then took her hands and held them tenderly. "Anne, we have to do something about the pills and the liquor."

She nodded slowly, her eyes slightly glazed.

"There's a place in Minnesota. A six-week program. You can leave tonight. I'll have Howard drive you there."

She released a weary breath, and he saw that she had no will to resist him.

When Howard arrived Owen escorted Anne to the car, placed her on the passenger side, then gave Howard the necessary instructions and watched, waving sweetly to Anne, as they pulled away. *See you soon,* he thought coldly, *both of you.*

A short while later Owen pulled his car across Highway 50 and waited. Howard would have to drive down this narrow, lonely road to get to Minnesota with Anne. Finally, he saw the lights, heard the country music playing on the radio as Howard brought his car to a halt.

Owen got out and walked over to the driver's side, where Howard sat, looking at him quizzically.

For a moment, he stood by the door, reminding himself of what it was all for, and that these were not the first to be sacrificed. Then he drew the pistol from his back pocket and fired.

Howard slumped to the right, a small hole in his forehead.

"He was always a little simple, that one," Owen said to Anne.

She stared at him, her eyes wide with terror. Then she jerked open the door and rushed down the deserted road. Owen stood in place, drew her calmly into his sights, and pulled the trigger.

She fell like something from a great height, crumpling lifelessly to the ground. He picked her up, carried her back to the car, placed the gun in Howard's dead hand and pulled the trigger a third time.

The blast seemed to echo among the mutely watching stars.

HILL AIR FORCE BASE, BOMB SHELTER

Jesse lifted the model of a spacecraft he'd fashioned out of small strips of torn paper plate. He didn't know how the design came to him, only that it had risen spontaneously into his mind.

He looked about the bare shelter, the wall of sandbags that rose to the concrete ceiling, and thought of his father, how sad it would make him to know that his son was here, alone, imprisoned, waiting . . . for whatever they were going to do to him.

He heard a whispery rustle, like the sound of wind through winter corn, glanced toward the far wall and saw the upper line of sandbags move slightly, as if rocked by earthquake. But the floor of the bunker didn't move. The earth was still, and yet a single sandbag suddenly shifted, tilted forward and fell to the floor, lifting a wave of dust into the air.

Jesse leaped to his feet and stood, powerless and

terrified, as another sandbag toppled to the floor, then another, and another, bright shafts of light shooting into the dark bunker, so that the interior now glowed softly, the light building steadily as one by one, the sandbags fell, a wall crumbling to reveal a medical room, stainless steel tables ready and waiting, with four small creatures facing him, their slender arms dangling far below their waists, and a tall figure in between, lifting his arms in welcome to his son.

PART FOUR

Acid Tests

Chapter One

The gleaming government car came to a halt beside a vast field of corn. Other cars lined the road, and everywhere, excited onlookers were scrambling to get a view.

"I really appreciate you taking me along on this, sir," Eric Crawford said.

"I thought it was time you . . . came on board," Owen replied.

"You won't regret it," Eric assured him. He glanced about excitedly. "This could be really big."

Owen said nothing, less pleased than irritated by Eric's enthusiasm. It was not Eric he wanted by his side, but Sam, who'd gone in the opposite direction, and was now in journalism school. Sam had had the mind and the will and the sheer energy to keep up with him. Eric seemed able to do little more than ride precariously on his old man's churning wake.

"We get these reports two or three times a week,"

Owen said dismissively. "It'll probably be nothing of real interest. Mutilated cattle. Dancing lights."

Eric persisted. "But for you to come personally . . . there must be some reason."

Owen shrugged. "Well, these particular reports are a little better than usual," he admitted.

Owen got out and surveyed the scene before him, a vast field of corn that waved green and lush in the spring breeze. People were streaming in and out of the field, eager to get in on the big news. He paused briefly, then pushed his way through the crowd and the waving stalks of corn, until he came into a clearing where the corn had been leveled and lay flat to the ground as if pressed down by a huge invisible hand.

A helicopter landed a few minutes later, bearing two fresh young government agents.

"Colonel Crawford, I'm Toby Woodruff," the taller agent said. "Defense Department. This is Ted Olsen. He's with the NSA."

They were low-level officials, Owen knew, and their lack of seniority reflected the low esteem to which he and the project had sunk. It should have been President Nixon in that helicopter, he thought bitterly, not two snot-nosed kids.

Owen pointed to the still whirring copter. "Let's go for a ride—take a look from the air."

In the air over Indiana, the leveled corn assumed the pattern of a perfect circle.

"It's a landing field if I ever saw one," Owen said, suddenly confident that the reports had been accurate, that something very noteworthy had happened in this cornfield. "This has happened before. Here and in France and

Germany. But the scale of this. The intent. Look at that formation. It's like a runway."

"A landing strip?" Eric asked. "If it's a landing strip then maybe they're going to be . . ."

"Landing?" Owen interrupted.

"Look over here," Eric cried as the helicopter banked to the right.

Owen stared out the window, down into the undulating corn, where a different pattern emerged, not a vast landing strip at all, but a huge peace symbol, and the single greeting, "Howdy."

"Landing field?" Woodruff scoffed.

Owen gave him a lethal stare, but couldn't rid himself of the mockery he saw in Woodruff's eyes, the way this pasty-faced kid seemed to be looking at a man who'd wasted his life chasing phantoms. He'd once had the proof in his grasp, he thought angrily, but Russell Keys and his tumor had gone up, quite literally, in smoke. And as for his son? The way he just vanished from a bomb shelter? How could he have followed a trail that disappeared in a beam of light?

Owen stared down at the earth beneath him. Jesse Keys might well be down there somewhere, he thought, but it seemed to him that the way he'd been taken was the most powerful argument so far that whatever the visitors were doing, he didn't have a chance against them.

"I think your control over this project has ended," Woodruff said with a smirk.

CHICAGO, ILLINOIS, APRIL 11, 1970

The rocket lifted from the launch pad, and Jesse Keys held his breath as it rose into the empty blue. Men were headed for the moon. The small screen seemed hardly able to contain the magnitude of the achievement, the sheer awesome nature of what was happening.

Willie slouched on the ratty sofa next to Jesse. "Hey, man, what's the weirdest thing you ever saw?"

Jesse shrugged, his attention still riveted on the rising rocket.

Willie tapped a small portion of brown powder into a spoon and began to heat it with a match. "I think I saw a flying saucer once."

Jesse wrapped a belt around his arm. "I've been on a flying saucer. More than once. One time I saw my father. He'd been dead for four days."

Willie sucked the solution through a cotton ball and poured it into the syringe. "Okay, my man." He handed the syringe to Jesse. "That is really and truly weird." He slouched back on the sofa, watching dully as the rocket continued upward. "Waste of frigging time and money, going to the moon." His gaze drifted over to Jesse. "You know what I always admired about you? When we were in 'Nam, I mean? That you were the only officer who walked point. Every single mission, you walked point."

Jesse shrugged, his attention on the few balloons Willie had placed on the table before him. "How's my credit?"

"Sorry," Willie said.

"I saved your life, Willie."

"Two times, man," Willie said. "Now I'll save yours. Get straight, Jesse."

Jesse released a despairing laugh. "I don't want to get straight."

"I know what you want. You want to get taken to that other world." He grinned. "Well, that costs money."

"I'm good for it."

Willie shook his head. "No, you ain't. You're like every other junkie. That's why it's strictly cash and carry."

Jesse gave up and returned his attention to the television. The rocket had disappeared into the empty blue by then. Well, not exactly empty, he thought. He reached into his pocket and pulled out a folded piece of felt, his father's medals inside it. "These were my dad's," he said. He handed them to Willie. "They should be worth something, right?" He closed his eyes wearily. "At least one balloon."

HAYSPORT, ALASKA, APRIL 11, 1970

Sarah, a young graduate student, set the canned beans and coffee on the store's plain wooden counter while Dr. Powell, her boss and lead archeologist, went to see if the telegram had arrived. The other people in the store watched them warily, unused to strangers.

"You're the people digging in the woods, aren't you?" someone asked.

Powell looked at the little girl who'd suddenly come over to him. "Yes, we are," he told her. "And who are you?"

"Wendy."

"Nice to meet you, Wendy."

The little girl cocked her head, her large eyes filled with innocent curiosity. "What are you looking for?"

"We're trying to find out about the Indians who used to live up there," Powell answered. He glanced at the other people in the store, took in their curious resentment.

"That's nice," a man said. "You gonna be getting the hell out of there any time soon?"

Sarah stepped back from the counter and turned to the other people in the store. "Why are you all so hostile to us?" she asked. "We're not doing anything but digging up a few artifacts from . . ."

"Maybe some things should be left buried," the man said.

"Like what?" Powell challenged. "What have we dug up that should have been left buried?"

The man hesitated, as if at the mouth of a tomb. "Word is, a mummy."

LAS VEGAS, NEVADA, APRIL 14, 1970

Sam Crawford sat in his father's study, his attention focused on an article in the *Anchorage Daily News*. The headline read MUMMY FOUND IN TSIMSHIAN VILLAGE. An accompanying photograph showed a certain Dr. Powell standing inside what appeared to be an underground chamber, the walls of which were covered with strange markings.

Suddenly the door opened and his father stepped into the room.

"Eric has just started working on the project," Owen said. "Did he mention that?"

"He might have," Sam said indifferently.

"I'd hoped it would be you," Owen said. "But I guess you've decided to be a reporter."

"I won a prize," Sam said. "Best coverage of an on-campus event."

Owen was not impressed. "I'm offering you a chance to be a part of history, Sam."

"I'm not going to live your life over again for you, just so you can make up for your mistakes."

Owen's voice turned chilly. "I never made any mistakes."

"Chasing . . . little green men your whole life?" Sam replied.

"You don't know what you're talking about, Sam," Owen said angrily.

"Evidently no one else does, either," Sam said. "Because now you've lost your job." He smiled. "I read about it at college. How this guy Tom Clarke fooled you with that crop circle. That's what did it, right? That's why you lost your job?"

"I was wrong about the crop circle, but I'm not wrong about this," Owen said. "Something is about to happen. Maybe next week. Maybe in thirty years . . . but these visitors are moving toward something." He walked to the safe, opened it and drew out the artifact. "I found this at a crash site in New Mexico," he answered. "What crashed . . . it was nothing man made." He paused to let what he'd just said sink in. "There were five . . . beings, in that craft. Three of them were dead. The fourth one died under observation. The fifth one . . ." He glanced upward. "Everything I've done since I found the wreckage has been about trying to understand who they were and what they wanted." He paused a moment, then added, "That fifth one. The . . . survivor that was never accounted for. I tracked him down to a small town in Texas. He had formed a bond there with a young woman. The woman's name was Sally. She was Tom Clarke's mother. The man who made the phony crop circle in order to destroy me. She had another son, as well. Named Jacob." He looked at Sam pointedly. "A strange boy. Not much emotion. I looked into this boy's eyes, Sam, and I saw . . . all my memories and all my fears . . . more than that . . . I saw them add up. Do you understand?"

Sam shook his head.

"I saw my own death, Sam," Owen said. "I saw how I would die."

HAYSPORT, ALASKA, APRIL 16, 1970

Powell came out of the store and handed Sarah the envelope. "Here are the test results. The body is only around six years old."

"Well, we knew it wasn't a mummy, no matter what the locals wanted to call it," Sarah said.

"I also got a letter from the people at the university," Powell told her. "The glyphs on the wall are indecipherable. No one in the language department has a clue as to what they mean or who could have put them there."

"Excuse me, Dr. Powell."

Powell turned to see a young man with long hair.

"My name is Sam Crawford," the man said. "I'm a journalism student at UC Berkeley. I was hoping to talk to you about your dig."

Powell shook his head. "I'm afraid our story's not going to turn out to be quite as exciting as you'd hoped."

"What do you make of the writings you found on the walls of the burial chamber?"

"They're no language we've been able to identify," Powell answered. "Probably no more real than our 'mummy.' And the 'mummy' . . . was only a few years old. Which makes our dig a crime scene."

Sheriff Kerby arrived at the dig a few minutes later. "Okay, so where's the body?" he asked.

"This way," Powell said.

At the tent, Powell opened the entrance flap and motioned the sheriff and Sam inside the chamber.

Sam came in just behind Sheriff Kerby, his eyes combing the interior of the tent, mainly a long table where the body had been laid out, but which was now bare.

"It's gone," Powell said, thunderstruck. He turned to Kerby. "The body's gone."

"Well," Kerby said sarcastically, "it didn't just get up and walk away now, did it? I want you and this whole bunch up and out of here by tomorrow morning."

Something caught Sam's eye. "Dr. Powell, there's something over here you ought to see."

"What?" Kerby asked.

Sam pointed to a distinct pattern on the inside of the tent, a four-fingered handprint, each finger with an extra joint.

Kerby stared at the print for a long moment, then turned to face Powell menacingly. His lips parted, but before he could speak, a patrol car ground to a halt just beyond the entrance of the tent. A woman sat inside, her gaze wild, desperate. "Wendy's missing," she cried. "She went into the woods behind the store and . . ."

"It's all right, Louise," Kerby told her. "Kids wander off all the time. We find them."

"Not in these woods," Louise said darkly.

"Don't you worry," Kerby said reassuringly. "We took care of that problem a long time ago."

Louise stared at him. "Do you really believe that, Kerby?"

CHICAGO, ILLINOIS, APRIL 17, 1970

Jesse Keys was not sure how he'd ended up in the Veterans Hospital, but only that the last surge of the drug had taken him far, far away, perhaps to the very rim of life, where things shimmered briefly then went dark.

For the last few days, he'd stayed in the ward, talking to three old vets, listening to their war stories. But it was a nurse named Amelia who'd cheered him, Amelia who'd seemed always to be there when he needed something, and who sat beside him now, the two of them together on the riverbank, eating hot dogs and watching a clown blow bubbles into the warm spring air while kids frolicked around him.

"Beautiful, aren't they?" Amelia asked.

"Yeah, those kids look really happy," Jesse said.

A few feet away, the bubbleman took a long wand and blew a bubble that seemed big enough to capture a small child and lift it up and up into the vast forever.

Jesse watched with horror as the bubbleman turned slowly, his face now clearly visible, a thin, emaciated face, with flinty eyes.

"The carny," Jesse whispered.

"What?" Amelia asked.

Jesse leaped to his feet. "No!" he cried. He dashed forward, charged toward the bubbleman and knocked him to the ground. "What do you want?" he screamed. "Why do you keep taking me?"

Amelia rushed up behind him and pulled him back. "Stop it, Jesse!" she cried.

The bubbleman looked directly into Jesse's eyes, and suddenly the features of the carny vanished into another face, tired, burned out, a street performer at the end of his rope.

Jesse released him and stepped away, Amelia at his side, her arm in his.

"You can tell me," she said as she gently drew him away.

Jesse nodded. "Maybe someday I can explain," he said.

HAYSPORT, ALASKA, APRIL 17, 1970

Sam stood alone in the woods. Several hours before, Powell had handed out whistles and led Sarah and several other people who worked at the dig into the woods to search for Wendy. Since then he'd heard that two of the searchers were now missing. It was as if the woods had swallowed them up.

He looked at the whistle, then at the engulfing woods around him. Even in daylight, the ground was beneath a veil of deep shadow, every sound frightening. He moved forward, determined to continue the search. Gradually the woods thinned around him, and he finally emerged into a meadow where waist-high grass rippled in the wind. He looked up. The sky was still faintly blue, but the light was fading. There was no choice but to return to the camp.

It was deserted when he reached it, all the others still moving deeper into the woods or making their way back.

First he walked to the tent where the body had been placed, examined the bare table, then the floor beneath, grassy, and covered with leaves. Nothing had been touched, not any other artifact from the dig, only the body. And nothing had been left behind, no bit of metal like the one his father had taken from the safe. Only the muddy print of a four-fingered hand.

For a time he studied the print, the extra joint of each finger. It was not a human hand, of course, and the more the studied it, the more he began to wonder if all the crackpot theories, all the weird sightings, all the fantastic tales were true.

He strode out of the tent and over to the earthen chamber where the body had been found. The strange markings he'd seen on the piece of metal his father had kept for so many years were clearly visible on the wall of the chamber. Powell had told him that they were not part of any human language. Nor could they be, Sam thought now. They weren't letters, as far as he could tell, nor numbers, nor drawings of any kind. Perhaps they were part of a funeral rite, but if so, it was not a human being who'd been buried here.

Suddenly he heard a rustling from the surrounding woods. He glanced about, looking for movement within the shadowy forest. His fear spiked, and he felt its edge like a finger down his spine. He imagined that finger with four joints, amazed at how quickly he'd absorbed his father's dread, the sense that they were . . . out there . . . waiting . . . watching . . . that no one was alone.

The rustling sounded again.

Sam wheeled around and thought he saw a shadow pass somewhere deep in the woods. He peered out into the tangled green where a figure suddenly staggered out of the shadows: Sarah, caked with mud, in tatters, her eyes staring wildly, her mouth wide open in a scream.

Chapter Two

CHICAGO, ILLINOIS, APRIL 17, 1970

Jesse felt Amelia's arm in his and it seemed to him that with each touch, some part of him gave way. To the right, the Great Lake swept northward and tumbled over the horizon.

"What happened?" she asked. "In the war, I mean." She stopped and looked him dead in the eye. "I heard you say to one of the other men that you thought you couldn't get hurt."

She had never approached him so directly, and Jesse knew he could not put her off any longer. "No, I *knew* I couldn't be hurt." He drew in a deep breath, like a swimmer preparing for a long dive. "We were in Quang Ngai Province. We walked into a trap. Knowing what I knew, knowing I was safe, I dared them. I said, 'Go ahead, take me! Take me out of this one.' " His eyes filled with wonder.

"And they did. They got me out. And they let twenty-seven men from my unit who were there with me die."

Amelia looked at him quizzically. "Who are 'they,' Jesse?"

He shook his head. "I don't know."

"Don't know, or won't tell me?"

"A little of both, I guess."

Amelia didn't press the issue. "Then I guess I'll just have to add that to the list."

"What list?"

"The list of things you're going to tell me someday," she said as she urged him forward once again.

He smiled and touched her hair. "Will you marry me, Amelia?" he asked.

She smiled and nodded.

HAYSPORT, ALASKA, APRIL 17, 1970

After depositing Sarah into safe hands, Sam returned to the site of the dig, drawn by a terrible curiosity. Taut with fear, he shined his light into the chamber, but saw nothing but a pile of rocks. The chamber was just as Powell and the others had left it, a pit nothing could come out of, save through the single entry where Sam stood.

He lowered himself into the chamber, moved past the altar, and faced the wall of rocks wedged in and around other rocks, almost like the stone walls of New England. He pulled one rock out, then another and another, until the rocks began to fall away, dropping to the floor of the chamber.

There it was.

He looked into the large shaft dug out of the ground behind the rock wall. He shined his light into the shaft, but the darkness rose solidly, blocking the beam.

Sam pulled himself into the shaft and the darkness closed in around him. It was thick and dense, and he felt a suffocating airlessness, as if the oxygen were growing thinner and thinner as he continued to drag himself deeper into the mouth of the shaft.

He was moving upward now, the floor of the shaft rising oddly, inching him toward the surface, where he could see the beam of his flashlight touch the open air. He followed the beam and pulled himself to the surface, rising out of the shaft like a man out of a foxhole.

He got to his feet and peered around.

And there it was—the "mummy"—laid out ceremoniously on a bed of leaves.

Sam knelt down and began to unravel the shroud that concealed the face. Shred by tattered shred, he unwound the shroud. The outline of the head emerged first, taking shape as he drew back the layers of cloth from a decidedly unhuman pear-shaped head and almond eyes.

"Proof," Sam whispered.

A sound, little more than a rustle of leaves.

Sam scrambled away, hid among the trees and waited.

At first he saw nothing, then a figure emerged from the woods, moved slowly to the body and brought it tenderly into its arms, weeping softly as its four-fingered hand stroked the creature's long-dead face.

Then, suddenly, the mysterious visitor turned and peered directly into Sam's eyes. Sam felt himself locked in the visitor's gaze, helpless, frozen, until a key turned, releasing him, and he fell into an engulfing darkness.

"Are you all right?"

Sam's eyes opened and he looked around in surprise.

An old man knelt over him.

"At first I thought you might be dead," the man said.

"Who are you?'" Sam asked.

"Name's Leo," the man said.

Sam sat up quickly, watching the man closely.

"My daughter's name was Nadine," the man said, his face in a curious trance, the story coming from him as if from a puppet. "She'd have been forty this year." He seemed to be looking into his past, watching it from afar. "She went off walking one night, wanted to get a better look at these strange lights we got up here. She come back a day and a half later. No idea where she'd been or what had happened to her." The old man stopped briefly, then continued, like a doll whose string had wound down, but been pulled again, loosening his tongue. "It was about four months after that she begun to show. Had twins in early fifty-nine. Died giving life to them. It was Dr. Shilling delivered them and he told me that Nadine saw her babies before she died." The string wound down and was pulled again. "I took the boys. Named them Larry and Lester. Strange boys. Grew too fast. Looked sixteen by the time they was eight. Had a way of peering inside a fellow. Spooked people doing that, so we moved out to the woods."

Sam heard another rustling in the trees, turned and saw Kerby emerge from the shadowy forest.

"Evening, fellas," Kerby said. He placed his hand firmly on Leo's shoulder.

The old man gave no response, but only faced Sam silently, a doll whose string had broken on the final pull.

Kerby looked at Sam. "You and I are going to go for a drive." He drew the the pistol. "Let's go."

On the drive Sam knew he was going to die. He knew because Kerby had brought a deputy along with him, but the car was not a police car. And he knew because Kerby talked freely, even boastfully, about his other crimes.

"Yes, I killed one of the twins," he said. He shook his head. "Larry was the worse of the two. He took to trying his 'abilities' when he was about sixteen. Did Leo mention that? All the dead dogs and cattle? The things he'd do to hunters in the woods." He glanced back to where Sam sat, the deputy beside him, in the backseat. "This town runs on hunting season and for close to ten years, we couldn't pay folks to go into our woods."

Sam glanced at the deputy, who was mindlessly humming "Jeanie with the Light Brown Hair."

"It's my job to keep the town safe," Kerby went on, "and that boy was a menace. I tried to talk some sense into him but . . ."

The deputy leaned forward and clapped his hand on Kerby's shoulder. "He come at you, Kerby. It's not like you had a choice."

"Maybe so," Kerby said. "Anyway, I buried him under a tree. How he wound up in that burial pit, wrapped up like that . . ."

The deputy's hand remained on Kerby. "You're just too kindhearted is what's your problem," he said.

"Maybe so," Kerby said again.

It was now or never, Sam thought. He steeled himself for an instant, then reached past the deputy, opened the door and lunged forward, knocking him out onto the road, then following after him, the two rolling in the gravel as Kerby slammed on his brakes and brought the car to a skidding halt.

Sam leaped to his feet, glanced about desperately, then bolted into the woods. He could hear Kerby and the deputy in pursuit, thrashing through the undergrowth like angry bulls. If they caught him, there'd be no more driving down the road. They would kill him where he stood.

He ran and ran, and the woods seemed to thicken around him, branches slapping at his face, the undergrowth clutching at his shoes and pants like tiny, entangling arms.

A figure suddenly darted in front of him, blocking his path. At first he thought it must be Kerby or the deputy, but he couldn't imagine how either of them could have managed to circle around and get in front of him.

He squinted hard, and the figure took shape, the head slightly pear-shaped, the arms elongated, and yet incontestably human.

"Can you . . . come with me?" Lester asked.

They walked together, through the trees, into the ever-more entangling forest.

Then the forest suddenly drew back, and he stood in a clearing where a small cabin rose in the distance, its lights blinking out of the darkness. At the door, Lester stepped back and motioned Sam inside, where he saw a little girl lying on a couch.

"She's hurt bad," Lester said as they moved toward the cabin. "Must have tried to climb a tree to see where she was and she fell. Her leg's broke in a couple of places."

Sam went over to her. She was breathing slowly, her eyes closed.

"I sneak over and leave food," Lester said. "I do it when she's asleep, 'cause I don't want her to look at me."

"What happens when people look at you?" Sam asked.

"I don't know exactly," Lester answered. "When my

brother and I were kids, we used to just scare folks mostly . . . but then it got worse. It's nothing I can stop from happening . . . I think . . . people look at us . . . they see too much."

"All their memories and all their fears," Sam said, almost to himself.

Lester nodded. "I guess you could say that."

Sam glanced about the room, his eyes lighting on another body laid out on a blanket, the unwrapped corpse of Lester's brother, Larry.

"Why'd you wrap your brother up like that?" Sam asked.

"My brother and I, sometimes we would draw in this weird language. We never knew what it meant, but I thought maybe if I wrapped him up like that, put him somewhere special with all that writing all around him then . . ."

"Maybe he'd come back to life."

"Kind of foolish, huh?"

"No, Lester," Sam said. "I don't think that's foolish at all."

Lester shook his head. "I never meant to hurt any of those people that dug up the grave. I was just trying to get help for the little girl." He seemed almost to shudder at the way people reacted to him. "And the lady, the one that was coming out of the grave . . . I only looked at her for a second."

"She's going to be fine," Sam assured him.

Lester looked at Sam with childlike helplessness. "My . . . whatever it is I do to people . . . I guess it got stronger after Larry left . . . I never really wanted anyone to get hurt."

Sam's gaze drifted toward the floor, where he suddenly

noticed spots of blood. "You're hurt too," he said to Lester. "We've got to get you to a doctor."

Lester shook his head determinedly. "No, just worry about the little girl."

Sam glanced back at her.

She stirred briefly, then opened her eyes.

"Hi," Sam said softly.

"Hi," the little girl said. "Are you the one who's been bringing me food?"

"No, sweetheart. What's your name?

"Wendy."

"Well, you're going to be just fine, Wendy."

Wendy looked at Lester. "Is that him? I want to say thanks."

Lester moved quickly into the shadows.

"Not now," Sam said, blocking her view of Lester. "Listen, I'm gonna pick you up. It might hurt a little. Can you be brave?"

Wendy nodded.

Sam reached to lift Wendy into his arms, and as he did so, a rock shattered one of the cabin windows.

"Bring him out, Lester," someone cried from beyond the window.

Sam crouched at the window, lifted his head slightly and peered out. In the clearing, a group of local people held torches while others emptied cans of gasoline all around the cabin.

"The little girl is in here," Sam shouted. He saw Wendy's mother step out of the crowd.

"Stop pouring the gas," she cried. "Wendy's in there."

"I'm coming out with the girl," Sam shouted. He looked at Wendy. "You ready, honey?"

Wendy nodded.

Sam drew her into his arms and headed for the door.

Lester stepped away, but not before Wendy caught him in her eye.

"Mister?" she said sweetly. "Thank you."

Lester touched her face with his strange hand. "You're welcome," he said.

Wendy's mother rushed forward as Sam came out of the cabin.

"Thank God," she cried, her eyes suddenly fixed on Wendy's injured leg.

"Did he do this to you?" she asked her.

"No, Mommy," Wendy replied. "I fell out of a tree."

A man stepped up to Louise. "Get Wendy back to the car," he told her. "We're going to finish this once and for all."

Sam felt a level of fear he'd never experienced before. He'd been surrounded like this, lost and helpless and utterly misunderstood . . . as Lester was.

"Why don't you let me take it from here."

The familiar voice came from out of the darkness, and Sam suddenly realized it was his brother, Eric.

Eric stepped forward, Kerby and the deputy and Dr. Shilling just behind him, keeping their pace with his, all three of them moving at Eric's command.

"What are you doing here, Eric?" Sam asked.

Eric lifted the copy of the Anchorage newspaper Sam had left in Las Vegas. "You weren't very hard to follow, Sam," he said. "And from everything the sheriff and Dr. Shilling have been telling me, you've got something here that's important to the project." He looked at Sam pointedly. "I'm here to keep you from doing anything . . . unfortunate."

Sam's face grew taut. "There's nothing here for you, Eric."

Eric smiled. "I think I'd like to see for myself." He stepped toward the cabin, but Sam blocked his way.

"You can't go in there," Sam told him firmly.

"You're going to stop me?" Eric said mockingly.

"You could be killed, Eric."

Eric released a mirthless chuckle. "You care about me? Sam, I'm touched."

Sam grabbed his arm. "I'm not going to let you take him."

"Get your hand off me," Eric snapped, pulling his arm away.

Suddenly Leo pushed his way out of the crowd and ran toward the house.

A man stopped him, a Zippo lighter in his hand. "Step back, Leo. We're going to put Lester out of his misery." He lit the lighter. "Stand back," he said, then tossed the lighter to the ground.

The porch ignited, flames rising greedily up the walls and supporting posts. Sam wheeled around and charged through the flames and into the cabin where Lester stood in the far corner, Larry in his arms.

A wall of flame separated him from Lester, but through that wall, Sam could see it playing like a home movie in the bottomless pools of Lester's two almond eyes: Eric as a little boy, running through the house, then his mother, spilling drinks over his brother's homework. Suddenly he was in his father's study, watching helplessly as his mother ransacked it, then again years later, his father standing at the safe, drawing something out of it, a small piece of metal.

He screamed, as all his memories flooded over him

in a sea of anguish, and suddenly he felt himself hurled back from the past, returned to the cabin in time to watch helplessly as Lester stepped into the flames, his own death now burning in him, reducing him to ash.

Chapter Three

LAS VEGAS, NEVADA, 1970

Owen had imagined happiness as such a simple thing, just the feel of his granddaughter in his arms, the way her large eyes seemed to study him, as if already yearning for his secret.

"Come on, Mary, say 'Grandpa,' " he said quietly.

"She's only a week old," Julie told him.

Owen laughed. "Of course." He looked at the baby tenderly. "I wish Sam . . ."

"Right," Eric blurted stiffly. He reached out and pulled Mary from his father's caress and handed her to his wife. "Julie, could you give Dad and me a minute?"

Julie rose, holding Mary to her chest, and left the room like an obedient soldier summarily dismissed.

"I bring my baby over to you, and you think about Sam," Eric said sourly.

"I'm worried about him," Owen explained. "I haven't heard a word from him since he left."

"You won't be hearing from him anymore, Dad."

Owen stared at Eric darkly. "What are you talking about?"

"Sam is dead," Eric told him brutally.

Owen felt his soul empty.

Eric's voice was as cruel as his eyes. "He went trying to find proof that would destroy you. He died trying to bring you down. He hated you that much."

Owen sucked in a cold breath. He felt something close inside him, the last open chamber of his heart.

"You never told me any of the things you told Sam . . . I would never have broken your trust and you never once gave it to me."

Owen slumped forward, then reared back, the room closing in upon him.

"Is this what you saw, Dad?" Eric taunted him.

Owen clutched his left arm. He felt one side of his face draw down, pain exploding everywhere, shooting tongues of fire through every vein and artery.

"Is this what you saw in that kid's eyes?" Eric sneered.

Owen dropped to his knees.

Eric towered above him, staring down in spiteful triumph. "A stroke, right? The moment of your death? That's why you always hated me. You knew I was the last thing you'd ever see."

In the fading light, as the curtain fell, Owen realized that it had all come to nothing, all his cruelty and lies, his long train of crimes. He had sown the wind, and reaped the whirlwind of a son who would do no better, reach no higher wisdom, find no better life than his own sorry round of days. Oh, he had made a mark in the world, he thought as he tumbled forward at Eric's feet, but it was only the mark of Cain.

K.G.B. TECHNOLOGIES, PALO ALTO, CALIFORNIA, APRIL 20, 1970

Tom and Becky Clarke stopped at the receptionist's desk. "We're here to see Jack Barlowe," Becky said.

A moment later, he stepped out into the room, a man who'd named himself Jack Barlowe, though Jacob's features remained unmistakable. He was twenty-eight years old now, but he looked much older, already frail and losing his hair.

"My, God, Jake," Becky breathed.

Jacob drew Becky into his arms, held her briefly, then did the same to Tom.

They sat down on a bench in the lobby.

"I read about your crop circle," Jacob said. "The peace sign. Very funny."

Tom smiled. "Not to Owen Crawford." The smile widened triumphantly. "I wanted him to know he'd messed with a good Texas family."

Becky touched Jacob's face. "We thought with him gone, we could risk coming to see you."

Jacob shifted the subject from himself. "How's Mom?"

"Still feisty," Becky replied. She glanced toward the reception desk, noticed how the woman behind it glanced away. "That woman, the receptionist."

"Carol," Jacob said.

Becky placed a finger at each side of her head. "I'm sensing something," she said, pretending psychic powers.

"Really?" Jacob said with a shy smile.

Becky looked at him knowingly. "So, Jake, how long have you been going out with her?"

GROOM LAKE FACILITY, APRIL 20, 1970

Eric stared contemptuously at the new sign that adorned his father's old office. *Lt. Colonel Marty Erikson.*

"Eric, thanks for coming," Marty said as Eric came through the door.

Eric gave Marty one of his father's smiles. "You're the boss."

"How's the new baby?"

"Fine," Eric said, faking a bright cheerfulness. "Mary gets cuter every day."

Marty's tone turned serious.

"Listen, Eric," he began, "I've got to say something here. This kind of thing has a way of coming out and I just want to clear the air between you and me about it." He paused briefly, then went on. "I was always, not to speak ill of the dead, I was always a little afraid of your father."

"He had that way about him."

"Yes, he did," Marty said. "You remember my friend Howard Bowen?"

"He was with my mother when she died."

"That night, Howard told me he was driving your mother to a clinic in Minnesota," Marty said. "For rehab."

"Well, Howard and my mother were . . . close."

"That's not the way I remember it," Marty said coolly. "Your dad took a car from the motor pool that night. When he returned it, the car had four hundred and seventeen new miles on it."

Eric lifted his head slightly, as if to receive a blow.

"That's the exact round-trip distance from Groom Lake to the spot where Howard and your mother were killed." Marty waited for Eric to respond, then continued when he didn't. "They were both killed with Howard's service revolver. He lost that revolver two days before he died. I remember him asking me if I'd seen it. He said he'd left it in his desk drawer and it just disappeared."

Eric felt it all come together, his father's work, his mother's murder. Almost to himself, he said, "She was drinking a lot. Threatening to expose his work."

Marty did not deny it, and in that lack of response, Eric felt that he'd finally reached the truth not only of what had happened to his mother, but also what had to happen next. "Thank you for telling me this, Marty," he said. "I appreciate it."

Eric left the office, but only after shaking Marty's hand with a hearty flourish.

It didn't take long to decide how to do it, and by nightfall, Eric had chosen the two MPs and put them in position.

He stepped out of the shadows when Marty approached. Once again, he offered his father's smile.

"I checked the motor pool records, Marty," he said. "The night my mother was killed, you checked out that car, not my father. That makes you an accomplice. Accessory before the fact."

Marty stared at him, stunned.

Eric motioned the two MPs forward. "These men will hand you over to the civilian authorities in Carson City," he added. "I'm sure your fear of my father will be taken into account, as well as your service record."

"And you'll be stepping up to take over the project," Marty said.

Eric nodded. "Who better?"

"The acorn doesn't fall far, does it?"

Eric's smile lay like a dagger across his lips. "Not this time, no."

seen so close. He told that mother two days before he
died, I remember that seeing me as a brother to the self
bedded, it naturally driven into near disappeared."

"He felt it all come together," he thought, work the
mottoed number. Anyone to himself, he said. "She was
thinking a lot. She may appease his work..."

Maybe did not deny it, word in that indeed together.
But felt that he'd finally reached the truth not only of
what had happened to his mother, but also what had to
happen next. "Thank you for telling me this, Miguel," he
said. "I appreciate it."

The father's voice, but with other shaking, started, and
with a heavy, he said...

"I didn't take long to decide how to do it, and by
Monday I'd had chosen the Vidal Espinal portiere in the
position..."

"He vanished but he the shadows when Miguel appeared. Once again, he offered his father's smile."

"I checked the motor pool records. Many," he said.
"On the night my mother was killed, you drove her out that
year, not my father. That makes you an accomplice. Accessory before the fact..."

Many stared at him, stunned...

Felt mediated, the two Miguel forward. "These men will
stand with over to the our district authorities in Calcutta City,
he added. "The statement is of of my father will be taken
into account, as well as your service record."

"And you may stop paying up a stake over the project,"
Marco said.

Tax nodded. "Who knew?"

"The account doesn't fall far down..."

"I'm a quite heavy like a supple motive in this line. Not this
time, no."

PART FIVE

Maintenance

Chapter One

Jacob Clarke felt his boyhood return to him as the old Pacer joggled along the dirt road that led to his mother's house. His brother Tom was at the wheel, and in the backseat, Carol, his wife, and their seven-year-old daughter, Lisa. A warmth came from each of them, one that reached out and touched him, palpable as a hand. A normal life, he thought. A normal life was a treasure beyond price, a life where things came and lingered for a time, then passed away according to the iron laws of earth. A life punctuated by the usual triumphs and misfortunes, within a fixed range both predictable and unpredictable, a life where darkness brought only night, and light brought only morning. It was all he wanted or had ever wanted, and briefly, as he closed in upon the old home place, he thought it might actually lie within his grasp.

"What are you listening to?" Tom asked cheerfully.

"What?" Jacob said.

"I was talking to Lisa," Tom said. He glanced toward the backseat, where Jacob's daughter sat, listening to a first-generation Walkman.

Carol laughed. "She can't hear you," she said, pointing to the headphones.

Tom mouthed the words slowly and with maximum expansion.

"The Ramones," Lisa answered brightly.

Tom turned back to the road and nodded toward the old farmhouse as it came into view

"Look like you remember it?" he asked.

Jacob nodded. "Exactly. It doesn't change much."

Once they parked, Jacob got out of the car and stared silently at the house. The years had taken their toll, as time . . . and experience . . . always did. It needed paint and new screens for the windows and the rusty gutters no doubt leaked badly. It looked like a thousand other run-down houses, and thus gave no hint of the unearthly things that had happened in its rooms, or within the old, tumbledown shed that still stood in the distance, or beneath the trees that edged its dusty grounds.

Becky rushed out of the house, the screen door slapping closed behind her, ran over to Jacob and hugged him fiercely.

"Mom's just waking up," she said. She looked at Carol. "I'm glad you guys came. Mom really wanted to see Lisa before . . ."

"I know," Carol said softly.

Sally lay in her bed, hooked up to an oxygen machine.

Jacob had never seen her this way, so wasted, and for a moment it left him unable to speak, so that he only stared at her, this woman now grown old and withered, but who'd once been so bold and determined, built "contactors" and yearned with all her heart to speak with other worlds.

"You grew up nice," Sally said weakly, her voice rattling with each word. "You all right?"

Jacob nodded.

She smiled, then closed her eyes for a moment, as if the nearness of her son after so many years was a pressure she could hardly bear. When she opened them again, Carol stood before her, Lisa huddled shyly at her mother's side

"Mom, this is my wife, Carol," Jacob told her. "And this is Lisa, your granddaughter."

Sally struggled to rise, urging herself up in bed. "Lisa, let me look at you," she said.

Lisa stepped up to her grandmother's bed.

"Say hello," Jacob told her.

"Hello, Grandma," Lisa said.

Sally peered into Lisa's face, and for a moment seemed to return to the past. "She has your father's eyes," she said to Jacob.

Jacob took Sally's hand, and watched as she lifted her eyes upward longingly, still searching desperately for the one who'd appeared that night so long ago, lingered briefly, then vanished. The effort appeared to exhaust her, and she sank back down into the rumpled bed.

"She never stops thinking about him, does she?" Jacob said later that night as he sat in the kitchen with Tom.

"I know who he was, you know," Tom said.

Jacob looked at him doubtfully.

"Back in the Cold War, the government experimented with soldiers," Tom explained. "It's all in documents you can get with the Freedom of Information Act. They were giving drugs to soldiers. I think your dad was one of them. He escaped from an Army base in Roswell. Owen Crawford came to get him." He leaned forward earnestly. "Your 'abilities' came from your father, Jake. From whatever drugs they gave him. Not because he came from outer space." His voice grew more grave. "The problem is, they're doing it again, with civilians this time. Same experiments. Mind control. Processing. Some of these people, they think they've been abducted by aliens, but that's just what the government wants them to believe."

"Alien abduction as a cover story?" Jacob asked skeptically. "It seems a little far-fetched, Tom." He drew in a cautious breath. "I mean . . ."

Just then Becky came into the room. "Mom's in a lot of pain," she said. "The morphine doesn't seem to be helping."

Jacob got to his feet and rushed to his mother's side. He took her hand and held it softly. "It's all right, Mom. It's all right."

Sally looked at him wearily. "I'm going now, aren't I?"

"Soon," Jacob answered.

"I want to sit up a little," Sally said weakly.

Jacob carefully supported her back as she rose, then fluffed the pillow behind her, before gently placing his hand on her brow. Then he concentrated on the vision, determined to bring it to her during these final seconds of her life. He knew the vision was forming as her eyes filled with wonder. She reached for her ear, plucked something from it, invisible to Jacob and the others but as real to her as the breath she drew. "John," she whispered.

Jacob knew that she was seeing him in her mind, Jacob's father as he'd been in 1947, perhaps the moment when she'd known absolutely that she was in love with him, the moment when she'd drawn her grandmother's lone-star earring from her ear and placed it in his hand.

Jacob reached to take Tom's hand, and Tom, too, turned in the direction of Sally's gaze. Tom placed his other hand in Becky's, and the vision was visible to them all now, not just to Sally. A figure emerged from the blinding radiance, a visitor to earth who had miraculously returned.

The figure stretched out his hand. "Come on, Sally."

Jacob looked at Tom and Becky and knew that they saw him, too. Then he looked at his mother, and saw that she had gone, her eyes closed now, her expression, for once, utterly serene.

HIGHWAY 375, NEVADA, OCTOBER 19, 1980

Eric sat back in the LTD as it sped toward Groom Lake. The voice at the other end of the bulky car phone was scratchy, but not so lost in distortion that he couldn't understand what was being said to him . . . and be angered by it.

"Listen to me," he fired back. "I need that funding shifted into biological research, Ted." He paused and listened impatiently for a moment. "Find the resources. What? None of your goddamned business. Ted? Listen to me. Do your job or lose it."

He slammed the phone into its cradle and glared out the window.

There they were again, the usual crowd, the nation's inexhaustible supply of gooney birds, all of them focused on Roswell now, the crack in every crackpot, America's number one lightning rod for morons and geeks and . . .

He shook his head at the hopeless idiocy of it. "We ought to put up a gift shop," he snapped. "Sell little bobbing alien heads for the jerks to take home." His mocking laughter held a bitter edge.

At the Groom Lake Facility, he leaped from the LTD and strode quickly through its growing field of Quonset huts and hangars to where he knew they waited for him, the scientists and technicians who belonged to him now, belonged to the project he oversaw, and which, unlike his father, he would never allow to slip from his grasp.

Inside the hangar, several men and women lay unconscious on stretchers, while other people, mostly in street clothes, catalogued them in preparation for removal.

Eric gave the scene a quick glance, sizing up the level of activity, who was working efficiently, who was not, and on that basis instantaneously deciding who would keep his job and who would lose it.

But he was not here to evaluate this part of the project, and so moved on, the heels of his boots clicking loudly across the concrete floor, until he reached his destination, a white room where Dr. Chet Wakeman waited.

"I have our people taking the test subjects out across the desert to avoid the . . . amateurs at the gate," Wakeman said with the hearty laugh of a man in his element—obviously feeding off the bustling amosphere's kinetic energy.

"The crowd gets bigger every day, Chet," Eric said as he stepped up to the table. "Like a damn circus."

Wakeman grinned. "Well, if you're going to be in a circus, best be in the center ring." Suddenly his tone became matter-of-fact. "We had to open up half a dozen people today before we got one," he said. "Like looking for pearls." He smiled proudly. "But what we did find is quite amazing." He turned to the right, where a glass wall looked out onto an observation room furnished with a single table upon which rested a small lead box. He reached for a microphone and spoke into it. "Send in the soldier."

The door to the observation room opened and a young Army private stepped inside.

Eric estimated the soldier's age at eighteen, his experience minimal, his mental attitude profoundly naïve. Perfect, he thought, as the soldier moved farther into the room, peering about until the door abruptly closed behind him and he startled visibly, then returned to himself and gazed about without concern, his attention not in the least drawn to the table or the lead box in which the specimen rested.

Suddenly he began to laugh, the laughter growing as the seconds passed, becoming ever more frantic and oddly desperate, the laugher of the madhouse. Then the laugher stopped, as if on command, and the soldier charged toward the booth where Eric stood watching. He crashed his head into the glass, then lifted it and slammed it against the glass once again and then yet again, turning his head into a bloody pulp blow by suicidal blow.

"In Buddhism we are taught that enlightenment is best attained through hardship and struggle," Wakeman said calmly. "A man will, for example, make himself angry because he seeks the energy of anger."

The soldier's head slammed loudly against the glass, but Wakeman remained oddly unconcerned. "We know that our little pals from the stars have found a very deep

and very real correlation between thought and energy."
He looked at Eric. "Seven seconds. That's how long it
took for exposure to that thing to completely destroy
this young man's brain." He tapped the blood-streaked
glass of the observation room. "That's what the implants
do. They pull out any thought, any memory, and play it
for us to see."

The soldier collapsed in a crumpled, lifeless mass.

"Of course, these devices can short-circuit in truly
fabulous ways," Wakeman continued. "But that's a by-
product of what they are."

"Which is?" Eric asked.

"Tracking devices," Wakeman answered without hesitation. "Tags. A sort of neurological fingerprint." He
shrugged. "We don't know how they work exactly. We
don't even know why the glass is keeping us safe." He
took a glass vial from his lab coat and poured a half-
dozen tiny implants onto the table. "We found these in a
sampling of brain tumor patients we've been monitoring
for the last couple of years." Eric stepped away from the
table nervously. Wakeman gave a dismissive wave of the
hand. "These particular devices are dead."

"Dead?" Eric asked.

"Like old batteries. They can't transmit anymore."

"Why did they stop transmitting?"

"My guess is that they stopped when the 'lab rat' was
no longer useful to our . . . visitors."

Eric studied the dead implants. "What if they come
back on?"

Wakeman smiled in a way that struck Eric as unset-
tlingly boyish and carefree. "Then we party hardy," he
said.

Chapter Two

Jacob stared out the window as Becky pulled a blouse out of her mother's closet and held it up to Tom. "Remember this one? Her favorite. She wore it to my graduation. Went all the way to Fort Worth to buy it."

"You should keep it," Tom told her.

Becky drew the blouse into her arms as if it were her dead mother. "I've been thinking about what the preacher said at Mom's funeral," she said. "About how a cruel death makes you wonder about God."

Jacob turned from the bleak landscape beyond the window, the vast sky that hung above the dry fields. "The ways of God are not the ways of man," he said. "That's a distinguishing tenet of modern science."

"How do you mean?" Tom asked.

"Science is just like religion," Jacob explained. "Only without the comfort. We tell you there's a plan, but part of that plan is for you to turn to dust."

Becky nodded. "Dust," she repeated, her eyes now on

her mother's blouse. "I just wanted her around to talk to a little longer," she said as she began to cry.

Tom hugged her gently. "I know," he said.

Jacob stood up, the grief closing in on him, driving him from the room. He walked out onto the porch and stood alone until Tom joined him there.

"You okay?" Tom asked quietly.

"Just a little tired."

"Is it what you did for Mom?"

"I'll be all right," Jacob replied. He looked at his brother closely. "You don't want to believe what happened to me, do you? Or to Mom?"

"No, I don't want to believe it, Jake," Tom answered quietly.

"But you always kind of did, didn't you?"

"Yes," Tom answered. "Kind of ironic. The country's number one debunker turns out to have a half-alien half-brother.

"What are you going to do now?"

"I want you to come forward."

Jacob turned away, now watching Carol and Lisa as they strolled along a line of crumbling fence. "I can't do that."

"But, Jacob," Tom argued, "this is something the world has a right to know. You are the proof that it really happened."

"What do you want me to do, go on TV and bend spoons? It would be a freak show."

"But after that, people would know."

"What would they know?" Jacob asked. "Not why they came. Not what they want." He shrugged. "Besides, I'm not the only one."

"How do you know that?"

"I don't really," Jacob admitted. "It's just a feeling I get sometimes. That there's . . . someone else."

"Like you?"

Jacob peered out over the barren land. "They're playing catch-up. The government. They're trying to figure out the same things." He looked at Tom darkly. "Owen Crawford knew about me," he said. "Maybe he knew about whoever else there is."

GROOM LAKE, NEVADA, OCTOBER 20, 1980

"Jesse Keys," Wakeman said excitedly, like a prospector who'd just stumbled onto a vein of gold.

Eric stared without enthusiasm at the black and white photograph of a teenaged boy Wakeman displayed on his computer monitor. "One of my father's many failures," he said dully.

"Failure?"

"I'd call it that," Eric said harshly.

"Your father couldn't have known what would happen when they took out Russell Keys' implant," Wakeman noted. "After all he . . ."

"I don't want to talk about my father," Eric interrupted sharply "Tell me about this one. This Jesse Keys."

"One thing's for sure about him."

"Which is?"

"That he mattered to them," Wakeman answered authoritatively.

"How do you know that?"

"Because they pulled him right through the wall of a bomb shelter in order to take him. They wouldn't have done that if they hadn't considered him vital."

"What do you think it all means?" Eric asked.

"Maybe nothing," Wakeman admitted. "But it's clear that some they chew on repeatedly, and some they spit out after one bite. They came for Jesse Keys and they took him. Now that we're looking more at the genetics, perhaps we'll figure out what he had that they wouldn't let us keep."

"Genetics," Eric mused. "What have you learned about those brothers in Alaska?"

"My guess is that they were failed attempts at cross-breeding," Wakeman said. "Like that kid your old man tried to bring back from Texas." His eyes sparkled suddenly. "You see what they're doing, don't you?"

Eric felt a jolt of energy. "What?"

"Everything they can," Wakeman said, and began typing rapidly, like a man seized by a vision. "This is an FBI 'aging' program," he explained. "Some fugitive has been underground for ten years and they want to make sure they'll know him if they see him." He punched the Enter key and waited as the pixels slowly revealed a computer-aged version of Jesse Keys. "I'll lay you diamonds to doughnuts this Jesse Keys is still alive. If you want to know what's so important about him, maybe we should ask the man himself."

STATE HIGHWAY 50, MISSOURI,
OCTOBER 21, 1980

The distress call cut in, and Jesse Keys yanked the microphone to his mouth.

"Yes?"

"Chief, we got a pileup on Old Cayton Road," the

dispatcher said. "Car full of college kids. Paramedics on the scene."

"I'm on my way."

When Jesse reached the site of the collision, the destruction amazed him.

The car had all but disintegrated around the telephone pole. A few other vehicles were strewn about, some involved in the accident, others belonging to motorists who'd stopped at the scene, backing up traffic in both directions.

"What have we got, Bobby?" Jesse asked the first EMS tech he saw.

"Kids coming back from Milton," Bobby answered breathlessly. "Two boys in the back pretty banged up. Already on their way to County. Girl's still in the passenger seat. Looks like a spinal. We're getting her out now."

Jesse raced to the car and looked in. The girl was pinned into the passenger seat, a neck collar already securing her neck. He adjusted the collar slightly.

"My friends?" the girl asked.

"On the way to the hospital," Jesse answered.

"Kevin?"

Jesse shook his head.

The young woman's eyes went blank and began to roll upward.

She was rapidly losing consciousness.

Desperate to keep her from going under, Jesse quickly snapped a pen from his pocket. "Listen, can you do something for me?"

The girl blinked rapidly. "What?"

"Can you keep your head straight and follow my pen with your eyes?"

He moved the pen slowly right to left, watching as the young woman's eyes labored to follow it.

"Good," he said, pocketing the pen. "We'll have you out of here in no time." He smiled. "You just keep looking at where my pen was, and keep your head straight."

He rose and moved through the wreckage, the usual scenes playing out before him, crumpled metal, gawking motorists, a landscape of flashing lights. Nothing drew his attention until he noticed Bobby standing off in a field, his shoulders hunched, head down.

"Jesus, I'm sorry, Chief," Bobby explained when Jesse got to him. "I just . . ."

"Don't worry about it," Jesse told him. "My first accident, I puked all over my chief's shoes." He patted Bobby's shoulder. "And remember this, when you come upon a bad thing like this, everything you do makes it better." He pulled out his pen and nodded toward the young woman in the car. "Keep her staring at this pen. Don't let her look at that hole in the windshield."

Bobby nodded softly and took the pen. "Thanks, Chief."

Jesse rushed away, still moving quickly among the wreckage, looking for anything that might have escaped the notice of the other police and EMS workers who'd gathered at the scene.

Within minutes, the chaos of the initial response had resolved itself in an orderly arrangement of activity.

Jesse stood within the flow of cars, watching as they whizzed past, getting glimpses of the far side of the road as he paced about, cars blocking his view as they passed, then revealing it again, a cop giving directions, an EMS worker standing by an ambulance, and finally a tall, slender man, hawk-faced and leaden-eyed, smoking a cigarette beside a large truck, its sides hand-painted, TRAVELING ATTRACTIONS.

Jesse froze.

It was him. He knew it instantly. It was the same man who'd chased him down the alley when he was kid.

The carny touched his baseball cap and nodded like someone greeting an old familiar friend.

But he was not a friend, Jesse knew, not a friend at all, and so he strode toward him determinedly, cars screeching their brakes as he stepped into the traffic, moving forward in a trance until something flashed and he awakened to find himself standing in the middle of a deserted road, nothing left of the accident save the occasional small bits of broken glass, the shadows deepening all around him as night fell.

The hours of missing time were still playing darkly in Jesse's mind the next day as he went through the routine motions of mowing his lawn. He'd not planned to mow that day, but after what had happened the day before, he felt drawn to the familiar, things he could do by rote, the safety of routine.

His nine-year-old son, Charlie, walked along beside him, his bare legs sprayed by tiny green flecks of severed grass.

"Did you know that twelve people have gone to the moon since 1969?" Charlie asked.

Jesse shook his head as he gave the mower a quick shove. "I didn't realize it was that many."

"My report is going to be on the first landing," Charlie said. "It's going to be a play."

"I'll be there," Jesse said.

Charlie looked delighted. "Even if there's an accident?"

"I'll get someone to work my shift," Jesse assured him.

Charlie gave Jesse a hesitant look. "That accident yesterday, are the people all right?"

"Most of them."

"Are you all right?"

Jesse stopped moving forward with the mower and looked at his son, wondering what change in his manner had given Charlie the idea that he was . . . different. "I'm fine," he said. He saw that his son didn't believe him, that he suspected something had gone wrong, or been wrong . . . or was destined to go wrong. He wasn't sure what his son sensed. He knew only that he wanted to avoid it. He unhooked the lawn mower bag and dumped the grass clippings. "Let's get this place hosed down before your mom gets home," he said.

He reached for the hose and turned on the water. The hose moved oddly, like something alive, a serpent wriggling in his hand. A blade of terror cut through him. He dropped the hose, and fixed his gaze on where it lay, half expecting it to rise, coil, strike.

"Jesse."

Jesse felt his insides leap.

Amelia was standing just behind him.

"Honey, what is it?" she asked. "What's the matter?"

Jesse stared blankly at Amelia, then at Charlie, unable to speak, his gaze riveted upon the hose as it wriggled wildly, spewing foamy venom across the glistening lawn.

He felt a strange itch in his chest, as if something had bitten him, and headed into the house. From the bathroom, he could see Amelia and Charlie talking worriedly on the front lawn, worried about him, about something . . . strange.

The itch struck again, sharp and painful, like a bite.

He lifted his shirt and his eyes widened in horror and disbelief, his mind barely able to take in what he saw, not a bite mark, as he'd expected, or a rash, but the boiling mark of a four-fingered hand.

LAS VEGAS, NEVADA, OCTOBER 28, 1980

Eric sipped his morning coffee and perused the newspaper. Reagan led in the polls, and there'd been no resolution of the hostage crisis in Iran.

"This hostage thing just shows you what happens when you let your enemy see your weakness," he said. "We should have gone in there and gotten our people, no matter what the cost."

His daughter Mary looked up from her cereal. "My teacher says if we'd done that, they'd have all been killed."

"Maybe," Eric told her. "But the Iranians would have been less likely to do it again."

Julie sat down at the table. "Can we talk about something else?"

Eric returned to the paper. For the last few days he'd been going over reports of "flying saucer" sightings in Maine. With each new sighting, he'd felt the pull of a change, a break from the arid land he had occupied nearly all his life, the desert wastes of Nevada. Except for the Roswell incident, the West had proven of little interest to the visitors. So what was the point of remaining in an area where those he sought rarely appeared, he asked himself. If you wanted to kill a polar bear, you had to go the Arctic, and increasingly in the last few days he'd determined that if he wanted to complete his father's

work, he could not remain where his father had remained. In a sense, he decided, Owen Crawford had
lived like a hunter in a duck blind, waiting for his prey to
show up, rather than actively pursuing it.

The decision came like a clap of thunder. "I think we
should move," he announced.

Julie turned this idea over, considering. "To somewhere a little farther out of town?"

"No," Eric replied. "Maine."

"Don't you think this is a bit too sudden?" Julie asked,
stunned by what Eric had just said.

Mary gave Eric a knowing look. "Is this 'cause there's
flying saucers in Maine?" she asked brightly.

Eric looked at Mary, astonished by her cleverness . . .
or was it intuition? "How did you know about that?" he
asked.

"Dylan Peters said that he and his family had gone
out to some mailbox and taken pictures of flying saucers
but the pictures didn't come out and that you were the
flying saucer soldier and you were in charge and all
that . . . like those guys in *Close Encounters* that kill the
cows."

"Smart girl," Eric said proudly. He turned to Julie. "I
don't think it's too sudden at all."

MISSOURI, OCTOBER 28, 1980

Jesse sat alone, reading, but hardly noticing what he
read as his mind returned to something that had happened a few days before. It had been a night like this,
clear and crisp. A terrible restlessness had seized him,
something invisible urging him from his bed. He'd got-

ten up, leaving Amelia asleep in their bed, dressed and gone for a drive, down the state highway, where he'd finally ended up near the accident site of a few days before, standing in a wheat field as the wind rippled through the tall green blades. He'd thought himself alone in the field, then a farmer had shown up, shotgun in hand, recognized him as the man who'd pulled his son from a sweep augur the year before, and lowered the gun. The farmer's question sounded in Jesse's mind, *You come to look at my glow-in-the-dark field?*

Minutes later, Jesse had seen the field for himself, a circle burned out of it, the farmer saying directly what Jesse had thought at the time, *Looks like a flying saucer, don't it?*

It did, yes, and now, as Jesse glanced up from his book, the night clear and crisp beyond the house, he felt oddly ready for what he saw: a light, bright and searing, reflected in the mirror above the fireplace.

He drew in a deep breath. They were coming for him, and he knew it. They were coming for him again, but this time it was going to be different. He got to his feet. This time he was going to fight them.

He knocked over a table as he rushed out of the house and into the street. The light was huge now, and steadily lowering, its bright glow intensifying as it descended.

"What do you want?" Jesse cried. "Leave me alone!"

"Dad?"

Jesse wheeled around to see his son standing a short distance away, his small hand lifted toward him imploringly. Amelia stood beside Charlie, a bag of groceries in her arms, the headlights of her car illuminating the scene. "Come back into the house, Dad," Charlie said.

Jesse nodded, his shoulders slumped, as if beneath the accusatory looks he saw in his neighbors' eyes.

Later that night, as he lay in bed with Amelia, he knew that the time had come, and so he told her everything, how they'd rescued him from the temple in Vietnam, how he'd thought of them as his dark guardian angels, and put himself in danger time and again to see if they would save him, the fact that they always had. But even all this was not enough. Everything had to come out, and so he went on, talking without restraint, the story pouring out of him in a flood of revelation, the way he'd been "taken" from a bomb shelter, the people who were after him, not aliens this time, but military people, how he'd assumed a false name and joined the Army in order to conceal himself. At last, he showed her the red imprint of the hand on his chest, though it was clear she saw only a rash.

"Maybe it's . . . all in your mind, Jesse," Amelia said cautiously.

"You don't see a hand?" Jesse asked.

She touched him softly. "We've been through a lot," she said. "And we'll get through this. But, please, see someone, Jesse. I want you to see someone."

He shook his head. "They'd just tell me I have a tumor. My father died of one. There is something in my head, Amelia, but it's not a tumor. It's something they put there. Something that tells them about me."

Amelia stroked his brow, a nurse again, only this time to a husband who was going mad. "Jesse, listen to yourself. You've got to see someone. If you won't do it for me, do it for Charlie."

He thought of Charlie, how much he wanted to stay

alive and healthy and watch his son grow up. "All right," he said. "I will."

He met Dr. Findlay the next day, went through every test the doctor suggested, then returned for the results. The doctor's diagnosis did not surprise him.

"The tumor is very small," Dr. Findlay said. "There's no sign of fluid buildup . . . but still, it could explain your recent behavior."

Jesse knew that it was not a tumor, but what was the point of saying so.

Dr. Findlay handed him a small card with a name and address written on it. "Dr. Franklin Traub. He's the best in the country."

Jesse took the card. He knew that Dr. Traub would recommend surgery, and that during the course of that surgery, he would surely die as his father had, bearing an unbearable secret to the grave. For a moment, that death seemed sweet, a way of escaping . . . and allowing his family to escape.

LUBBOCK, TEXAS, OCTOBER 29, 1980

Jacob and Becky watched the television screen where Tom appeared, sitting in a chair like a real celebrity, talking to the host, explaining his certainty that people were being abducted by aliens, even displaying a picture of the aliens themselves, creatures he estimated as being about four feet tall with pear-shaped heads, almond-shaped eyes, elongated arms, and long, extra-jointed fingers.

"Any minute he'll do a card trick," Jacob said.

Becky looked at him somberly. "I always knew, Jake. I always did. But I never thought that contactor Mom was building in the garage was going to get . . . your father's attention."

Jacob concentrated on the screen. Tom was now declaring that although he'd once been the nation's foremost debunker of alien abductions, he had recently come to accept such stories as entirely true, a change he attributed to a "personal experience" he was not "at liberty" to discuss.

Jacob shook his head. No one would believe him, he thought. No one in the world save a few "crackpots" who were actually looking for the proof. And the price to Tom would be enormous. He would be ridiculed ceaselessly, caricatured and lampooned, the butt of a thousand cruel jokes. Ordinary people would cross the street in order to avoid him.

Jacob glanced across the room to where Carol sat with Lisa in her arms, reading to her quietly. It was a frail world, he knew, one he could blast into a thousand pieces with a single word.

He glanced back at the television. The audience was laughing.

Not me, he thought, *not me.*

RIVERS CLINIC, ST. PAUL, MINNESOTA,
OCTOBER 30, 1980

Jesse and Amelia took their seats in Dr. Traub's wood-paneled office and waited for the test results.

The doctor remained behind his desk, his hand on a slender folder.

"You were right," he said to Jesse. "That thing in your brain is not a tumor."

Jesse could hardly believe that Dr. Traub had actually confirmed what he'd always known, but never expected anyone to believe, that the thing in his brain had not been formed by his body, not a malignancy of flesh . . . but of intent.

"It's very small," Traub went on. "It looks metallic." This last remark seemed almost physically to yank Traub forward in his seat. "Where did you grow up?" he asked.

"Illinois."

"Any exposure to chemicals?"

"Heroin," Jesse admitted.

"And you say your father had a similar tumor?"

"Not similar."

"No?"

"Identical."

"I see." Dr. Traub smiled reassuringly. "Well, for the record, we see such deposits occasionally in people who work with unusual chemicals," he explained. "They're usually made up of some kind of foreign matter that got swept into a little pile because your body couldn't figure out how to get rid of it." He clasped his hands together. "The important thing is that we can treat it without surgery. We can use localized ultrasound therapy to break it up. Once that's happened, you'll pass it in a matter of days."

Jesse glanced at Amelia, then back to Dr. Traub. "No surgery?" he asked with great relief.

Dr. Traub nodded.

"So, if you get this thing out of my head," Jesse asked tentatively, almost afraid to hear the answer, "then it might make . . . them . . . go away?"

"Them?"

Jesse shook his head. "It doesn't matter."

Traub looked at him gently. "You don't think you've got a metallic deposit in your head, do you, Jesse?"

"You've got your ideas about what's in my head. I've got mine."

"Why are you here, if you don't think I can help you?"

"You have to help me," Jesse said, his desperation rising to the surface. "You have to make this thing go away. I don't care what it is anymore. I have a nine-year-old son. I don't want to see him hurt . . . because of this thing in my head."

Dr. Traub smiled quietly, though in some way, as Jesse noticed, his eyes remained oddly calculating. "Don't worry," he said. "You'll soon be fine."

LAS VEGAS, NEVADA, NOVEMBER 1, 1980

The house was chaos, and all Eric wanted to do was escape it. There were boxes and packing crates everywhere, and Mary was screaming that she didn't want her Cabbage Patch dolls put in boxes for the move, and Julie was screaming at Mary to *do it now,* and everything was in such intolerable disarray that Eric heard the knock at the door as sweet relief from the disorder within the house.

Chet Wakeman stood on the front porch. He was beaming. "We've had a fantastic stroke of luck, Eric," he said. "Jesse Keys is in a clinic in Minnesota."

"How do you know?" Eric asked, astonished.

"I have a contact there," Wakeman answered. "A Dr. Traub. In seems that Keys came to see him about some odd behavior. Traub found the same kind of 'tumor' that was in Keys' father." He clapped his hands together delightedly. "We've got him!"

"What do you want to do with him?" Eric asked.

Wakeman smiled. "I'm thinking. I'm thinking."

"Well, while you're thinking, don't lose him," Eric said impatiently. "I'm not going to make the same mistakes my father made."

Wakeman looked at him. "Your old man's been dead what, eight years?"

Eric nodded.

"So don't you think you can stop trying to kick his ass?" Wakeman asked.

Eric frowned darkly.

Wakeman shrugged. "We're not going to lose him," he said. "One of our researchers was going through some of the old files, looking for research that we might have missed. He found these."

Eric looked at the papers Wakeman handed him. They were transcripts of the markings that were identical to the metal artifact his father kept in the safe in his study, but Eric betrayed no sense that he'd ever seen such markings.

"Any idea what they are?" Wakeman asked.

"They look like the glyphs from that excavation in Alaska," Eric replied. "The one where my brother died."

"That's what I thought too. But these are dated 1947, and that burial chamber in Alaska wasn't opened until 1970."

"Did you translate it?"

"Can't be done," Wakeman said. "But we may be close, what with Jesse Keys under wraps. The genetic guys are finding out more and more about the implants. I think we're near a breakthrough." He stopped and looked at Eric darkly. "Is there something you're not sharing?"

"You know everything that I know."

Chet Wakeman looked at him, considering, then his gaze fell to Eric's desk, two books by Tom Clarke. "What's this?" he asked.

"Did you see him on TV the other day?" Eric asked. "Talking about a government conspiracy to cover up the presence of aliens here on earth?" He laughed. "Suddenly he's the Woodward and Bernstein of alien abduction."

Wakeman held his eyes on the books. "Hmm. Tom Clarke."

"Tom Clarke," Eric repeated. "The same guy who thought our entire program was a lie. The one who made that peace sign in the corn that cost my father his job. Now he's suddenly a believer?"

"Evidently," Wakeman said.

Eric turned Clarke's inexplicable conversion over in his mind. "I think I'll find out what made him change his mind."

CENTERVILLE ELEMENTARY SCHOOL, DALLAS, TEXAS, NOVEMBER 2, 1980

Eric stood, half-hidden by the morning light as Becky's car drew to a stop before the traffic light. He knew the moment had come, and so he quickly approached Becky's car and yanked open the door. "Don't be afraid," he said. He flashed his Army Intelligence identification. "Just drive to the park."

"Who are you?" Becky demanded.

"Just drive," Eric told her. "When we get to the park, I'll tell you."

Becky eyed him apprehensively.

Eric smiled. "If I were planning to hurt you, would I have you drive me to a public park?"

At the park, Eric escorted Becky to a bench in the open.

"You're much prettier than I expected," he told her. "Your surveillance photographs don't do you justice."

Becky stared at him edgily. "Is this visit about something more than good looks?"

"My name is Eric Crawford. I'm here because I understand that your brother Tom has switched sides—that now he's a believer."

Becky didn't answer, only peered out into the park, her hands in her lap.

"You look a lot like your mother," Eric told her.

Becky faced him. "That's what they say."

"My father was a bastard," Eric admitted. "What he did to your mother was unforgivable. But he had a reason for doing it. He found a spaceship in the desert in New Mexico. There were four bodies in that ship. But there were five seats in the craft. He came to your home looking for the visitor who was sitting in the fifth seat. He never stopped looking. And when he died, I started looking." He leaned forward slightly and his voice took on an unmistakable gravity. "This planet has been visited thousands of times since my father found that ship. People have been taken from their homes. Things have been done to them. But we still don't know what they're doing here, or what they want from us."

Becky nodded softly, and he could see that she no longer feared him.

"My father was a ruthless man, Becky," Eric added. "But the things he wanted to know were reasonable because these aliens are the greatest threat the world has ever known." He lowered his voice like one confiding a deep secret. "You don't have to tell me what changed your brother's mind. At least not for now. There's something else you can do instead."

"What?" Becky asked.

The Crawford smiled slithered onto Eric's face. "Have dinner with me," he said.

RIVER CLINIC, NOVEMBER 2, 1980

Dr. Traub glanced up from his desk as Wakeman entered his office.

"There's something new," Wakeman said. He dropped a file on Traub's desk. "My guys have found the signal the tracking devices give off. It's incredibly weak, and so it has to be amplified somehow before it can be transmitted back to . . . our little buddies."

"You mean to their transmitter?" Traub asked.

"Perhaps an organic one," Wakeman said with a clever grin. "For example, a brain." He sat down in the chair opposite Traub's desk. "The energy of thought . . . of mind. That's why Jesse Keys is so important to them. He's their transmitter. Of course, there's only one way to find out if he really is a transmitter."

"How?"

"Shut him off."

Dr. Traub was clearly shocked by Wakeman's suggestion. "You mean, kill him?"

"Sooner or later the man had to go," Wakeman answered casually. "A question of security, you know."

Traub sat back in his chair and looked at Wakeman determinedly. "You're not going to do that here."

Wakeman laughed and waved his hand. "Oh, don't get all hot and bothered, Doctor. I'm going to take him back to Nevada."

"Good."

"But I'd like you to pave the way a little, if you don't mind," Wakeman said.

"In what way?"

"Just tell him that you've done all you can for him, and that you think he should go to the Brazel Clinic."

Traub nodded. "But if he's a transmitter and you shut him down, do you really think our visitors might show up?"

Wakeman's smile grew into a dark chuckle. "Wouldn't it be a gas if they did?"

DALLAS, TEXAS, NOVEMBER 3, 1980

Becky was already waiting for him when he came to pick her up, and Eric took that fact as a sure sign that he'd already won her over.

"Nice blouse," he said as he came up to her.

"It was my mother's favorite," Becky said.

He motioned her over to his car and opened the door. "I have a plane waiting for us."

"Why would I get in a plane with you, of all people?" Becky asked him.

"I'll have you back by two A.M.," Eric replied with a

joking smile. He knew that she wanted to resist him, but couldn't. "Spook's honor," he assured her.

In the plane, a table had been set with food and champagne. Becky looked at it, then back at Eric. "You know how to show a girl a good time."

The meal went quickly, and there was a lot of laughter, and with each glass of champagne, Eric could see that Becky was falling deeper and deeper beneath his spell. She laughed about the government, about the law, and even about some of Tom's strange theories.

"Growing up in Las Vegas then, you met a lot of weirdos," Eric said.

"I guess so," Becky told him. She looked at her plate. "I'm used to leftovers."

Eric laughed briefly, then grew serious. "I got married really young. First girl I slept with. First time I slept with her. She's pregnant. I'm married. Anything to show my father I was grown up."

"I just needed my own identity," Becky said. "Someplace where I wasn't Tom Clarke's little sister."

"The brother shadow?" Eric asked. "Me, too. The sun rose and set on my brother, Sam."

"I guess a lot of people do that," Becky said. "They're just kids trying to get away from home and they wind up smack dab in the middle of their lives before they know what hit them."

The plane landed on a deserted airstrip with only a few Quonset huts surrounded by the desert waste.

"I want to show you something," Eric told her.

They exited the plane and walked across the airstrip to a large building. The interior corridor was brightly lit, and at the end of it, Eric opened a door and ushered Becky inside.

"This is what I wanted to show you," Eric said as he switched on the light.

Becky stared in disbelief at a large specimen jar, the small body trapped inside it, with pear-shaped head and almond eyes, now closed in death, so that it seemed to sleep on a cloud of unknowing.

"It's breathtaking, isn't it?" Eric whispered. He drew Becky nearer to the jar. "I come here sometimes by myself. I sit and stare at him. I keep feeling that if I stare at it long enough, I'll be able to understand."

Becky's hand lifted to her throat. "Thank you, Eric, for showing me this."

He touched her hair. "I wasn't going to, but . . ." He trailed off, drawing her into his arms.

"What's happening to us?" she asked.

"Listen, Becky," Eric told her. "I want you to come with me."

"Where?"

"I've got a spot picked out in Maine. The gawkers will still come to the desert. They'll see the same experimental planes and think they're seeing flying saucers." He drew his arms more tightly around her. "The trucks leave Groom Lake tomorrow. They'll sneak across the desert to avoid your brother and his friends."

She looked at him seriously. "Tom says you've taken people. Experimented on them."

His embrace tightened.

"I swear to you, Becky," he said. "I have never in my life done anything to harm anyone."

The first kiss was tender, the second more passionate, the third so blinding in its hunger, that he could tell that

Becky had lost track of where she was. The odd and un-expected thing was he felt himself lose track too, and not only of Becky, but of the room around him, the lights and machines, and even the small creature in the clear glass jar, who watched him now with open eyes.

Chapter Three

It had all happened so fast, and even now, as Jesse sat in the passenger seat, watching the unfamiliar landscape, he could scarcely comprehend the series of events. First Dr. Traub had told him that his deposit was not disintegrating as quickly as he'd hoped. Then he'd introduced a Dr. Patterson from the Brazel Clinic, the place Traub said he had to go in order to have the tumor removed. Patterson had given him only enough time to call home, speak to Charlie and hear the frantic voice of a young boy who missed his father terribly.

"Big country," the driver said. He was tall and very thin and wore a wrinkled sweatshirt, which seemed strange for a guy who claimed to be a doctor.

"Yeah," Jesse answered dully

"We'll take care of that thing in your head," the driver assured him. "And once that's done, no more little gray men."

"I'm ready," Jesse said wearily.

They drove on in silence for a few moments. Jesse once again went over the last few days, the accident, the lights, the way he'd told Amelia everything, how she'd taken him to Dr. Traub, the whole story of his . . .

He stopped. Little gray men? He'd never told Dr. Traub anything about "gray" men.

He turned to the driver. "Little gray men? I never said anything to Traub about little gray men."

The man shrugged. "Educated guess."

Jesse nodded, steeled himself for what he had to do, and then did it.

The blow came hard and fierce and the man's head slammed into the side window, his sweatshirt flapping up to reveal the forty-five tucked in his belt.

Jesse grabbed the pistol, wheeled the car around in a wrenching turn and headed back toward Missouri, thinking only of Charlie now, determined to get back to his son, before his son was . . . taken.

Charlie stood before his class, reciting proudly. "That's one small step for mankind . . . I mean for man . . . one giant step for mankind." He looked out over the other children in his class, his eyes on the empty chair where he imagined his father sitting, beaming proudly.

Then the door opened, and he was there. His father.

"I can't believe you came," Charlie said excitedly. He rushed down the aisle and leaped into Jesse's arms.

"We have to go now," his father said, lowering him to the ground, then tugging him swiftly out of the classroom, down the corridor and finally into the car.

"Where are we going?" Charlie asked.

His father didn't answer, but only pressed down hard on the accelerator, the car now hurtling down the highway until it reached a place Charlie recognized from pictures in the paper, the place where the accident had happened, and where his father suddenly pulled the car over, slammed on the brakes, and brought the car to a screeching halt.

"Dad?" Charlie asked. "Why are we stopping here?"

His father took his hand and quickly urged him out of the car and toward the adjoining field, a wall of wheat undulating weirdly in the distance, his father moving fast now, as if under some invisible lash.

Another sound. Another car.

Charlie looked back over his shoulder and saw his father's car slide to a stop on the side of the road, then another man get out, identical . . . his father!

"Dad?" Charlie asked, glancing up at the man who held his hand in a tight grip.

Jesse ran toward him. "Charlie, get away from the field," he called frantically. "Come over here to me."

The other father stopped dead and wheeled around to face Jesse. "He's not your father," he said to Charlie.

"Don't listen to him," Jesse cried.

Charlie looked from one to the other.

"Charlie, it's me," the man who held his hand said.

"He's not me," Jesse called to him desperately. "It's going to be all right. Charlie, he's not me."

"Charlie, I'm your dad," the man holding his hand said firmly.

"No," Jesse shouted. "He's making me from your head, from your picture of me."

Charlie glanced back at the man who stood a few yards away begging him not to go into the field.

"Remember last month?" the man called to him loudly. "I cut myself shaving and I didn't know it. I came down to the breakfast table with blood all over the side of my face, and you and mom . . ."

Charlie glanced up at the man who still held his hand. Blood had begun to drip from a cut on his cheek. "You're not . . ." Charlie began, then stopped, as a group of men suddenly emerged from the wheat.

"Dad!" Charlie screamed, trying to tug free of the man's grip.

But the man held him tightly.

"Leave my boy alone!" Jesse screamed. He drew the pistol and fired, the blast so loud it shook the earth and seemed to tear from the sun a blinding orb of light.

Jesse came to in a hospital room, his eyes barely able to focus, as if they'd been seared by the light. Through the blur he made out Amelia and Charlie beside the bed.

"They'll be coming for Charlie now," he said weakly. He felt a trickle of blood ooze from his nose, then a small sliver of something carried on its flow. The sliver dropped to his chest in a small pool of blood, and he knew it was the thing they'd planted in his brain when they'd taken him years before.

Amelia looked at the device, then frantically at her husband, and Jesse felt a deep wave of vindication pass over him. For he could see that at last she knew that he was not some hopeless paranoid, locked in an insane vision, but simply a man who'd always, and in everything, told his wife the truth.

He started to speak, but a squeal of tires silenced him. He glanced out the hospital window, and they were there, several men in sweatshirts, all of them rushing toward the hospital. He turned to Amelia and with his eyes told her what she had to do.

"Charlie," she said, acting now on his unspoken command. "Come on."

He saw her press Charlie urgently out the door, then from the window, watched her emerge again, dressed as a nurse, pushing Charlie in a wheelchair while the men in sweatshirts darted back and forth among the cars. She gave them no notice, but simply moved forward determinedly, this woman he had loved and married and dared to tell the truth, a truth she had at last understood and acted upon, and thus, in the hour of her departure, granted him the hope that his son might yet live an earthly and unbroken life.

STATE HIGHWAY 93, EASTERN NEVADA, NOVEMBER 7, 1980

Eric could not believe what he saw. Tom Clarke and Becky standing in the middle of the road, facing him squarely, a squad of reporters behind them, ready with their camera. And so he had failed, he realized. Becky had never truly surrendered to him, and he was hit with the surprising fact that for a moment he had surrendered to her.

Eric got out of the truck, walked over to Tom and faced him sternly. "You and your friends here will be driven to Las Vegas. You'll be detained for seventy-two hours, then released." He looked at Becky and understood that despite himself, he still loved her, that the full power of that kiss still held him in thrall.

"Detained for what cause?" Tom asked.

Eric returned his attention to Tom. "Detained because you're interfering with a scheduled movement of Air Force personnel."

"Bastard," Becky snapped.

Eric couldn't bear to look at her and so continued to stare directly at Tom. "It's over. Get in the damned trucks."

Tom's eyes shifted to the right, and peered just over Eric's shoulder. "Still don't know how it flies, do you?"

Eric turned around to see four helicopters hovering in the distance, the spacecraft hanging between them, nearly motionless in the dark air.

"How much longer do you think you can hide this kind of evidence?" Tom asked.

Eric wheeled around. "For as long as I have to," he said sharply. He nodded, and a crowd of armed men suddenly appeared, the two groups now facing each other, both equally determined to stand their ground.

A silence fell over them as the two groups glared at each other.

Then a soft hum sounded in the distance, barely a rustle of air at first. But its steady drone grew louder with each passing second, as the lights of the enormous craft engulfed them. They stood frozen, staring upward in stunned amazement, as the humming craft held weightlessly above them, encasing them in a light more radiant than earthly light, their ears vibrating with the steadily building hum of an engine without gears or straining levers, the sound of pure propulsion, unhindered and streaked with light, the cosmic energy of a foreign cosmos.

Then both light and sound vanished and they stood,

watching in astonished silence as the air went black around them with such blinding speed that all the world suddenly seemed no larger than a cramped, windowless cell in which the last candle had abruptly guttered out.

Eric's lips parted in stricken awe, leaving him mute, deaf, and very nearly blind, as if he'd been stripped of all sensation save wonder.

Then, slowly, the world returned to him in little particles of sound and vision, and he saw the milling crowd again, the trucks and soldiers, Tom and Becky as they were led away, and finally Wakeman beside him.

"They took your proof," Wakeman said. "The bodies and the craft. Every bit of proof."

Then Wakeman walked away, and Eric stood alone in the darkness, watching as the men and women Tom and Becky had brought with them were loaded onto trucks and driven away. When the last of them had been taken, he walked to his jeep, glanced about, careful that no one was nearby, picked up his briefcase and opened it.

The artifact winked up at him from the dark interior of the case. "Not everything," he said as he gazed at the only proof of unearthly worlds that still remained on earth.

PART SIX

Charlie and Lisa

Chapter One

In the solitude of his study, Eric thought of Becky Clarke, the unexpected love he'd felt for her, the willing gift of her body, then the bitter reality of her betrayal. He knew there was no explanation for the feeling that had swept over him during that one evening he'd been with her. It had been a new experience, and it had shaken him to the bone. Now he thought of her as a part of life he'd missed, a treasure lost and irrecoverable. At times, when he sat alone in his study, the irony was almost more than he could bear, the painful and irreducible fact that he'd spent his life in search of an alien presence when it was a human presence he most powerfully desired.

In the other room his daughter Mary was busily working on a scientific paper for school, but for Eric, the whole vast world of science was reduced to the one thing he could truly claim as his, the one thing that had not been taken from him either by aliens or by humans. The artifact.

The artifact was the unassailable evidence that he had not lived in vain. The artifact was the solid ground in which his life was rooted, and if he gave up his search to decipher it, he felt that his soul would shatter, and he would be as empty as the space from which it had come so many years ago.

He walked to the safe, dialed the combination and removed the artifact. In the gloomy half-light he preferred now, he stared at the indecipherable markings inscribed upon it in the language of another world. *This much I have,* he thought, *this much is mine.*

There was knock at the front door, but he left Julie to answer it. It was Chet Wakeman, and he could tell that Mary was suddenly excited, her voice pealing though the house as she greeted her "Uncle Chet."

After that, he listened to the usual greetings, then Wakeman's inevitable question.

"So, where's Eric?"

"In his study," Julie answered.

Eric hurriedly returned the proof to the safe and closed the door just as Wakeman came into the study.

"Hey, Eric," Wakeman said brightly. "Jesus, turn on some light in here, will ya?" He hit the switch beside the door and the shadows retreated into the far corners of the room. "That little girl of yours is really something," he said. "You should check in with her once in a while, Eric. She's a great kid."

Eric slumped down in the chair behind his desk.

Wakeman gave him a penetrating look. "Whatever happened to you, you need to get over it."

"You have news?" Eric asked, almost curtly.

"As a matter of fact, I do," Wakeman said. "They pulled the plug on the project, as expected."

Eric's eyes reflexively shot to the safe, then back to Wakeman. "Because all our evidence . . . all our research is gone."

"That's right," Wakeman said. He laughed. "I thought I had a pretty good argument. Told this senator that the reason we didn't have any evidence is because it was all taken by a flying saucer. He said when they brought it back, he'd restore the funding."

"It's too bad we could never find Charlie Keys," Eric muttered.

"And you know what really burns my ass?" Wakeman said. "That if we had had any funding at all, I could have gotten that positioning system running, and we'd have tracked Charlie Keys by that thing in his head. We could have found him, or anybody else who'd been taken, in twenty-four hours."

Eric nodded dully. "So what do you do now?"

Wakeman plopped down in the chair across from Eric's desk. "I thought I might go out to California. Couple of buddies of mine from Yale are going into biotech."

Eric's face soured. "I keep picturing Tom Clarke smiling that smug smile of his and saying 'Still don't know how it flies, do you?'" He looked at the safe again. "I want to know what made Tom a believer all of a sudden."

"You were supposed to get that out of his sister, weren't you?" Wakeman said with a wink.

"But I didn't," Eric said.

Wakeman looked at his friend knowingly. "What you keep picturing is Tom's sister dumping you. I think that's what turned you all gloomy, old buddy."

Eric's stare was lethal. "My personal life is none of your business, Chet. But just for your information, I'm not finished yet. Becky or no Becky, I still want to know what changed Tom Clarke's mind."

LOS ALTOS, CALIFORNIA, FEBRUARY 28, 1983

The baseball in his hand felt like a small, densely packed planet, so heavy Jacob Clarke could barely lift his arm. But he had to lift it. Lisa was at the plate, bat in hand, waiting to swing. And so he summoned his strength, made his mind and will provide the power his body lacked, wound his arm, and sent the ball hurtling toward his daughter.

She swung and with a loud crack the ball lifted higher and higher, into the vast blue where Jacob followed it with his eyes, a terrible weariness falling upon him again, like a long-distance runner at the end of his run, with the finish line retreating from him as quickly as the rising ball, impossible to reach.

The ball hit the fence, and Jacob saw the disappointment in Lisa's eyes.

"It's a game of inches," he explained.

Lisa shook her head. "I swung too late. I thought it was going to sink."

"That's why I like baseball," Jacob told her as he came over and knelt beside her. "You can never make assumptions."

Lisa punched him playfully. "I thought you liked it because it was impossibly hard and there were all these useless statistics to memorize." She gave him her best "gotcha" look.

"Well," Jacob admitted. "That too."

He returned to the mound, picked up another ball,

no less heavy than the first, closed his eyes, as if in a prayer for strength, then felt the weight descend upon him, wrap around him like a leaden shroud, leaving him strangely encased and immobile within his own body.

"Are you all right?"

It was Carol's voice, and with all his strength he managed to pry open his eyes.

"We'd better get you home," Carol said gently.

Yes, Jacob thought, home.

At the car, he suddenly stopped before getting in. He felt an urgency in his blood, something deep within him crying out a last instruction. He reached into his pocket, pulled out the small jewel box, and opened it. "It was your grandmother's," Jacob told his daughter. He drew out the lone-star earring and placed it around his daughter's neck. "I love you, honey," he said. "Every day and twice on Sundays."

Lisa peered at the star, and watching her, Jacob saw that she sensed its importance, the legacy it bore, the terrible mission she had just been given.

"Some guy will meet you one day," Jacob told her. "And with one look, he'll tell you that there's no other place he wants to be."

Lisa caressed the earring, her eyes upon it wonderingly. Then she looked up and nodded, and at that instant Jacob knew that he had passed it on, done what remained of his duty. And on that thought, his legs buckled under a heaviness beyond human weight and he fell to earth like a dying star.

BAKERSFIELD, CALIFORNIA, MARCH 1, 1983

The lights of the pizza parlor burned garishly, flooding into the car, the passenger seat where Charlie Keys should have been, where his mother had left him sleeping soundly only minutes before.

Amelia stared helplessly at the empty seat, the pizza dropping from her hand and slamming down upon the pavement as she searched the darkness of the parking lot, peeling back the shadows, looking for her son.

Then suddenly, he was there, standing behind her, looking strangely dazed, like one awakened from a deep sleep.

"Charlie," she said, "you can't just go off like that. Where were you? Where did you go?"

Charlie peered at her silently, his hand lifting to his throat where she saw three small scars in a triangular pattern.

"What happened to me?" he asked.

"I don't know," Amelia answered.

"The men we're running from . . . does it have to do with them?"

Amelia shook her head. "I really don't know, Charlie."

Charlie stared at her worriedly, a look of terrible abandonment in his eyes, like a boy who'd been left behind on the street on in the railway station, and who could not find his way home. "Dad could tell us," he said.

Amelia drew her son into her arms. "I don't know if your dad will ever be able to tell us anything," she said.

NEW YORK CITY, MARCH 16, 1983

Eric stood next in line as Tom Clarke scribbled his name hastily into the book, while the line of people twining through the bookstore's cramped aisles steadily grew longer.

"Why do you think the aliens took all their stuff back?" the man in front of Eric asked.

Tom grinned. "How do you know they took it all?" He grabbed the next book from the stack and signed it as the man moved away.

Eric stepped up to the table. "Quite a turnout."

"What do you want?" Tom asked dryly.

"I find I have a lot of free time on my hands," Eric replied.

"Imagine that."

"How's Becky?"

Tom got to his feet, knocking over a stack of books. "Becky is not your business."

Eric casually gathered up the fallen books and returned them to the table.

"We're not enemies anymore, Tom," he said quietly. "I'm a private citizen now. Our 'friends' saw to that when they took back all the evidence."

Tom peered at him warily. "What do you want, Eric?"

"You went from skeptic to believer in a nanosecond," Eric replied. "I want to know why."

"Maybe I just saw the light," Tom answered cagily.

"If you're talking about the lights in the Mojave, you changed months before that," Eric said. His gaze bore down upon Tom. "What do you know that you're not telling me?"

"I might ask you the same question."

Eric shrugged, giving up any further effort to win Tom over. "Say hello to your sister," he said, as he turned and walked to a nearby aisle where Wakeman waited for him.

"Well, what do you think?" Wakeman asked.

"Tom Clarke will never give us anything," Eric told him.

Wakeman smiled. "You know what I love about chaos theory? It's about systems that can't resist outside influence. Something happens somewhere, and the system changes. Which means that at the moment, all we can do is watch the skies."

Eric shook his head determinedly. "You can watch the skies, Chet, but I'm watching Tom Clarke."

LOS ALTOS, CALIFORNIA, MARCH 4, 1986

The apartment still felt empty, and curiously lifeless, as if a strange, invisible energy had been drained from it. Lisa peered at the lone-star earring and thought of her father, how he'd seemed strangely resigned at the end, a man who had done his best and had no more to give. She looked at her mother, the red-rimmed eyes, how bereft she was now, more alone that she'd ever been or dreamed of being.

"He'd been . . . getting weaker since your grand-mother died," Carol said. "I kept asking him to see some-one, but he wouldn't." She shook her head. "He was so resigned."

"He understood what was happening to him," Lisa said, offering what little comfort was possible for her mother.

"That sounds like something he would say." Carol

touched Lisa's face. "He loved you so much. He was so proud of you."

Lisa knew that, and never doubted it, so in the months that followed, and even after her mother had found a simple, kindhearted guitar player named Danny and married him, she still felt that her father was with her in some way. By then, she'd begun to wear her grandmother's earring around her neck. It was the last thing he'd given her, and she found a strange comfort in keeping it so near.

She was wearing it the day she started classes at Morrison Junior High School three years later, the earring still hanging from a chain around her neck.

"Do you know anybody here?"

Lisa glanced at Nina, took in her shocking pink hair and Husker-Du T-shirt. "No," she admitted.

"Okay," Nina said brightly. "So, you wanna be friends for life?"

Before Lisa could answer, a waterfall of paper slid from one of Nina's notebooks. As she helped her gather them up, Lisa noticed that the drawings were quite good, and decided that Nina was not the frivolous fourteen-year-old she appeared to be.

"I don't show my stuff," Nina said self-consciously. She smiled. "I worry about . . ."

"You shouldn't worry about what people think," Lisa said decisively. "If someone doesn't like them, so what?"

They moved toward a van that rested at the nearby curb, a dusty, beat-up VW.

"That's my stepdad," Lisa said. "His name's Danny."

Nina looked at Lisa knowingly. "An old hippie?"

"He's a guitar player," Lisa told her new friend for life. "He lived near us when my father died. I guess my mother just . . ." She shrugged. "My mom's at Berkeley, taking a course in alternative nutrition."

"So it's just you and . . . Jerry Garcia?"

Lisa nodded. "For now," she said.

But it wasn't all that bad, Lisa told herself that night as she and Danny prepared pork chops, the two of them listening to the television as President Reagan talked about how the people of the earth had a lot in common, and that if the planet were ever attacked by aliens, the whole world would unite.

After dinner, Nina dropped by. They talked a while, and Lisa demonstrated the drum set Danny had bought for her. Nina won Danny over almost instantly, despite her earnest vegetarianism, and the lack of interest in the pork chops he so proudly offered.

Once Nina left, Lisa took her dog Watson on a walk through the trailer park. She could hear the usual sounds of early evening, couples talking, kids playing, the steady drone of televisions and radios. The trailer park was not a bad place, but on these walks in the evening, Lisa thought of her other home, the one she'd had with her father, and how, during the last few years she seemed only to miss him more, and yet to feel that he was not actually gone at all, but remained around her, she still the object of his loving, but now distant, gaze.

Suddenly Watson stopped and began to growl.

"Watson?" Lisa asked. "What is it?"

Watson bolted forward, racing among the trailers and then into the woods, Lisa in full pursuit, rushing through the undergrowth, catching Watson in brief glimpses ahead of her as he darted through the shadows.

"Watson, come back," Lisa cried.

But the dog continued to dart through the woods, the

lights of the trailer park suddenly extinguishing behind her, Lisa running tiredly, growing exhausted, the woods steadily thinning as she neared a clearing where she saw a man sitting on a log, smoking, his crooked body framed by the side of old carnival truck marked TRAVELING ATTRACTIONS.

The carny sat entirely still as Lisa broke into the clearing. Then his eyes shifted over to her, his face wreathed in smoke. "Lisa," he said. "Today you are a woman."

MADISON, WISCONSIN, MARCH 4, 1986

Charlie turned onto the darkest stretch of Madison Street. A faint breeze scattered bits of litter across the pavement and rattled the tin signs that lined the deserted street.

He stopped, as if by a hand at his arm, drew in a long breath and steeled himself. If you let this street scare you, he told himself, then you'll live in fear your whole life long.

He stepped forward resolutely and headed down the street, the breeze at his back, pressing him forward like an invisible hand to where the street made a slow curve toward a bus stop. He could see a man sitting on the bench at the stop, his crooked profile in silhouette beneath the streetlamp, a dusty old carnival truck rooted in the distance, traveling attractions that seemed to have traveled very far.

Charlie stopped, felt a spike of fear, and kept his eyes on the man before him, watching fearfully as he continued to smoke idly, the ghostly curls from his cigarette rising skyward into the darkness like souls released from their long travail.

LOS ALTOS, CALIFORNIA, MARCH 17, 1986

Lisa wasn't sure why it had come over her, this sudden interest, only that it grew more intense with each passing day. Now she was reading *The Mojave Desert Sightings,* by Tom Clarke, a book she'd hardly have noticed before . . . what? She didn't know. It had simply come upon her, this need to explore the far-fetched notion that strange beings walked the earth, or hovered above it, looking down, waiting to be discovered.

Carol glanced at Danny worriedly, then across the table to where Lisa continued to read intently, her food untouched before her.

"Are you reading that for an assignment?" Carol asked.

Lisa did not look up from the book. "No."

"Then why are you reading it?"

Lisa shrugged, her eyes riveted to the page. "I don't know," she answered. "I just got curious."

Danny looked at the book, the photograph of Tom Clarke on the back cover.

"Tom Clarke," he said to Carol. "That's Jacob's brother, right?"

Carol nodded.

"Kind of a fruit-loop."

Lisa tensed. "I'll be in my room," she said.

In her room, she was not sure why she'd suddenly felt so hostile to Danny, or so defensive about Tom Clarke. After all, Danny had always been good to her, and she hardly knew Tom Clarke. And yet, she'd bristled visibly when Danny had made light of Tom. It was almost like he'd insulted her as well, called her a fruit-loop, too.

Strange, she thought, as she sat down on her bed, reading intently once again, her eyes fixed on the page, her mind so focused on the account of the Mojave sightings that she barely noticed when her mother stepped into the room.

"What's going on, Lisa?" Carol asked.

"Nothing," Lisa answered. She could see that her mother wasn't buying it. "I'm fine," she added reassuringly. "Really."

Carol sat down on the bed beside her. "Your uncle Tom has a lot of weird ideas, Lisa." She glanced at the book apprehensively, as if it were a loaded gun. "You're not starting to . . . have the same ideas, are you?"

"What if I am?" Lisa replied, a touch of defiance edging into her voice.

"Lisa," Carol said softly, "you come from a . . . special family. Your father had an amazing mind. He could look at things and figure them out. With people too. He could see things other people couldn't see." She touched Lisa's hand. "Honey, your life is changing because you're growing up. You're not being abducted by a spaceship, you're being taken into adulthood." She released a short, awkward laugh. "Of the two, I'd say that's far and away the scarier proposition."

Lisa listened as her mother continued, but found her mind continually drawn back to the Mojave sightings, her uncle's book, so that by the time Carol left her room, she had made up her mind to contact him.

Chapter Two

Wakeman gave Eric a boyish wink. "So, what's this all about?" he asked.

Eric didn't know. He knew only that he and Wakeman had been summoned to the Office of Science and Technology for what had been described as an important briefing.

The briefing began with the solemn description of a disturbing event.

"About three weeks ago we sent a manned mission into space," Hinkle told them. "This launch was unannounced. The purpose of the mission was to put certain very sensitive equipment into orbit." He glanced at General Beers, as if for approval to go on. The general nodded silently, and Hinkle continued. "It had to do with President Reagan's Strategic Defense Initiative."

"Star Wars," Wakeman said in a carefree tone Hinkle did all he could to ignore.

"As you probably remember," Hinkle said. "There were some questions about whether or not this program was feasible. Before President Bush revisits the project, we need to know if it is . . ."

"So what did you send up?" Wakeman asked. "A reactor?"

"One of the major issues was finding a compact power system that put out enough kilowatts to power both particle-beam weapons and rail guns."

"So, a reactor, like I said," Wakeman said happily.

Hinkle looked at Wakeman irritably, but continued. "Our payload was highly classified. The capsule has been in orbit for fourteen hours. It was two hours away from the position where the payload was to be . . . delivered when . . . well . . . the astronauts went dark for almost two and a half hours."

"They disappeared," Eric said dryly.

"There was no contact," Hinkle confirmed. "Nothing. Then they came back, clear as day. They had no idea that they'd lost two and a half hours of their lives."

"What happened to the payload?" Eric asked matter-of-factly.

"Gone," Hinkle replied.

"And the astronauts?"

"We've debriefed them extensively, used hypnosis and drugs, but they simply have no recollection of this . . . missing time."

Wakeman sat back and grinned. "So, gentlemen, what have you come up with for an explanation?"

General Beers leaned forward. "Let's get something straight," he said to Wakeman sternly. "The people in this room represent seven billion dollars a year in defense spending." He glanced from Wakeman to Eric. "We need your help, gentlemen."

"What do you need from us?" Eric asked.

"What you know about whatever might be . . . out there," Beers answered. "Who they are and what they want."

Eric and Wakeman left the room a few seconds later.

"We're back, baby," Wakeman said cheerily.

Eric stopped and looked at him seriously. "You get started." He smiled. "I'm going to keep working on this Tom Clarke thing."

"Tom Clarke?" Wakeman asked.

"He keeps getting calls from someone in Los Altos, California," Eric explained. "The phone is registered to a guy named Danny Holden. I thought I'd run out there and take a look."

Wakeman looked at him and smiled. "For a while, I thought this was all a bluff. I thought you had something big and you were holding out on me."

Two weeks later Eric arrived at Los Altos, all the other trailers in the park little more than a blur beside the one he came toward like a bullet.

At the door, he presented his ID as a census taker.

The man at the door gave it only a cursory glance, then swung open the door and let him in.

"Let's begin with your name," Eric said as he took a seat in the trailer's cramped living room.

"Danny Holden."

"Do you rent or own?"

Danny laughed. "Who would rent a trailer?"

Eric smiled. "And you wife is?"

"Carol."

"Children?"

"One daughter. Carol's. Her name is Lisa."

Eric wrote the names down on his form.

"She's my stepdaughter," Danny added. "From my wife's first marriage."

At that moment, Lisa entered the room, lugging her drums.

"Lisa, this is Mr . . ."

"Jones," Eric said.

"Mr. Jones. He's from the census."

"Pleased to meet you," Lisa told him.

Eric offered his hand. "I'm very, very glad to meet you," he said. He saw the odd look in her eye, the lightning glint of her suspicion. It was pure intuition, a way of knowing more than the simple facts revealed. It was not unusual to see it in people, this intuition, and he'd have thought nothing of it had Lisa's particular form of it not struck him as far more powerful than any he'd seen before, like steel made stronger by some alloy from another world.

SEATTLE, WASHINGTON, SEPTEMBER 5, 1992

The apartment was small and modest, but no more so than the trailer she'd lived in almost all her life.

"Homey," Tom said, though with a wry expression on his face.

"I think it's nice," Lisa told him. "Thank you."

She'd called Tom a few days before, told him about the man from the census who'd suddenly turned up at the trailer. Tom had responded immediately, told her to come to Seattle, that he would make arrangements for her to stay there.

And so now she stood in a new apartment, embarked upon what she thought must surely be a new direction in life.

"You said you'd tell me," she said to Tom. "About these people, and why you think they're looking for me."

Tom's expression turned serious. "From your description, I'm sure that the man who came to see you was Eric Crawford. His father was an Army colonel named Owen Crawford. It was Owen who came after your father."

"Why was Owen Crawford looking for my father?"

"Because he thought he might be . . . proof."

"Of what?"

"That people had been . . . taken," Tom answered.

"By . . . ?"

"Yes," Tom said.

"And my mom, does she know about all this?"

"She knows that your father was very . . . special. But this alien thing? No. She thinks I'm out of my mind."

Lisa suddenly felt strangely burdened, like one who'd been given a deadly secret she could not share.

Tom touched her face. "Listen, if you need me, put a personal ad in *The New York Times*. 'Drummer seeking gig with Texas country band.' "

Lisa nodded.

"You're going to be all right, Lisa," Tom assured her.

He hugged her, then headed for the door.

"Thanks," Lisa said.

"And believe me," Tom added. "No one's going to find you."

She waved good-bye as he left the room. She knew that he'd believed everything he'd just told her, especially that she was going to be fine, that no one was ever going to find her, not the people from the government, and certainly not the aliens. She could only hope that he was right.

MILWAUKEE, WISCONSIN, SEPTEMBER 6, 1992

Charlie had not been able to stop thinking about his father since his death, and now, with the war medals in his hand, he felt closer than ever, as if his father were with him, standing over him, watching from some great distance.

"Your dad never kept his own medals," his mother told him. "These are your grandfather's from World War II." She looked at them lovingly, as if they connected him to Jesse rather than his grandfather. "He carried them every day of his life. They were in his pocket when he died."

Charlie looked down at the box that had held Russell Keys' medals. A photograph lay at the bottom of the box. He took it out and looked at it closely.

"It's a picture of your father," Amelia said. "When he was eight years old. I think the guy with him is his step-father." She studied the photograph and Charlie could see a dark recollection form in her mind. "Oh yes," she said quietly. "This was the time your father went to the carnival. His stepfather took him. He said it was the most terrifying thing he ever went through. Worse than any-thing in Vietnam." Her fingers held the photograph gin-gerly, like something that might at any moment burst into flame. "It was one of those . . . traveling carnivals," she added, "with rides that spin you around."

"Is that what scared him?" Charlie asked. "The rides?"

Amelia shook her head, her gaze fixed on the picture,

staring at it as if through a rent in time. "No, it was the carnies," she said. One finger slid over to a tall slender figure who slouched, smoking, beside a ticket booth. "Like him."

She handed Charlie the photograph, and as he peered at it, his hand reflexively moved to the red scar behind his ear. "What was wrong with Dad?" he asked.

"He had a . . . brain disorder. He believed certain things."

"What things?"

"He's dead, Charlie," Amelia said. "Do you really want to remember that part of him?"

"I want whatever I can get."

"All right," Amelia said. "He believed that he'd been taken by aliens. Lots of times."

Charlie glanced at the photograph, the carny whose face he recognized. "But the people we're hiding from, they're not . . . aliens."

"No," Amelia said. "They believe in them, though. They believe that your father was taken by them and that's why they wanted him."

"How about you?" Charlie asked. "What do you believe?"

"I don't know," Amelia said. "Your father thought that the aliens were his guardian angels. That they protected him. Because they wanted something. He believed that they saved him in Vietnam." She hesitated a moment, then added, "And he believed that they were coming for you."

Charlie's eyes fell upon the carny. "They have come for me. More than once," he said. He saw the terror crawl into his mother's eyes. "But you know what, Mom? None of this scares me anymore. It just makes me mad."

She smiled, and he could see the pride she had in him, and the pride his father would have had.

"If they come for me again," Charlie added determinedly, "I won't go without a fight."

SEATTLE, WASHINGTON, SEPTEMBER 8, 1992

Lisa set the drums down just inside the door. She'd lugged them for blocks, but it had been worth it, because she'd actually gotten a job with a band. The band wasn't much, and she'd been the only drummer to show up for a tryout. She hadn't been very good either. In fact, the leader of the band had told her that she "sucked," but that if she could "unsuck" in a week she could join them for a hotel gig.

Lisa started to close the door, then was startled to notice the band's guitar player standing behind her, his eyes on the "I Married a Monster From Outer Space" poster she'd tacked to the wall.

"I remember the night before I left home," he said. "I was sleeping in the bed I'd slept in since I was nine. All my stuff still on my walls. I'm lying there thinking how weird it is, this is exactly like it's always been and tomorrow it will be different forever. Do you know what I mean?"

"Oh, yeah," Lisa said.

"You do?"

"That's exactly what happened to me." Lisa smiled. "I expect to wake up any minute in my old room." She made a slow turn, taking in the cramped, but oddly cozy room, and as she turned the old walls changed into something bright and gleaming, and she was . . . now back in her room, staring first at the poster, then at the doorway, which was empty now, the guitar player abruptly vanished . . . if he'd ever been there at all.

ELLSWORTH, MAINE, OCTOBER 28, 1992

Eric pulled up to the fish cannery, observed its rusty tin roof and dilapidated exterior. He smiled. Very good, he thought.

Inside the cannery, banks of monitors lined the walls, their screens gleaming brightly as people bustled about, the whole atmosphere so feverishly active and intently focused that it reminded him of Houston Mission Control.

"Welcome back," Wakeman said as he made his way through the welter of machinery and technicians. "How was California?"

"Sunny," Eric replied. "Very sunny."

Wakeman turned serious. "I've got earth-shattering news, Eric. Are you ready?"

Eric nodded.

"I was wrong," Wakeman said with a delighted laugh. "I took all the money the generals threw at us and I told my guys to build me something that will pick up the impulse signals from the implants. Remember, those faint little beeps that were amplified by the transformer? The transformer I said was the body we had stored at Groom Lake?" He pointed to a large monitor that displayed a map of the United States peppered with lights. "Okay, so we build the thing and we turn it on, and, see there, it lights up like a Christmas tree because those signals are big and bad and boosted."

"Which means what?" Eric asked.

"Which means there's still a transmitter and that we can track any implant, Eric," Wakeman told him proudly, motioning him over to the monitor. "Suppose we want to find Alan, the guy loaded with a chip from that Cleveland girl. Guy works for the Department of the Interior, thinks he went in for a root canal." He looked at the map, then pressed a button on the console. The map enlarged and closed in on Medford, Oregon. "So, okay, there's Alan," Wakeman said happily as the letters appeared on the screen. "Motel Six. Nine seven six Apple Street, nine seven five oh two." Wakeman grinned broadly. "Shall I check in on him, Eric?"

Eric shook his head. "How does this help us, Chet?"

"How does it help us?" Wakeman asked broadly. "How does it help us the man asks." He motioned toward the screen. "Here's how. It provides us with our very own galaxy of abductees."

"I can see that," Eric said coolly.

"Well, here's what you don't see, evidently," Wakeman said. "We can cross check the implants we made, eliminate each one, and what are we left with, my good man? We're left with the unidentified abductees."

"Like Charlie Keys?" Eric asked

"Exactly," Wakeman said delightedly.

"And someone else?" Eric asked, a note of challenge in his voice.

"Just give me the name," Wakeman said confidently.

"Lisa Clarke."

Wakeman sat down at the monitor and typed in the name.

No light flashed.

"She's not coming up," Wakeman said disappointedly.

"Looks like you still have a bit of work to do on your system," Eric said.

"The system's fine," Wakeman shot back. "She doesn't have an implant." He thought a moment, then said, "And why would she? She's part . . . them. They don't need an implant to track her."

"So how is she . . . connected?"

"Probably by some sort of psychic link," Wakeman answered. He tapped a few keys and the image of a brain appeared on the screen. "This is a brain section from the sample we recovered in Alaska."

Eric studied the image, noting the internal structure, the uniformity of color, everything he'd expect to find, but with something added, a green spiral of neutrons.

Wakeman sat back, convinced of his analysis. "Antennae," he said. He looked at Eric. "Lisa Clarke probably has a set just like them."

Eric nodded. "I think the time has come to find out."

SEATTLE, WASHINGTON, NOVEMBER 1, 1992

Lisa saw him as soon as she walked out of the club, a man in a dark jacket, leaning against the wall. He lifted the hood of his jacket, and there was something in the way he did it, the odd concentration of his eyes upon her, that raked a blade of fear down her spine.

She picked up her pace, now focused on a woman in a yellow parka who stepped away from a pay phone as she approached. She glanced behind her. The man in the dark jacket had fallen in behind her.

She continued to move head, the woman in the yellow parka now closing in behind her too.

A lighted bus stop beckoned from the far end of the street, and she headed for it immediately, almost trotting now, her apprehension building. The bus stop seemed very near, yet very far. She could hear the footsteps growing louder and more insistent behind her. They were closing in, and she knew it, but she did not look back.

Then, suddenly, her fear spiked, and she bolted forward and began to run, heading for the cross street now, the footsteps clattering at her rear, so that she knew that the woman in the yellow parka and the hooded man were now running too, rushing after her in full pursuit.

She reached the cross street just as a car sped into it and skidded to a stop, blocking her way. She stopped and glanced behind her. The woman and the man were running toward her at full throttle, the man now with a pistol in his hand.

She whirled around and faced the car.

The window on the driver's side was down now, and she saw a man sitting behind the wheel.

"Lisa," the man said. "How are you doing?" He smiled. "We have so much to talk about."

She stared at him, stunned that he knew her name. Behind her, the man and woman were closing in. She was trapped, and she knew it. There was no escape.

Then, suddenly, five beams of lights converged into a single shining brilliance that swept around her protectively. The light was impossibly bright, and yet she could see through it, as if she were encased in a vase of shining crystal. Through a veil of sparkling light she saw the woman and the man freeze instantly, as if blinded by the very light that held her. She turned and saw the man in the car. He was smiling oddly, and looking up. She followed the direction of his upward gaze and saw a shimmering craft hovering a hundred feet above her, the protective beam shooting down from its base. From inside her tube of light, she could see five globes of blue light, dancing and coming together, the underside of the craft barely visible beyond them.

She lowered her eyes and peered out through the shimmering wall of light. The woman in the yellow parka was very near now, almost touching the rim of light, so that the light itself began to sizzle. The woman jerked away suddenly, and Lisa saw that her face was badly burned.

Her eyes shot over toward the hooded man. He was standing beyond the light, his eyes frozen in stricken awe, the pistol still in his hand, but useless to him now.

Then the light began to move, and Lisa felt herself move with it, floating inside the beam, carried by it like a small child, and she knew that she was being taken home.

She was safe, and she knew it. She saw the hooded man lift his pistol toward her, then the man in the car, nod for him to put it down. Another car arrived, and she saw the man who'd come with the census forms get out and stare at her through the light, helpless to reach her, his eyes locked on hers as the light swept her on and on until, abruptly, it vanished, and she stood alone in her apartment.

She drew in a deep, calming breath, then knew what she had to do, walked determinedly to the phone and dialed the number.

"Information," a man said.

"The national edition of *The New York Times*," Lisa said.

The man gave her the number and she dialed it.

"I'd like to place an ad in the personals, please," Lisa said, when someone answered in New York.

Chapter Three

The photographs scrolled by in two columns on the monitor, scores of human faces that had been collected in the database.

"These are matched repeaters," Wakeman explained. "We started with anyone who'd been taken more than once. We noticed there was a subset. People who were repeatedly taken on the same day as others. These are the eight-timers. Taken eight times since childhood, all on the same day, every time. Fifty men and fifty women. They seem to take them when they're young. Again when they hit puberty."

"Breeding pairs?" Eric asked.

Wakeman shrugged. "It makes about as much sense as anything else they're doing." His eyes suddenly sparked when Charlie Keys' photograph scrolled onto the screen. "Stop," he cried. "Russell Keys' son."

Eric nodded.

Wakeman indicated the picture just beneath it. "And this, of course, is Lisa Clarke." He considered the two photographs briefly, then said, "They were both taken on September eighth of last year. That's the most recent simultaneous abduction. In fact, they're the only one among the fifty pairs in the last year and a half."

"You think they're being bred?" Eric asked, returning to his earlier idea. "Keys with a girl who's one-quarter alien?"

"You know, maybe I've been looking at this the wrong way," Wakeman said, almost to himself. He looked at Eric. "I'm used to looking at genetic engineering as a way of breeding out certain traits. What if our friends are interested in breeding in?"

"Meaning what?" Eric asked.

"Well, think about Russell Keys. He was a pilot, right? Brave, courageous and bold, so to speak. His son Jesse had the same characteristics. That is, when they were taken, they fought back."

"And the Clarkes. I know Jacob could . . . do things," Eric offered.

"But what are they breeding for?"

"It could be anything," Wakeman said. "Maybe they're trying to create a superweapon." He shrugged. "Or a supersavior." He returned his attention to the photographs on the screen. "Either way, we should have the answer in another couple of months," he said.

SEATTLE, WASHINGTON, APRIL 7, 1993

Lisa stood at the stove, making tea for her mother and Nina.

"What do you think?" Nina asked, displaying the spiraling conch tattoo on her shoulder.

"I think it must have hurt a lot," Lisa said. She glanced over and caught her mother looking at her silently.

She knew what her mother was thinking, that her little girl had moved to Seattle, gotten a dingy little apartment, and was now pregnant. Not very impressive.

"Come home," Carol said.

"I can't," Lisa told her. "I'm safe here."

"Why?" Carol said, her voice laced with anger and frustration. "Because beings from another world are looking out for you?"

"Yes, Mom," Lisa answered, daring her mother to say otherwise. "And if you'd seen what happened to me, you'd . . ."

Carol got to her feet. "Enough, Lisa."

"But it's true," Lisa pleaded. She rose and drew her mother into her arms. "It's going to be all right, Mom," she said. "I can feel it."

Carol looked at her, and Lisa saw that she was seeing her father also, the terrible burden of what he'd known, the long years of his suffering.

"I never wanted to believe any of this," Carol said. "Your father let me see some things, but I really couldn't accept that any of it was real. I just thought it was his way of dealing with his own life, the fact that he never knew his father."

MADISON, WISCONSIN, APRIL 9, 1993

Charlie startled at the knock at the door and grabbed the ball bat before answering it.

Naomi glanced at the bat, then at Charlie. "What are you doing?"

"Nothing," Charlie said. He put down the bat. "I'm sorry."

Naomi stepped into the room, surveying its disarray, the piles of paper, library copies of articles, magazines, books. "So this is how you've been using your leave of absence," she said. "Sitting in the dark, reading with a baseball bat by the door in case anyone drops by."

Charlie closed the door. He could imagine what his friend was thinking, that he was a nut, the sort of crazy eccentric who ended up talking to himself on street corners or in parks, destined for the mental hospital. "I just needed a little time to myself," he said lamely.

Naomi faced him squarely, her stern middle-aged face a perfect vision of the no-nonsense disciplinarian. "I've been principal at Lincoln for ten years, Charlie," she said. "I taught there before that, and let me tell you something, you're the best teacher I've ever seen and I'm not going to lose you without a fight." Her gaze fell on one particular book. She picked it up, stared at the illustration of a little gray space creature on the cover and read the title skeptically. "*Arrival,* by Tom Clarke." She looked at Charlie. "What's this?"

"Nothing," Charlie said, embarrassed.

Naomi read the subtitle. "The alien agenda—what the abductions really mean." She let the book slip from her hand, then snatched up another. "*Compendium of Alien Races.*" She looked at Charlie in stunned disbelief. "Charlie, you think you've been abducted by aliens, don't you?"

Charlie knew that he had no answer to give her. She thought he was crazy as a loon. Everyone did. Or would, if they knew the . . . what he . . . his . . . it was all so use-less, he thought, so utterly futile, and yet he knew the truth.

"Do you have any idea how many people say they've been abducted every year?" he asked.

Naomi looked at him as if he were a small child in need of serious correction. "Charlie, people believe in these things because they want to believe in something."

"If that's true, then why are all the stories so similar?"

"Because we all see the same movies and read the same books," Naomi answered emphatically. She picked up the first book and turned the cover over to the face on the back. "For instance, this guy, Tom Clarke. He's every-where, Charlie."

Charlie felt something break inside him, the last re-serves of his argument, leaving him nothing but the raw edge of his pain, the heartbreak of the pariah. He saw the sadness in Naomi's eyes, how much she wanted to help him, and how helpless she felt in the face of what she had to believe was his madness.

"They've been taking me since I was nine years old, Naomi," he said quietly. "They came again seven months ago. I fought back. I kicked and bit and . . ." He stopped and stared into Naomi's fretful eyes and more than any-thing yearned simply to *be believed!* "I'm not crazy," he said. "And so I'll find the proof."

SUPERIOR FISH, ELLSWORTH, MAINE, MAY 31, 1993

Eric peered at the map of the world that Wakeman had displayed on a huge board. It was filled with lights, and in each light Eric saw the nature of the encounter, the fear and wonder of it all, the news both dreadful and awe-inspiring, that we were not alone.

"Always the same story," Wakeman said. "A woman in Siberia. Another one in Norway. A third in Alaska. All over the world. Zanzibar. Australia. One hundred and forty-four multiwitness, confirmable reports."

Eric kept his eyes on the map. Something had changed, he knew.

"When did all this start?" he asked.

"Six weeks ago. One big rush, then zilch. No activity since then."

"What do you think it means?"

"It's the calm."

"The calm?"

Wakeman returned his attention to the map. "The one before the storm," he said.

SEATTLE, WASHINGTON, JUNE 22, 1993

Lisa stared out the window of her room in the maternity ward, listening to the radio as the reports came one after the other, lights in Grand Teton, in Coeur D'Alene, Idaho, lights seen by all manner of people, farmers, workers, doctors, cops . . . and now here, in Seattle, where she could see them, radiant orbs that hung silently in the night sky as the radio reporter breathlessly narrated the scene, all the wild speculation, the government's unwillingness to confirm or deny anything.

"Are you focused?" Nina asked.

Lisa felt the cramp draw in like a belt yanked tight around her.

Nina pressed her hand on Lisa's sweat-spattered fore-head. "Listen, I have a great idea for a tattoo for the baby," she said with a nervous laugh. "Nothing too big. Just a little snake."

The cramp subsided, and Lisa once again stared out at the night sky.

"When the next contraction comes," Nina told her, "take in a deep breath."

The cramp came again, fierce and searing, but Lisa continued to gaze into the sparkling night.

"She's fully dilated," one of the nurses said. "Stop pushing."

Lisa was not aware that she'd been pushing. It was the baby who was pushing, being born at its own pace and of its own free will.

"Stop pushing," the nurse cried.

Lisa watched the heavens. "I can't," she said.

The nurse's voice was tense. "Call Dr. Catrell."

Lisa's eyes swept over to the nurse. "What's wrong?" she demanded. "What's going on?"

She heard the nurse give her blood pressure. "She's having seizures," the nurse said, but Lisa felt no seizures. She turned her eyes back to the window, where scores of lights sparkled brightly in the night sky. One, two, three, she said to herself, counting the lights as rapidly as she could. Six, seven, eight . . .

"She's preeclamptic," the nurse called.

"Let's stabilize her."

The lights were coming together, and Lisa's eyes widened as the dazzling display began to move in upon itself.

"Four grams magnesium."

The beauty of the lights bloomed like a flower in her mind, but she continued to count.

"Five milligrams hydralazine."

From the corner of her eye, she saw Dr. Catrell draw near, his lips at her ear. "What's happening is called eclampsia," he said.

Lisa watched the sky, the lights moving in upon each other, drawing in as if toward the nucleus of some great cosmic soul.

"BP's down to one twenty," the nurse called.

"It's coming," the doctor cried.

"So much blood," the nurse said.

"She's DIC," the doctor said.

Lisa held her gaze fixed on the sky, all the lights in their final convergence, becoming one dazzling ball of light.

"She's bleeding out!"

And the light flashed in a huge magnificent radiance, an explosion in the vast night sky, but silent, utterly silent, so that all Lisa heard as the light engulfed the room was the faint cry of her newborn little girl.

A blackness settled over her, then rose in a slowly building light. When she opened her eyes, it was morning, and Nina sat beside her bed.

"Hey," Lisa said softly.

"Hey," Nina said. She smiled. "You weren't supposed to be here, you know. You were bleeding to death."

"What happened?"

"The bleeding stopped," Nina answered. "No one knows why."

"My baby?" Lisa asked fearfully.

Nina stepped over to a bassinet, picked up the baby and brought her to her mother. "She's beautiful, isn't she?" She placed the child in Lisa's arms. "Seven pounds three ounces of perfect little girl."

Lisa nodded. "Yes."

"What are you going to name her?"

She hadn't considered a name, but one sprang into her consciousness so quickly it seemed to have been there always, as if long ago implanted in her mind.

"Allison," she said. "Allie. Her name is Allie."

ELLSWORTH, MAINE, AUGUST 2, 1993

Eric stirred the lone olive in his martini and looked admiringly at a daughter he'd rarely seen since the divorce. His bright little girl had grown into a lovely, intelligent woman with intense, determined eyes. Looking at her, he felt a vague sadness for the inevitable passage of time, the way fathers grew weak as their children grew strong, shrank as they developed. Becky came to mind again and he wondered how his life might have been different if he'd simply met her on a spring day, just an ordinary guy, a doctor or a scientist perhaps. Had he been only that, she might have loved him. But he was Eric Crawford, Owen Crawford's son, the dark legacy of his father like a stain on his soul.

"So," Mary said with her usual directness. "Why did you want to see me, Dad?"

Eric smiled. Right down to business. That was Mary. No time for sentiment, for idle conversation, a simple inquiry into his health.

"There's something I want to show you," Eric said. He opened the drawer of his desk, took out the artifact and handed it to her. "Your grandfather found this in Pine Lodge, New Mexico. He found it at a crash site."

Mary turned the artifact in her hand, and he could see the way she was drawn toward it, almost mystically, a power pulling her in.

She looked at Eric. "It's all true then," she said finally. Her eyes swept back down to the artifact, and he saw that she believed it, and was suddenly, miraculously in league with him.

Then he told her everything, the whole history of his involvement with the artifact, as well as her grandfather's. The artifact she held in her hand was the one proof in all the world that the kooks and crackpots had gotten it right, that out there, somewhere in space, there was another world, that creatures from that world had visited the earth, taken people and in some way used them. He told her about the implants, his theory that people were being bred in some way and for some purpose he had not yet been able to discover. He told her about Charlie Keys and Lisa Clarke. Chet Wakeman knew all of this, Eric said, but he knew nothing of the artifact. That, and that alone, was a secret she must keep to herself.

"Chet's coming by in a few minutes," Eric said in conclusion. "He says he has some news. From now on, we'll all be working together."

Mary said nothing, but Eric saw her eyes flash with excitement.

When Wakeman came into the room a few minutes later, Eric noticed that Mary's fingers instantly curled protectively around the artifact.

"Hello, thrill seekers," Wakeman said as he stepped into the study. His gaze immediately leaped to Mary.

"Well, look at you," he said. "All grown up and beautiful. How's the quest for the Nobel Prize coming?"

"I came close to coming up with a genomic-mismatch scanning technique," Mary answered proudly.

Wakeman smiled. "And you're only in graduate school." He looked at her admiringly for a moment, then turned to Eric. "Well, ready for the news?"

Eric nodded.

Wakeman sat down in the chair opposite Eric. "Well, here's the latest. Lisa Clarke has had a baby. A little girl."

"Are we going to try to pick them up?" Eric asked immediately.

"What would be the point of that?" Wakeman asked.

A few hours later, Mary lay in Wakeman's arms, her eyes moving along the walls of the small motel room.

"God, I've been waiting a long time to do that," Wakeman said.

"Me, too," Mary said. She leaned over, kissed him, then drew away. "Why don't you pick up the baby?"

Wakeman smiled. "You don't waste any time, do you?"

"She's clearly important," Mary said. "In fact, I'd say, she's the point of this."

"Definitely."

"So pick her up. Take her."

Wakeman shook his head. "They'd just take her back . . . and they're way better at that than we are."

"So what do we do?"

"We watch and wait," Wakeman told her. "And we work on a way to take her that will work."

"'Watch and wait,'" Mary repeated. "That sounds a lot like my father."

Wakeman chuckled. "I'm nothing like your father."

Mary kissed him softly.

"I have a theory about who she is," Wakeman said. "Want to hear it?"

Mary nodded.

"Evolution tends to eliminate, or at least, subjugate emotion," Wakeman said. "The limbic brain is still down there." His eyes slid over to Mary. "Imagine their . . . abilities combined with the energy of our strong emotions."

"They'd be cherry bombs," Mary said, her eyes lifting toward the ceiling as if picturing the terrible force of such a combination. "But she'd be a thermonuclear weapon."

PART SEVEN

God's Equation

Chapter One

Charlie lay naked on the bed, his body glistening with sweat. Or was it sweat? In the dream he'd been suspended in a tank of translucent liquid, floating upside down, his arms spread. Through the thick liquid he'd seen figures scurrying about, slender, with elongated arms, their pear-shaped heads and almond eyes continually glancing toward him.

He sat up and stared around the room, his gaze moving over the vast amount of testimony he'd gathered over the years, tapes and transcripts, printouts from alien abduction sites he'd found on the Internet. None of that seemed as real as the dream, however, none of it actual proof of what had happened to him, or that it had ever happened to anyone else, proof that he wasn't crazy, proof that he was not alone.

SEATTLE, WASHINGTON, PRESENT DAY

Allie knew that they came to her because they sensed that she could calm them, give them direction, Denny and Milo and even Nina. Her eyes moved silently from one face to the next, all of them in a circle around her. There was something about them that made her think of the fairy tales her mother had read to her. People were like characters in those tales. They were abandoned in the woods. They were locked in towers. They couldn't reach each other. They went after things they thought were valuable or important or would last, but they couldn't be sure that the things they went after had any of those qualities. Half the time they seemed lost and desperate, as if some horrible monster were chasing them, and they were growing tired, and it was closing in.

"You guys want to get enlightenment, or you want to play some rock and roll?" Lisa asked as she came into the room.

Denny and Milo got to their feet and headed for their guitars. Allie took her place near Denny, who'd told her that his rhythm improved when she was near him. She wasn't sure this was true, but during her nine short years of life, she'd gotten used to people saying strange things to her, expecting strange things from her. She had a power, people said, and she knew that this was true.

She recalled the time, three years before, when her mother had taken her to see the dolphins, how she'd stood before the tank, lifted her arms without knowing why, then stood, oddly unsurprised, as the dolphins had turned and drifted toward her, their many faces finally near hers, their noses nearly touching the glass, suspended there, as if waiting for instructions. She had a power, yes, but all she really wanted was just to be a little girl.

SUPERIOR FISH CANNERY, ELLSWORTH, MAINE, PRESENT DAY

The video showed a soccer field, kids frantically at play, Allie in the forefront, pursuing the ball.

"That's Lisa Clarke's daughter, and yes, she can block a shot on goal," Eric said. "But other than that, she hasn't demonstrated anything like the kind of power we were expecting. Which is good, because once she demonstrates, we might not be able to pick her up." Eric held his eyes on the video, Allie now closing in on the ball. "Lisa has joined some kind of therapy group for people who claim they've been taken. We've placed an agent in that same group." He shrugged. "Just a way of keeping an eye on things."

Wakeman and Mary continued to watch the video until it froze with Allie still on the soccer field, her eyes sparkling with competitive drive.

"She's still a little kid," Wakeman said. "Give her time."

"Chet's right," Mary said. She gave Wakeman a curiously charged glance. "A lot of genetic traits don't demonstrate until right before adolescence. Schizophrenia, for example."

She smiled at Wakeman, and Eric caught a glimmer in her eyes. It was no longer the look of a little girl who admired her "uncle," he realized, but of a woman flirting with a man.

"Well, we can't pick her up anyway," Eric said with a

shrug. "They'll just take her back, like they did when we tried for Lisa."

Wakeman returned Mary's flirtatious smile, then turned to Eric.

"That used to be the case," he said.

"Used to be the case?" Eric asked.

Wakeman could hardly contain his billowing self-confidence. "Want to see what we can do?" He pressed his hand at Mary's back and gently urged her over to a small microwave oven attached to a computer.

"Microwave radiation," he said as Eric joined them at the oven. "Part of the light spectrum." Wakeman stared at the small hamster that scurried about inside the oven. "In the case of the oven, twelve point five centimeters to be exact." He hit the oven's switch. "Don't worry, my dear," Wakeman added with a laugh. "We're not going to fry our furry little friend." He smiled. "At least . . . not yet."

Eric watched as the hamster continued to move about inside the oven, ears up, whiskers twitching, large round eyes peering back at him from the other side of the glass.

"When we block that wavelength, our little friend is on easy street," Wakeman said. He reached down and tapped a command on the computer keyboard beside the oven.

Instantly, the hamster exploded, its hair and entrails slammed against the glass in a gooey, red mass.

"In meditation we learn the oneness of all things," Wakeman said, his gaze on the bloody pulp that was all that remained of the hamster. "The harmony that flows through nature. These are the same ideas, only stripped of the comforting notion of divinity that we get from science, and more specifically, from mathematics." He took a pad from the desk, scribbled a few numbers and handed the pad to Mary.

"The Fibonacci sequence," Mary said. "Each number added to the one before it makes the next number in the sequence." She looked at her father, she now the teacher, he the student. "The Fibonacci sequence gives us the golden mean," she told him. "They're everywhere, these numbers. Shells. Nebulae. The spiral of a pinecone. Beehives. DNA."

"Is this going somewhere?" Eric asked impatiently.

Wakeman turned to him. "Their crafts hold five," he explained. "The number of confirmed sightings in Mexico last year was 1,597. They have three fingers and one thumb."

"The number of breeding pairs you charted when you were figuring out who Allie was, 55. 1 . . . 3, 5 . . . 55 . . . 1,597," Mary said. "They're all Fibonacci numbers."

"And it goes on," Wakeman said, winking at Mary. "How many lights on board? Forty-six thousand, three hundred and sixty-seven, and with our little friend, Allie . . ." He wrote the number on the pad and turned the pad toward Eric. "46,368. The twenty-fourth Fibonacci."

"So," Mary said grandly. "How do you take our revelation and use it to make an effective block so that we can grab little Forty-six thousand, three hundred and sixty-eight, our little Allie?" She looked at Wakeman, turning the narrative over to him now.

Wakeman gestured toward a young man who lay unconscious on a gurney. "That's Peter Miller. Mr. Miller has been taken thirteen times." He smiled. "Don't worry, Eric, I'm not going to splatter dear Peter all over the room. Janitorial would never forgive me."

He pointed to the huge tracking board that covered the opposite wall, a enormous map of the United States, its surface scattered with colored lights.

"Mr. Miller has an implant," he said. "We're monitoring that implant. You can see by that light on the map that Mr. Miller is currently residing right here in the lovely, peaceful fishing village of Ellsworth, Maine."

Wakeman took a five-sided device from the table and placed it like a hangman's hood over Miller's head. "The implants broadcast on a spread spectrum. They're all based on the hydrogen hyperfine transition line. The most fundamental wavelength in the universe." He took a studied, theatrical pause, then said, "Fibonacci again." He smiled. "We block those frequencies in a way that will ensure that . . . shall we say . . . the 'hamster' doesn't splatter." He pointed to the map. "As you can see. Mr. Miller's light is no longer shining. That means that his implant isn't registering, and *that* means that we can pick someone up without having them grabbed right back."

Eric stared at Peter Miller. "Will this work on the girl?"

"Allie doesn't have an implant, remember?" Wakeman said. "Just that neutron spiral, if you recall. The one she no doubt inherited from her mother."

"So we can't . . ."

"Yes, we can, Eric," Wakeman said. "Because the same principle applies. We can block her frequency, too."

HARRIET PENZLER'S OFFICE, SEATTLE, WASHINGTON

Charlie moved around the room, his camera pausing at each face. Dale Adler, a middle-aged man whose grief lay upon him like a black veil; Ray Morrison; a married couple, Ben and Nora; a tough-looking young woman named Cynthia; Dorothy, who claimed to have twelve cats; and an older man named Adams.

"Contrails are messages," Ray said. "When they appeared in the sky above St. Paul, the incidence of severe upper respiratory infections quadrupled."

"What are contrails?" Dorothy asked.

"Those white trails jets leave behind," Adams said.

"Messages," Dale repeated. "I think we're reaching here."

"We're not here to judge," Harriet cautioned. "Just to listen."

"There is a base," Ray went on adamantly. "A landing strip at the bottom of Lake Superior. I was taken to this landing strip on my third abduction."

"How come you didn't drown?" Nora asked.

"They did something to me that made me able to breathe under water," Ray answered.

Dale gave a doubtful shrug.

Ray glared at him. "But I'm supposed to believe your story about seeing your dead son in a spaceship, right?" he demanded. "So why is it that you can . . ."

"Could you share the story of your son with us, Dale," Harriet said, cutting Ray off.

"We lost our boy, Luke," Dale began. "In the Gulf War. It was about six months later when they came for me. One night, I woke up and there were these five young men standing by my bed. Soldiers, like Luke was. They asked me would I like to see Luke. Then there was this big light, and Luke was there and we talked. And after that, they'd come for me every night, these same soldiers, and there'd be Luke, and we'd talk, and then he'd be gone." He shook his head. "It was like they wanted to make me grieve for him all over again."

Ray shook his head. "You're just having bad dreams, Dale."

Dale leaped to his feet, his eyes flaring. "Does this look like dreams to you?" he asked as he pulled down the collar of his shirt, revealing several slender red lines on his neck, each knotted with what appeared to be joints.

Ray looked at the marks on Dale's neck. "That could have happened any way at all. You could have done that to yourself."

"Please now," Harriet said. "You're all here because you believe you've experienced something. This is hard work. Painful work."

The door opened and Charlie saw a slender, dark-haired young woman enter the room. "Sorry I'm late," she said, glancing at Charlie.

"Lisa, we have a guest today," Harriet explained. "This is Charlie. He's taping the session for a documentary he's doing. Charlie has spent years talking to people who've had experiences like yours. The others have agreed to being taped but if you're not comfortable . . ."

"No, I'm not," Lisa interrupted. She looked Charlie dead in the eye. "I like to keep my private life private," she said.

Charlie lowered the camera. "Sorry," he said. "I understand."

Throughout the rest of the session, Charlie noticed that Lisa continually drew her eyes toward him. They were knowing eyes, and what they knew was something fierce and dreadful, that a human being could vanish into a white light, then reemerge hours later in a completely different place, be taken again and again in sudden, nightmarish seizures, never told why you'd been chosen or if they would ever leave you alone.

Later that afternoon, as they sat together in a coffee shop, Lisa made no effort to conceal what had happened to her, or what she knew had happened to Charlie.

"How long have they been taking you?" Lisa asked.

"Since I was a kid," Charlie answered.

"Me, too."

"But they don't take me anymore," Charlie added. "Not in nine years. Since then, I've been trying to prove that it really happened. I want to know why they did it and why they stopped."

Lisa considered this briefly, then said, "Did you like your abductions?"

"Like them?" Charlie asked, astonished.

"Yeah," Lisa answered. "As in enjoy them. Look forward to them. I used to get this energy thing. This buzz. It felt great. I believe this whole abduction deal is going to turn out to be a positive event. Right now, people think we're whacked, we're fringe-dwellers, but that's going to change. We've been chosen for something."

"For me, it was never a buzz," Charlie said. "I didn't know what was happening to me . . . and I fought back as hard as I could."

For a moment they peered at each other silently, then Lisa began to gather up her things. "I have to get home," she said. "I have a daughter."

Neither of them stood up. They just stared at each other, neither of them able to shake the eerie feeling that they'd already met.

Charlie reached for his wallet, and as he did so a picture fell onto the table between them. "That's my dad," he said when he noticed Lisa staring at it.

"The carny," she whispered, her eyes lifting slowly toward Charlie. She seemed almost to shiver. "Things just got a lot more weird," she said. "We need to talk to Dr. Penzler."

Minutes later Charlie sat a few feet away as Penzler prepared to do what she called a regression. Lisa lay on a sofa, her eyes watching him, so strangely familiar, he felt they'd watched him all his life.

"Are you ready?" Dr. Penzler asked.

"Ready," Lisa said.

And suddenly the walls of Dr. Penzler's office dissolved into panels of radiant light, and she felt her body lift and turn and float upward toward the top of a huge glass canister. Revolving slowly, she saw small creatures with almond-shaped eyes. Then another canister came into view. Inside the canister, a naked man floated in the same thick liquid. Suddenly both canisters began to close in upon each, getting nearer and nearer until, in a moment of radiant energy, they touched, held briefly, then drew apart, each turning more rapidly now, the velocity building steadily, until she felt herself spinning wildly, everything a passing blur as if she were being shot through a tunnel of light at terrific speed, away and away, back to something far below, something added to her from the journey, a thrilling spark of life.

"Lisa!"

She opened her eyes and saw Charlie standing over her, Dr. Penzler at his side.

"What did you see?" Charlie asked.

"It wasn't quite my 'new age' dream," Lisa answered quietly.

"What was it then?"

Lisa looked at him softly. "It was about you and me."

"What about us?"

Lisa shook her head.

Charlie stared at her urgently. "What was it?" he asked insistently.

Lisa's eyes fled toward the window, held briefly, then returned to him.

He could see how oddly shaken she was, how reluctant to reveal what she'd seen.

"I'm not ready," was all she said.

Charlie met Allie an hour later, a little nine-year-old girl with large, penetrating eyes who seemed to reside in an otherworldly calm. They sat in the small living room of Lisa's apartment, Allie framed by her mother's poster of "I Married a Monster From Outer Space."

"You're in the fourth grade, right?" Charlie asked.

Allie nodded.

"I taught fourth grade," Charlie added. "You're doing state history, reading *Sarah, Plain and Tall,* and this is the 'big ideas' year in science. Electricity and magnetism."

"We read *Sarah, Plain and Tall,* last year," Allie said, her voice spirited and energetic, a little girl so eager to learn that time itself seemed her only obstacle. "This year it's *Island of the Blue Dolphins.*"

"Good one," Charlie said with a quick smile.

Allie's expression grew oddly serious. "So this is the year I find out how everything works? The 'big ideas?' "

"Pretty much," Charlie answered.

"So then what happens, they all forget?"

Charlie laughed. "I never thought of it that way," he admitted.

Nina arrived before Charlie could ask another

question, and he saw that she was surprised to find a stranger in the house.

"Who are you?" she asked.

Lisa laughed. "We've been trying to figure that out all afternoon."

Nina's eyes remained on Charlie. "I can't hang around to find out more," she said, "But it looks to me like I'll be seeing you around." She rushed over and gave Allie a kiss. "Gotta run. Bye sweetheart."

At dinner, Allie paused a moment, as if considering the right approach, then said, "You've been on spaceships too."

It was not a question, Charlie recognized, but a statement of fact. "Yes . . . I have," he said.

"Was it scary?"

"Kind of."

"Did it make you mean?" Allie asked.

"I don't think so," Charlie answered. "How come?"

"My mom didn't get mean either," Allie told him. "But some of the people she knows did . . . I think people get mean when they're scared."

Charlie recognized himself in her words, recalling the ferocity of his battle, how he had swung at them, kicked, screamed, all of it done in the grip of terror.

Allie smiled. "I have a journal," she said. "I write down things I think of and stuff."

"That's a good idea," Charlie told her. "I always wish I'd done that."

"Maybe some time, I could read you mine," Allie said.

Charlie smiled. "That would be great." He turned toward Lisa, and saw that she was watching him somberly.

"You're up next, you know. With Harriet. Your regression. You've never done it before, have you?"

Charlie shook his head.

"Sometimes it can be . . . there can be a lot of information."

"Okay," Charlie said softly.

Lisa seemed hesitant to continue, but determined to do it. "During the regression, I saw us," she said.

"Us?"

Lisa glanced toward Allie, then back to him. "Us, yes," she said significantly.

Charlie's gaze swept over to Allie, and he knew that she was his and Lisa's, conceived in a tunnel of light, a kind of star child, yet an earthling too, precious beyond measure, rare beyond imagining, and so a creature others were surely hunting down.

SUPERIOR FISH CANNERY, ELLSWORTH, MAINE

Mary strolled with Wakeman along the dock in the early morning light, water lapping softly on the wooden pylons. She'd never seen this particular look on his face, oddly dreamy, and somewhat pensive, a man in love, she thought, but also a man who seemed to be taken by a sudden insight.

"Maybe they want to make us better," Wakeman said after a moment. "Enable us to move to the next rung of the ladder. And in doing that, they'll better themselves as well."

Mary shook her head. "I have a different idea. Say it began as a research project. . . a project on a scale totally beyond our comprehension. A detailed accounting of our entire planet."

Wakeman smiled. "I like it."

"Now, imagine this," Mary continued. "While doing the research, they inadvertently come across an incredible insight. Something that utterly rearranges the way they see the universe."

"And that's what Allie is," Wakeman asked. "The result of this insight?"

"Evolution comes at a cost, Chet," Mary said. "Every choice is the death of all other possibilities. Maybe something was lost along the way."

Wakeman nodded. "Probably something very simple." He thought a moment, then added, "All I've ever wanted was to understand them . . . not even understand, just catch a glimpse, see through their eyes." He glanced up toward the heavens. "We're getting close, Mary. We'll have the girl. Through her, we'll be able to talk to them." His eyes glistened. "I've been waiting for this moment all my life." He drew Mary into his arms. "What I never knew was that I'd find someone to share the moment with me." He started to kiss her, but the ring of Mary's cell phone stopped him.

"Yes," Mary answered. "Dr. Penzler. Hello." She looked at Wakeman significantly. "Thank you very much. I look forward to seeing you again soon." She smiled. "Yes, it is unexpected . . . but that's one of life's happy accidents." She closed the phone and returned it to her pocket. "There's a new wrinkle," she said gravely. "Allie's dad just showed up."

Charlie and Lisa sat together, the others in Dr. Penzler's group seated around them, Dr. Penzler near the center, her notebook open, pencil at the ready.

"I just can't stand this feeling that my life is out of control," Adams said.

Ray waved his hand. "Welcome to my world," he scoffed.

"They're more advanced," Ben complained. "But that doesn't make them God."

Adams seemed hardly to hear Ben. "What makes me furious is that the government has cut a deal with them," he said. "They know about this, but they cover it up."

"You people make me sick," Ray blurted out. He glared at the others. "You're all victims. It's time someone took charge."

The others stared at him motionlessly.

"They come into our homes," Ray cried angrily. "They . . . do things to us. And we just sit there and take it."

"You talk like there's something we could do," Ben said.

"There is," Ray shouted, his temper flaring. "We can fight back."

Dr. Penzler shifted uneasily in her seat. "Have you ever fought back, Ray?"

Ray shot a piercing look over to Dr. Penzler. "I've . . . yeah, I'd like to think I have. But that's not what I'm talking about. There's us, here in this room. Fine. But the people out there in the world, they treat us like we're crazy." He glanced from face to face among the group. "If we're all alone, there's no fighting back. But if we were believed . . . if there was proof . . ."

Dr. Penzler turned toward Charlie. "That was your idea, too, wasn't it, Charlie? To get proof?"

Charlie shifted nervously, suddenly on the spot. "It was . . . yeah."

"Not anymore?" Dr. Penzler asked.

Charlie looked at Lisa, smiled quietly, then turned to Dr. Penzler. "Some things have come up that kind of . . . rearranged my priorities," he said.

"This is so romantic," Ray scoffed. "Charlie and Lisa. Soul mates. Destined to find each other in the stars. It's enough to make me puke."

Charlie felt his anger rise. "Why don't you lighten up, buddy?" he warned.

"Why don't I lighten up?" Ray snarled. "Maybe because I'm tired of all this cosmic whining."

"You know what, Ray?" Cynthia said. "All you ever do is shout down everyone else's story. So, what's your story?"

Ray glared at her. "You want my story?" He jerked a pistol from behind his back. "Here's my story," he said.

Charlie stepped forward. "Give me that gun, Ray."

"Not the whole thing," Ray said quietly. "Just a piece of it."

Then he fired.

SEATTLE, WASHINGTON

Mary rubbed a smudge from the windshield for a clearer view, then sat back, her hands on the wheel. In the soccer field beyond a line of trees she could see Allie darting along, kicking at the ball. She glanced at her watch. Three-thirty.

"They should be here by now."

"Don't worry, these guys are very punctual." Wakeman smiled, his gaze following Allie as she moved across the field. "Pretty little girl," he said.

Mary nodded as a dark car pulled up near the goal-post, two men in sweatshirts in the front seat. "There they are," she said.

Wakeman watched a third man move along the edge of the field, a jogger in a sweatshirt. "And the rest of the team, right on time."

"Yes," Mary said. She opened the door and looked at Wakeman. "Ready, Chet?"

"Ready."

Wakeman pulled himself from the car and joined Mary, the two of them now heading across the field to where Allie continued to chase the ball until she abruptly stopped, peered at them intently for a moment, then whirled around and began to run.

"Let's go!" Mary cried as she bounded forward, running with all her strength, joined by the others, all of them converging as Allie fled into the adjoining woods.

Mary could see her racing toward a break in the trees and into the speeding traffic beyond the woods where . . . the air suddenly congealed and she felt as if she were moving through a thick invisible gelatin, Wakeman lurching ponderously at her side, encased in the suffocating air, everything slowing as if some mysterious force had been drained from the earth, leaving nothing free to move save the little girl she could still see darting deerlike and unencumbered through the otherwise numb and exhausted realm of earth.

Charlie lay on the sofa in Dr. Penzler's office, grimacing in pain as Lisa applied the tourniquet. He stared at the others herded together around him, pale with fright, watching as Ray paced back and forth before them.

"He needs a hospital," Lisa said.

Ray shook his head. "I need to talk to the FBI." He picked a cell phone from one of the pile he'd taken from the group and tossed it to Dr. Penzler. "Call the FBI. Tell them that I'm armed and that I'm going to have to start shooting people if my demands aren't met."

"What are your demands?" Dr. Penzler asked.

"Tell them that I want to speak to someone in charge," Ray answered. "The extraterrestrial project. I want to talk to whoever's in charge of that. I want him here, in this room, so I can look in his eyes."

Dr. Penzler opened the phone.

Suddenly the door burst open and all eyes turned toward where a little girl stood breathlessly.

"Allie," Lisa said.

Ray moved the pistol, directing Allie to join the others. Then he looked at Dr. Penzler. "Make the call," he said.

Dr. Penzler dialed a number, then said. "This is Harriet Penzler. I'm a psychologist in Seattle, Washington. Yes. Yes. This is very urgent. I have a patient who . . . well . . . who has to speak to whomever is in charge of the extraterrestrial project. Yes, that's what I said. Yes, and this is no joke." Dr. Penzler waited a moment, then returned to the phone. "And there are hostages," she said, her voice now very grave. "Seven adults." Her eyes swept over to Allie, settled upon her a moment, then returned to the phone. "And . . . one . . . little girl." She returned her gaze to Allie as she listened. "Yes," she said. "That's right . . . exactly."

"All right, I'm here," Mary said as she stepped into Dr. Penzler's office a few minutes later. She lifted her arms to show that she was unarmed. "Are you the one who asked for the FBI?" she asked, her eyes locked on Ray.

"Yeah," Ray said.

"I'm here. You can talk to me."

"Did anyone explain to you what this was all about?" Ray asked.

"Man in therapist's office holding eight hostages . . . demands FBI agent."

"I asked for someone from the FBI extraterrestrial project."

"You mean like *X-Files*?" Mary asked. She smiled. "I'm the person you want to see."

Ray glared at her. "I want the FBI to go public," he said. "I want the FBI to tell us everything it knows about . . ."

"I'm sure everyone here would agree," Mary said. "I can't tell you how many times I've wanted to . . . go public." She glanced at the other hostages one by one until her gaze finally settled on Allie. "Give me the little girl and I'll do what I can for you."

Allie looked at Mary closely. "She was in the park," she said to Lisa. "She tried to grab me."

Mary's eyes swept back to Ray. "Let the little girl come with me," she said.

Ray strode across the room, yanked Allie from Lisa's grasp and put the pistol to the child's head. "I've got something you want, don't I?" he said to Mary. His eyes narrowed menacingly. "Well, you'll never get her," he added as he drew the gun away and let Allie go. "She's staying with her mother." He smiled. "Now get out!"

Mary eased herself from the room, then quickly made her way across the street to where she found her father, the building's blueprints spread out on a table in front of him.

"What's the situation?" Eric asked.

"He's going to kill the girl if we don't tell the whole world that we're not alone."

"You two were going to pick her up. This was supposed to be easy."

Mary ignored the accusatory tone in her father's voice. "We have to make sure that little girl doesn't get hurt." She glanced over to where a gas company truck rested at the curb, the snipers she'd already put into position now taking aim, awaiting her signal.

"No one's getting killed here today," Eric warned her, his eyes now on the same snipers.

Mary nodded, and suddenly, the snipers fired, smashing through the windows of Dr. Penzler's office.

For a moment, there was silence, then the phone rang, and Mary quickly picked it up.

"WHAT DO YOU THINK YOU'RE DOING!"

It was Ray, and he was screaming.

"It was a miscommunication," Mary told him urgently. "It won't happen again."

"YOU'RE DAMNED RIGHT IT WON'T! NEXT TIME ANYTHING LIKE THAT HAPPENS, THE LITTLE GIRL IS COMING OUT THE WINDOW WITH A BULLET IN HER HEAD!"

Mary put down the phone, and stared at the window of Dr. Penzler's office, where Ray now stood, Allie held like a body shield in front of him, angrily repeating his demands.

"He's going to kill her," Mary said. "The proof. We can't let that happen."

"I will not be a party to any more killing," Eric said firmly. "I'm done with that."

"I don't think you are, Dad," Mary said darkly. "You know who's in there, right? Besides the little girl, I mean. Her mother . . . and her father. That means he knows. That's a lot of information in the hands of two people who have had some very bad experiences with us over the years." She returned her gaze to the shattered window. "They have to go. And Dr. Penzler, too. I can't risk a leak. Allie's too important." She shook her head. "None of the others matter anymore. It's all about Allie."

"You are not in charge here, Mary," Eric reminded her. "I am. Take a step. Calm down."

Mary smiled, but her eyes remained cold. "I'm sorry," she said. "You're right."

Eric stared at her warily. "On your way out, tell your personal gunmen that their services will no longer be required."

Mary stiffened like a soldier called to attention. "Yes, Dad," she said as she left the room.

Allie looked softly into Ray's tormented eyes.

"It's easier, isn't it, Mr. Morrison," she asked. "Blaming it on them."

Ray sucked in an exhausted breath. "What?"

"It's easier to say that 'they' did it to you," Allie answered. "That 'they' came down and took you."

Ray's fingers tightened around the pistol grip. "Shut up."

"It's a whole lot scarier when the monsters are us," Allie continued.

"I told you to shut up," Ray said.

"Nothing you do is going to change what happened, Mr. Morrison."

"And what was that?" Ray challenged her.

"That man in the woods when you were eight," Allie answered. "The one who took you in the shed. He wasn't from another planet. He was just mean and crazy."

Ray leaped to his feet. "Shut up!"

"You're just going to hurt a lot more people, that's all."

Ray lowered the pistol, his hand shaking, but his face curiously serene, as if he'd lived the life of one condemned, but whose death sentence had suddenly been lifted. He looked at Allie without fear or malice. "What should I do now?" he asked.

Allie smiled quietly. "I think you already know."

Mary eased back behind the gas truck as the door to Dr. Penzler's building opened.

"They're coming out," she said. "The girl said she'd come with us."

The sniper nodded.

"Remember what I told you."

"Good as done," the sniper assured her.

Mary edged back to the rear of the truck. She could see Allie in the lead, the others behind her, all walking slowly, keeping their pace with hers. One, two, three, she began, counting the seconds for the moment, five, six . . .

She stopped as her father abruptly appeared, striding across the street, waving his arms, his voice higher and more desperate than she'd ever heard it.

"Get away!" he cried. "Take your little girl! Run!"

She nodded to the sniper.

He promptly took aim and fired.

The sound of the blast seemed to shear away the night. In the distance, Eric spun around as the bullet pierced him, then fell heavily to the ground.

Mary stepped out from behind the truck, her gaze lethally fixed on Allie. The proof, she thought, watching as Allie stood in place, her gaze focused no less intently on Mary.

Wakeman took his place beside her, and together they moved forward, intently . . . then strangely . . . then impossibly as the street and buildings dissolved and they found themselves in a broad green field where nothing stood around them but a happily grazing cow.

"I'm ready to go with you."

The pasture vanished and Allie stood before them, the street deserted now, the hostages departed, nothing but the eerie silence that follows a violent storm.

"Screening," Wakeman said, his voice filled with awe.

"What?" Mary asked.

"She threw up a screen, and everyone escaped while she kept us behind it," Wakeman said, his gaze resting quietly on Allie. He smiled. "Little girl," he said gently, "I love the way your mind works."

Dropping the Dishes

Chapter One

Allie sat silent as the truck sped through the cold New England night. She stared straight ahead but saw everything around her, Mary on one side, Wakeman on the other, busily assembling a five-sided helmet.

"Do you know who I am?" Mary asked.

"Not exactly."

"Our families go way back," Mary told her. "Mine and your mom's and your dad's. I kind of think that you and I might be the end of all this."

"We might be just the beginning," Allie said. She looked at Mary. "Your grandfather wasn't a very happy man. Why are you trying to be like him?"

Before Mary could answer, Wakeman said, "We're almost at the airstrip. We better get this thing in place." He nudged Allie forward and placed the helmet over her head and secured it with a strap. "What can you see?" he asked.

Allie didn't answer. *Everything,* she thought.

SEATTLE, WASHINGTON

Lisa's scream split the air, "Allie! Allie!"

Charlie and Nina darted from the kitchen to where Lisa lay furiously rubbing her eyes.

"I can't see!" she cried.

"I'm right here in front of you," Charlie told her. "With Nina."

Nina slapped Lisa hard, and suddenly the room was visible, Charlie and Nina's faces hanging like moons above her.

"I don't know what happened," she said, staring around. "It was like I was somewhere else, and wherever I was, I couldn't see a thing. There was something covering my eyes."

Charlie took her in his arms.

"Are you okay," Lisa asked. "I mean your . . ."

"It's completely healed," Charlie told her, thinking now of Allie, of the miracle she had so clearly performed. "Twelve hours ago there was a bullet in my lung. I should be dead."

Lisa looked at Charlie pointedly. "She stopped time, Charlie. Allie stopped time for two hours. She was trying to keep us safe."

"I know."

Nina shook her head. "I should have been closer to her at the soccer field," she said mournfully. "I should have . . ."

"No," Lisa said. "I should have known something was . . . happening. We always had this connection, Allie and me, we always . . . ." She stopped and looked at Charlie. "Where is she, Charlie?" she pleaded. "Where's my little girl?"

SUPERIOR FISH CANNERY, ELLSWORTH, MAINE

From behind the observation glass, Mary watched as Allie sat alone in the adjoining room, the helmet securely on her head. Wakeman stood beside Mary, his eyes on the little girl.

"She knows we're in here," Mary said. "She knows we're watching her."

Wakeman nodded. "We haven't had a chance to talk, Mary."

Mary held her gaze on Allie. "What do you want to talk about?"

Wakeman opened the door of the room and ushered Mary out into the corridor. "Your father," he said.

"The craft," Mary said coldly. "The bodies. He lost them."

"He couldn't have stopped what happened," Wakeman told her.

"He could have tried," Mary said. She stared Wakeman directly in the eyes.

Wakeman nodded.

"You think I have no remorse, right?" Mary asked him.

"I think you did what you had to do," Wakeman said.

She could see how deeply he loved her. "Really?"

"Really," Wakeman said. He leaned in to kiss her, then saw General Beers striding down the corridor.

"You've got the girl?" Beers asked.

"Yes," Mary answered.

The general stepped inside the observation room and stared through the glass to where Allie sat alone, the helmet still on her head.

"You really believe that thing you put on her head is blocking a signal?" General Beers asked.

"Right now they're in their ship scratching their little gray heads and wondering where in the world their little girl could be," Wakeman said lightly. "Believe me, the minute we take that shield off, here they come."

"And you're confident we can take them down?" Beers asked.

"Wherever they come from," Wakeman answered. "The minute they enter our time and space, our reality, they are confronted by the laws of our physics. Remember, in 1947, in Roswell, New Mexico, a ship came down when it collided with the Mogul spy balloon. Just a balloon, but it brought down their ship"

General Beers was clearly satisfied. He motioned Mary and Wakeman to follow him, then led them out of the building.

"You've done a fine job," he said to them. "We will always be indebted to you."

Mary saw an odd glint in the general's eyes. "Always?" she asked.

General Beers' face stiffened. "That's right."

"You mean . . . ?"

"I mean you've done your part, Ms. Crawford," the general interrupted. "The little girl is part of a military operation now."

"A military operation?" Mary shot back angrily. "General, for three generations my family has been preparing for this day. I've given my career, no, my whole life over to this."

The general smiled thinly. "And don't think we don't appreciate it," he said. He looked over Mary's shoulder, where several trucks were moving toward them. "You're benched. Go sit down."

"In a matter of days, we may be able to step inside one

of their craft," Mary protested. "We may be able to meet these . . . beings. Do you honestly think I'm going to stand by while you take that opportunity from me?"

"You don't really have a choice," the general said confidently. He nodded as the truck came to a halt and several soldiers piled out of the back, arms at the ready. "Except for a few clean-up details. Like that doctor in Seattle. And the little girl's parents."

"We have people for that," Mary said.

General Beers' features hardened. "Don't think I don't know what happened to your father," he said threateningly. Then, with a flourish, he wheeled around to face Wakeman. "You can ride with me, Doctor," he said.

Wakeman didn't move. "Ride with you?"

"We need your expertise," the general explained.

Wakeman looked helplessly at Mary, then back to General Beers.

"I'm not giving you a choice here, Doctor," Beers told him as the soldiers came forward, surrounding them. "Now let's get the girl," he added. "As you can see, her transport is ready." The general turned his back to Mary. "Just how powerful is this little girl, Doctor?"

"She has demonstrated powers beyond anything we imagined," Wakeman replied. "She's capable of manipulating time. She has amazing abilities to screen . . . to project images from our minds."

The general looked at him doubtfully.

"She made an entire group of people see something that wasn't there at all," Wakeman said. "That's how powerful she is."

Mary stepped away as the soldiers entered the building, the general in the lead, Wakeman at his side. She waited in the bright light until they emerged again, Allie with them now, the shield still in place on her head. Within minutes she was gone, and in the wake of her leaving Mary felt a terrible heaviness descend upon her, everything she'd worked for gone, vanished the way the craft had vanished and the bodies had vanished, the way everything had vanished but . . .

She whirled around, walked quickly to her office, opened the safe and took it out, a small metal artifact, oddly marked, which, as it rested in her hand, suddenly began to glow.

Chapter Two

Allie sat on the bed of the farmhouse where they'd taken her. She could feel the metal helmet, but during the long drive through miles and miles of farmland she'd learned to balance its weight, which was part of the way you had to live, she supposed, dealing with burdens that came out of nowhere and gave no sign of going away.

A nurse had hooked a tube to her arm, and the little pinch of the needle still ached slightly.

Private Pierce seemed to sense her pain.

"How are you doing?" Pierce asked her.

Allie could feel that something lay buried within the chambers of his mind.

"I'm all right," she said.

Pierce smiled. "You like to read? I keep a copy of *Huckleberry Finn*. It was my mom's favorite book. She'd bake us Toll House cookies, and we'd share a whole plate of them while she read."

"If it wouldn't make you too sad to remember her, I'd like to hear the story," Allie said.

Pierce shook his head slowly. "No, it wouldn't make me sad at all."

Allie listened attentively as Pierce began to speak. Outside a vast array of military vehicles was assembling, soldiers scurrying into positions where they lay in wait, a whole army in full alert, but for all their weaponry still only men whose fears Allie sensed, fears of death and loneliness, of height and water, of bugs and snakes, and everywhere the fear of being afraid. Wakeman was standing among them, watching all this immense preparation with what Allie sensed, as she drew her mind toward his, a terrible foreboding.

Suddenly, Pierce leaped to attention as Beers entered the room.

"That'll be all, soldier," Beers commanded.

"Yes, sir," Pierce said. He glanced at Allie, and she saw that he didn't want to leave her alone with these men, but had no choice.

Beers turned to Wakeman. "Are you ready to proceed?"

Wakeman turned toward Allie and smiled. "Magic time," he said as he removed the helmet and her hair fell loosely to her small shoulders.

SEATTLE, WASHINGTON

Charlie knew nothing else to do, no place else to go. And so he was at her door now, standing with Lisa, waiting for Dr. Penzler to answer his knock.

When she opened it, he knew she had something to hide . . . or something to fear.

"Come in," she said, then led Charlie and Lisa into the room, carefully closed the windows and drew the curtains. "You don't have to worry," she told them. "No one's coming here."

"What do you mean?" Charlie asked.

"I work for them, Charlie," Dr. Penzler said. "I was the one who called them."

"Tell us where they are," Lisa demanded. "Tell us where they took Allie."

Dr. Penzler hesitated a moment, then shook her head. "I don't know," she said. "I know you don't believe me, but I really don't know. I've been calling people. At numbers I was given. But all the numbers have been disconnected." She glanced from Charlie to Lisa, then back to Charlie. "I have no way of finding them."

"We trusted you," Lisa said.

"They told me that I was helping," Dr. Penzler explained. "That they had proof people who had been taken were in great danger. I thought I was helping."

Lisa glared at her. "You told them Charlie was here. You told them that Allie was with us and now they have her."

Dr. Penzler nodded. "Lisa, I'm so sorry," she said.

Lisa glanced at Charlie, then back to Dr. Penzler. "I want you to regress me," she said. "Allie and I have this link, and in regression I've had these moments where I feel Allie . . . sense where she is. I want you to help me find her."

"We'd have to go pretty deep, Lisa," Dr. Penzler warned.

"Can you get me there?" Lisa asked desperately.

"Are you sure you're ready?"

"I'd go anywhere to get Allie back."

Dr. Penzler rose, her face full of resolution. "All right," she said. "We'll do it."

She moved over to Lisa and placed her hands on her forehead. "Close your eyes and take a deep breath."

Lisa did as she was told.

"And another."

Lisa drew in a second deep breath.

"And a third."

Lisa took the third breath, even deeper than the previous two, and let it out very slowly.

"Now I want you to go to that place where you and Allie find each other," Dr. Penzler said. "It's in your heart and in your head. Can you find it for me?"

"Yes," Lisa said softly.

"Good," Dr. Penzler said. "What do you see?"

"Darkness," Lisa answered. "All I see is darkness."

"Go ahead. Tell me more."

"It's very dark," Lisa continued. "It smells kind of moldy. But I feel something. There are people waiting. Soldiers."

"Waiting for what?"

"Waiting," Lisa began, then stopped. She heard clamps being loosened, felt a strap beneath her chin fall away.

"Waiting for what?" Dr. Penzler repeated.

"They want something," Lisa answered. "They're waiting for something."

"Do you know where you are?"

"It's a room," Lisa said. "License plates on the wall. Peeling paint. A calendar with a tractor on . . . Wallington's . . . Feed . . . and . . . Grain."

"The license plates, where are they from, Lisa?"

"Peace Garden State. ND. North Dakota."

"Tell me more," Dr. Penzler said urgently. "We're getting to that place, Lisa."

Lisa flinched violently and felt something splatter onto her chest. She opened her eyes and saw a stain, red and glistening, then, at her feet, Dr. Penzler's body, curled and bloody. She looked up and saw a man standing a few feet away, his pistol now aimed at her.

Charlie rushed forward, grabbed a lamp and brought it down on the man's head, then gathered Lisa into his arms. "We've got to get out of here," he said.

Wakeman stood beside General Beers in the observation room, his eyes on Allie.

"What happens now?" the general asked curtly.

"We wait," Wakeman answered.

"How long should it take?"

"I don't know."

"You believe they'll come?"

"Absolutely," Wakeman answered. "But then again, I believe a lot of things."

ELLSWORTH, MAINE

Mary walked to the phone in her father's study and dialed the number.

"Superior Fish," the technician answered.

"This is Mary Crawford," she said. "Look at the map. Any new lights?"

A pause, then, "There's one new light."

"Where on the map?"

"North Dakota. Benson Country. Just outside of Brins-made."

Mary quickly wrote the name on her notepad. "Thank you," she said.

BRINSMADE, NORTH DAKOTA

The roadblock appeared almost out of nowhere, a truck strategically parked, soldiers all around it.

Charlie lifted his foot off the accelerator, and looked at Lisa. He saw her answer in his eyes, that they had no choice but to go on. He pressed down on the accelerator and continued on until he reached the roadblock.

A soldier walked up to their window. "Where you headed?" he asked.

"Brinsmade," Charlie answered.

"Are you from there?"

"No. We're visiting a sick cousin."

"Brinsmade's been evacuated," the soldier told him. "You'll find your cousin at the high school gym over in Leeds."

Lisa leaned over to get a better view of the man. "Why has Brinsmade been evacuated?" she asked.

"Toxic spill," the soldier answered. "Truck collided with a train."

"What kind of spill?"

"They don't tell me," the soldier answered. "They just say to keep the cars out."

"You're not afraid you're standing downwind of something?" Charlie asked.

The soldier's voice hardened. "You folks need to turn

around now," he said. "Like I told you, your cousin is in Leeds."

"Okay," Charlie said. He wheeled around and headed away from the roadblock, the soldier now in his rearview mirror, reaching for a field telephone, talking into it. "I have a really bad feeling about this," he said.

"So, what do we do?"

"We have to get around the roadblock."

"How?"

"Not alone, that's for sure."

They drove to Leeds and stopped at a small bar to think things through. Several men, in hunting clothes, sat at one of the wooden tables. Charlie eyed them a moment, then rose and walked to the bar.

"I need someone who knows the area," he said.

The bartender nodded toward one of the men at the table. "Dewey Clayton," he said.

"Thanks," Charlie said, then turned and strode over to the man the bartender had indicated.

"You're Mr. Clayton?" he asked.

"That was my dad. I'm Dewey."

"I'd like to hire your services."

"You want a guide?"

"I'm told you're the best."

"You want to go hunting?"

"In a way, yes."

"You're out of luck. We're shut down. Damn government's locked us out of our own woods."

"We know that," Lisa said as she stepped up beside Charlie.

Dewey looked at her closely, then at Charlie. "But you've got some reason you want to go up there anyway?"

"Our daughter," Charlie said.

"She's lost in the woods?" Dewey asked.

"The Army has her."

"This have something to do with that 'toxic spill' that didn't happen?"

Charlie and Lisa nodded.

Dewey smiled. "We'll find your little girl," he said.

Chapter Three

Mary flashed her most winning smile at the approaching soldier.

"How are you?" she asked brightly.

The soldier smiled. "I'm all right, ma'am."

She indicated the Humvee that blocked the road, the soldiers gathered around it, arms at the ready. "So, what do we have here?"

"Some sort of toxic spill, ma'am," the soldier answered.

"I'm here to see General Beers," Mary told him.

"Do you have a clearance?"

"No, I don't," Mary said. "But what I do have is information that General Beers needs. It could save thousands of lives."

The soldier wavered for a moment before responding. "Sorry, ma'am. Not without a clearance."

Mary looked at him coolly. "I was going to try to run the roadblock. But why don't you just arrest me?"

"What?"

"Arrest me and have me taken to General Beers."

The man shook his head. "No one goes in. We detain people here."

"Then detain me," Mary said without hesitation. "Detain me and get someone on the phone to General Beers and tell him that Mary Crawford is at the roadblock with some important new information about the project."

"I'm afraid I can't do that without provocation," the soldier replied.

Mary smiled girlishly, and with a lightning fast movement grabbed his crotch.

The man's eyes bulged. "Jesus," he groaned.

Minutes later she stood before General Beers, Wakeman beside him, clearly both pleased and astonished to see her.

"You just don't know when to quit, do you, Mary?" the general asked.

Mary laughed coldly. "You son of a bitch," she sneered. "What did you think, that you'd just take the project away from me?" She wheeled furiously toward Wakeman. "And you sold me out," she cried as she lunged forward and slapped his face. "You worthless bastard!" She slipped the artifact into Wakeman's hand.

"Take her away," the general said.

Mary looked at him angrily as two soldiers stepped forward and grabbed her arms.

A few minutes later, just as she'd known he would, Wakeman came out of the building and walked to where she stood, under guard, behind a Humvee.

"I need to talk to Ms. Crawford," Wakeman told the soldiers.

He waited until they'd left, then said, "It must be their

transmitter." He opened his hand and looked at the artifact. "This is how they send the implant signals up."

"It's a lot more than a transmitter," Mary told him. "I've looked at it several times, and it's changed, Chet. Some of the markings were there in 1947, but some of them are new."

"New?" Wakeman said, astonished.

"Yes. I think it gathers information. And the way it's glowing, they must have left it behind for a reason."

"How long ago did you take the shield off?" Mary asked.

"A day and a half."

"Nothing's happened?"

Wakeman shook his head.

"We have this," Mary said, referring to the artifact. "And we've got the little girl. In a way, it's as if they left both of them."

"It would be interesting to see what would happen if the two were brought together," Wakeman said.

Mary smiled. "I was thinking the same thing."

Moments later Mary knocked at the door of the farmhouse.

Pierce opened it.

"I'm Dr. Crawford," Mary told him. "The general asked me to take a look at Allie."

"I wasn't told anything about it," Pierce said.

"No, you weren't," Mary said authoritatively. "But I'm afraid you'll have to wait outside."

"But . . ."

A child's voice called from inside the farmhouse. "It's all right."

Pierce looked into the room's dark interior. "You sure?"

"She's not going to hurt me."

Pierce motioned Mary inside the room, then stepped outside.

Allie sat on the bed, her hair falling freely to her shoulders. So small, Mary thought, and yet so powerful.

"It must be strange for you," she said. "Finding out how strong you are. All the things you can do."

"It is a little," Allie said softly.

"I've frightened you a lot," Mary said. "I'm sorry. I don't mean to scare you."

"You don't care if you do," Allie said.

"That's not really true," Mary told her. "I'm not the kind of person who takes any pleasure in frightening people. In hurting them."

"But you do all those things."

Mary saw it in her eyes and in the serenity of her posture, an eternal solitude. "They're not coming, are they?"

"I don't know," Allie answered.

"Maybe that's for the best."

"Maybe."

"Would you like to go home?"

"Yes."

Mary drew the artifact from her pocket. "This is something that belonged to my grandfather," she said. She held it out to Allie. "Tell me what it says."

Allie stared at the softly glowing piece of metal.

"You can read it, can't you?" Mary asked. "Tell me what it says."

Allie's gaze lifted from the artifact. "What do you want it to say?"

Mary's mouth twitched into a snarl. "Pick it up and read it!" she snapped.

"I can't," Allie said. "Not yet."

Mary stared at the glowing metal. The letters were moving now, some information fading from it as other information formed, new symbols rising to its glowing surface as others vanished.

Mary wheeled around and strode out of the farmhouse and back through the woods, where she found General Beers and Wakeman standing by a Humvee, a group of MPs just behind them. The general pushed Wakeman over to Mary's side.

"If either one of them tries to leave the area," he said to the soldiers, "shoot them, is that clear?" When he received no response, the general turned. "What . . . ?"

The MPs were standing motionlessly, staring up at the sky, watching as balls of blue light descended toward them.

The general grabbed the field telephone. "We have the enemy in sight," he shouted, his eyes riveted on the sky, where the lights now came together to form a single, brightly glowing spaceship.

For a moment, the general stared at the ship, transfixed.

Pierce rushed forward urgently. "Sir, we've got to get the little girl out of here."

"Get back with the other men," the general commanded.

"But . . . sir."

"Do it now!" the general shouted. He brought the field telephone to his lips. "Fire!" he shouted.

On the hill above the farmhouse, Charlie and Lisa watched in stunned silence as the missiles rose into the dark air. They rose toward the craft in wide arcs, then disappeared into its bright light.

The explosion seemed to come from the depths of the universe, huge and deafening, filling the air with sparkling light that glittered briefly then dissolved to reveal the craft again, its smooth exterior now rippling wildly with wave after wave of oddly shivering light.

"Allie!" Lisa cried.

She glanced, terrified, at Charlie, then raced down the hill toward the farmhouse.

Charlie bolted forward and followed behind her, his eyes still skyward as the craft shook and tottered, as if on the edge of some impossible precipice, then nosed downward in a sharp decline, light spewing in a gleaming mist from its wounded side as it fell and fell, and finally crashed to earth, burying itself in the ground beneath the farmhouse.

"My God," Lisa said as she stopped dead. "Allie."

Charlie came to her side, and drew her into his arms. "We can't go down there"

"But we have to," Lisa cried.

Charlie held her tightly. "We can't, Lisa. Wait!"

"But Allie's in that farmhouse," Lisa said desperately. "I know she is."

He watched the soldiers that had begun to move in toward the farmhouse. There were far too many of them. And they were well armed. It was impossible.

"What are we going to do, Charlie?" Lisa whimpered.

"I don't know," Charlie answered.

Down the hill, he could see Mary Crawford, staring at the craft, transfixed as it began to glow, slowly at first, then with increasing brightness, until the light was almost blinding. Squinting into the light, Charlie could just make out the figure of Mary Crawford. For a moment, she stood utterly motionless, frozen in awe at the sight before her. Then, suddenly, she bolted toward the craft, running wildly toward the light, her figure growing faint as she approached its most far-flung rays, but running still, moving deeper and deeper into the ever brightening light until she vanished into its blinding shield.

PART NINE

John

John

Chapter One

The darkness was thick and impenetrable, and it seemed to Charlie that Lisa's eyes floated in that blackness, small blue orbs, moist and curiously intense, staring out into the woods and down the slope to where the craft still lay buried in the earth, the lights of the farmhouse shining softly just beyond it.

"I should have gotten her out of there," she said to him. "My daughter's in the farmhouse. I need to get down there."

Charlie noticed that she'd said "my" daughter, not "their" daughter, though he knew that is what Allie was. He looked at Dewey, who stood, still transfixed, as if replaying what they'd all seen only a few minutes before, the descent of the craft, then its crash, and finally the light that had swept out of it, rolled over the woman who'd fled across the field, a light that had somehow . . . taken her.

Dewey shook his head. "You're on your own," he said determinedly. "I'm just a hunting guide."

Charlie saw that he meant it, that the courage Dewey

had shown earlier had been wrenched from him, taken, it seemed, by the same light that had swept over Mary Crawford.

"Just show us how to get down before you go, okay?" Charlie asked.

Dewey nodded.

Charlie turned back to Lisa, and noticed that her eyes had changed, that they seemed powerfully focused on something he could not see at all. "What is it, Lisa?" he asked.

Before she could answer, Charlie heard a rustling all around him. He looked up and saw a group of soldiers closing in.

"Put up your hands," one of them shouted.

Charlie rose slowly, his hands in the air.

"You're under arrest," the soldier shouted.

Lisa got to her feet with a strange grace, and Charlie saw that she was no longer crying, no longer afraid.

"What is it?" he asked desperately.

"Allie's all right," Lisa said. Her voice seemed to come to him from far away, and there was a strange wonder in her eyes. "She's all right, but she's doing something . . . very . . . very . . . hard."

"She's working really hard at something," Wakeman said. He watched the monitors that lined the wall of the trailer, the evidence they showed of the raging torrents of Allie's brain, a storm that for all its force and fury, remained locked inside her, so that her face gave so sign of it, but remained as motionless as the eye of a hurricane. "I've never seen anything like it."

General Beers stood beside him, his gaze moving from

monitor to monitor, from the image of Allie that flickered on one of the screens, a little girl, seated in the bare
room of a farmhouse, locked in dark concentration, to a
second screen that showed the exterior of the craft, surrounded by armed men who seemed poised to enter it.

Wakeman glanced again at the first screen. He could
almost see the volcanic intensity of Allie's mind, the way
it seemed at the edge of explosion.

"It's time to get her," he said.

Beers picked up the microphone, gave the order.

On the monitor, Wakeman watched as the soldiers began to close in upon the craft. Their movements were
slow and hesitant despite their lethal arms, as if they
sensed that their weapons were useless against the force
they confronted, archaic as bows and arrows, the primitive armor of a primitive creature. "They're scared to
death," he said.

Beers' eyes fixed on the monitor as the soldiers moved
forward, slowly tightening the circle around the craft.
They took short, cautious steps, their fingers gripped
tightly to their weapons, as if they were moving in on a
trapped and wounded animal of ferocious strength, a
tiger that might at any moment charge toward them at
inhuman speed.

Then, suddenly, the craft began to glow, and the soldiers stopped, and crouched low on the ground, as if mo-
mentarily blinded by the building light.

Beers snapped up the microphone. "What's happening?" he demanded.

"This is Walker, sir," a voice called back. "Some kind
of opening has appeared in the craft."

Beers' eyes shot over to the monitor. The glow had
intensified, as if the craft were readying itself for some

terrible defense. "Enter with extreme caution," he ordered.

"Yes, sir," Walker answered.

On the monitor, Beers and Wakeman watched as the soldiers closed in upon the craft, then moved beneath it, toward the opening.

Then, abruptly, the monitor went blank.

Wakeman's eyes shot from one monitor to the next, each of them now going blank in turn, as if switched off by invisible hands. "We're blind," he said.

Beers snatched up the microphone. "Walker, what's going on?" he demanded.

Walker's voice came through the scratchy dissonance. "We're in the craft," he said, his voice locked in unearthly wonder. "And there's this woman."

"What?" Beers cried.

"An old woman."

"What are you talking about?"

"With cookies," Walker said. "Pierce says . . ." His voice bore a world of awe on its quiet whisper. "Pierce says it's his mother, sir."

"Walker," the general barked. "Listen to me, I . . ."

"I know she isn't real," Walker stammered, "but . . ."

Suddenly a quiet voice came over the microphone. "Would any of you nice people like one of my Toll House cookies?"

"Dear God," Wakeman whispered.

"Just keep moving!" Beers ordered.

"Yes, sir."

Suddenly one of the monitors flashed on, revealing the craft, still glowing softly, but now around a central core of light that seemed to lead into it beckoningly, like a door.

"Sir, we're in some sort of corridor," Walker said. "It's all light in here."

"They're flying blind," Wakeman said.

The monitor flickered briefly. "We're losing you," Beers said.

Suddenly a wild scream broke through the static.

"Cockroaches!"

Beers glared at the still flickering monitor. "What the hell is going on there, Walker?"

"They're all over," Walker screamed. "Get off! Get off!"

Then, suddenly, the screaming stopped.

"Walker, they're not real," Beers cried. "Walker, it's in your head. Walker?"

Walker's voice was filled with dark amazement. "They're gone," he whispered. "They ran away . . . into the light." He laughed lightly, a man trying to regain his courage. "Did I mention I was scared of rabid dogs and cobras?" A pause, then, "Okay, we're going on now."

"What are you seeing?" Beers asked.

"Light," Walker replied. "Like a corridor . . . of light. Then a room . . . and . . ."

"What?"

"A kitchen. Pierce is having cookies with his mother."

Mary watched as the glass door slid open. She smiled at the man who stepped into the room, carrying a plate of Toll House cookies. "Have a cookie," he said. "They're very good."

Mary stared at him, amazed.

The man's gaze was very soft and sweet, as if, in this light, all the great tumult of his life, all the evil he had

done, had evaporated, leaving only the best part of himself behind. "I see your father in you, but not enough to
ruin things," he said.

"Grandfather," Mary said quietly.

"You've done all right to get this far," Owen said.

"How is this happening?"

"They go into your head and pull things out," Owen
explained. "You've seen pictures of me. You have an idea
of how you want me to be. In my day, we called them
projections. Now you call them screen memories."

"There's so much I want to ask you," Mary said. "But I
suppose I'd just be asking myself."

"Give it a try," Owen said. "You might find something
out about yourself you never knew."

Mary nodded gently, her eyes suddenly moist. "I've
done terrible things," she said.

"You had to."

"Why? To learn about them? To see them?"

"Because of your overwhelming sense of their power.
Because you know, you truly know, that the future lies
with them."

Mary shook her head.

"You've got another idea?" Owen asked.

"They made this girl . . ." Mary said. "Allie. Because
they weren't complete without us . . . without something
that we could give them."

"Either way, their power is what compels you. You
want to be part of that power . . . at any cost." He smiled.
"You don't need that doctor boyfriend of yours anymore,
Mary. You know more than he does. Trust your gut in-
stincts, and you'll be fine."

"You're me," Mary said. "You're saying what I want
you to say."

"I'm saying what you know."

She looked at him pointedly. "What I see is a man who couldn't live up to his dreams."

"What do you mean?"

"You had this all in your hands. The whole thing. You had Jacob Clarke. You had him and you let him go."

"You don't know what happened."

"He scared you," Mary told him. "That little boy scared you so badly that you let him go."

"It's not that simple."

"You saw something that scared you, and you ran."

"You want to know what scared me so badly, Mary?" Owen asked. "Is that what you came to find out?"

"Yes, damn it," Mary exclaimed. "That's what I want to know."

Owen smiled thinly, a dark purpose crawling into his eyes. "Then look at me, Mary." His eyes narrowed darkly. "Look at me."

The soldier opened the door of the trailer and pushed Charlie and Lisa inside.

"We found these two in the woods not far from the farmhouse," the soldier said.

Charlie glanced up, taking in the wall of flickering monitors that rose just behind General Beers and Wakeman.

"My God," Wakeman said.

"You know these people?" the general asked.

"They're Allie's parents."

The general glared at Wakeman, then turned back to the soldier. "Find some place for them where they won't get in anybody's way," he commanded. His eyes shifted to Wakeman, then back to the soldier. "Take him, too," he said.

Within minutes they were in a small shed, an armed guard posted at the door.

"So, you're Charlie," Wakeman said with a strange smile. "You don't use the last name Keys, do you?"

Charlie said nothing.

"My name's Wakeman. And I happen to know that a great deal of money and technology went into looking for you."

Charlie glared at him.

"You'd like to knock me on my ass, wouldn't you?" Wakeman asked. "That's what they liked about the Keyses. That you guys had 'tude."

Lisa moaned and Charlie turned toward where she lay, dazed, beside him.

"All these voices," she said exhaustedly. "More and more . . . it's too hard . . . just a little longer."

He could see that Lisa was in some other place, far away, and that in some impossible way, she was with Allie.

"A lot of work," Lisa said, almost frantically. "This is too hard!"

Mary sat in front of a wall, soldiers all around her, but keeping their distance, afraid to move in. Her eyes were eerily vacant, the light that had once danced in them, now part of the larger and more brilliant light that encircled her. She sat in silence, utterly indifferent to the subtle movement that rippled through the surrounding light like ghostly fingers beneath a luminous veil. She could see the soldiers shrink back as the radiant walls began to weave and churn, giving birth to the thousands of small creatures that hung on the luminescent walls, wriggling like neon worms on hooks of light. She sensed the terror in the fleeing men . . . and she smiled.

Lisa could feel the desperate concentration of Allie's mind. "Very hard," she repeated softly. "She is doing something very hard."

Charlie brought his face close to hers. "What are you seeing, Lisa?"

She seemed not to hear him. "Come on," she whispered urgently, and with a strange note of encouragement, as if offering the full measure of her own will to the fierce needs of her daughter. "Come on, come on."

"Jesus," Wakeman said as he looked out the small window of the shed.

Charlie rushed to the window and stared out.

The soldiers who'd been guarding the shed were now frozen in awe, as the craft, glowing brightly, began to lift out of the scarred earthen pit that held it, inching backward and upward . . . rising!

"There are men in there," Wakeman said.

The craft continued to rise into the enveloping darkness, rising and rising until it reached high above the farmhouse and the awestruck men who surrounded it. Then it paused, as if to enjoy the view from the high aerie of its power, and leveled off, all its lights whirling rapidly, a vast engine brought back to full throttle, a wounded craft miraculously restored.

"Allie," Lisa whispered.

The craft continued to hover silently. Then a beam of light, brighter than any emitted before it, fierce and blinding, shot down to the farmhouse with laser-sharp perfection, carrying a crystalline beauty to the earth, sweeping around the farmhouse and tugging it upward from its ancient foundation.

Lisa moaned, as if the weight of the farmhouse were on her shoulders. But Charlie knew that Lisa's burden was only a reflection, light and unsubstantial, compared to the vast weight Allie bore upward, huge and crushing, as Atlas bore the world.

He stepped outside the shed, his eyes fixed on the unreal and impossible vision beyond it, a farmhouse tearing away from its foundations, rising slowly upward as if drawn into the sky by huge, but invisible cables.

"They're taking it," Wakeman breathed.

And instantly they did, the farmhouse now encased in a shimmering wrap of light that suddenly coalesced into a single, fiery ball and vanished into the upper sky, away and away, fleeing the earth as if it were a dark stranger of terrible intent.

Lisa moaned again, then collapsed in utter exhaustion.

Charlie hurried over to her and drew her into his arms.

"It's all right," Lisa said. "It's all right."

She struggled to her feet, and with Charlie's help, gazed out at the dark field, a few figures now standing, dazed, beneath the very place from which the craft had disappeared: Mary, surrounded by soldiers, all of them thunderstruck and staring about, as if looking for what was missing.

Chapter Two

Mary sat inside General Beers' trailer, holding a blanket snugly around her shoulders. Outside, the entire base was being dismantled. She knew what that meant. Soon there would be no sign that anything had happened here. It would all be explained as a "toxic spill" or some other such idiotic explanation the public would no doubt accept.

"Want to tell me what this is?" Beers asked, pointing to the alien artifact.

She nodded. "It's theirs," she said.

"No kidding," the general said facetiously. "What else do you know about it?"

Mary shook her head.

"You won't tell me?"

Mary stared at him silently.

Beers nodded crisply then turned to the MP beside him. "Get me Wakeman," he said.

Wakeman came into the room a few minutes later, an MP on either side.

"Mary, you all right?" he asked. "What happened? What did you see?"

Beers interrupted him. "What can you tell me about this, Doctor?" he demanded.

Wakeman looked at the scrolling artifact. He smiled.

"Nice," he said, as if he were viewing nothing more than a curious piece of jewelry. "Very nice."

"What is it?" the general asked.

"It gathers information," Wakeman answered. "A recording device of some kind. A brain."

"You and Ms. Crawford withheld valuable evidence," Beers said. "In my opinion, your actions are directly responsible for the failure of this mission."

Wakeman shrugged. "Nice to have someone to blame when things go wrong, isn't it, General?"

Beers glared at him. "Maybe the ride back to Ash will give you a little time to consider the consequences of being uncooperative."

He motioned Mary to her feet. "Take them to the truck."

The soldiers stepped forward and led Mary and Wakeman out of the building. In the distance she saw two people, a man and a woman, standing beside a Humvee. Allie's parents, she recognized, no doubt distraught that their precious little girl had been taken. They had made an enormous effort to save their daughter, traveled hundreds of miles and risked their lives. It was a strangely human thing to do, she thought, throw everything else to the wind, risk it all for . . . just a child. She couldn't help wondering if her father would have done the same for her.

"Get in the back of the truck," an MP commanded.

Wakeman offered a hand, but Mary didn't take it.

Without help, she climbed into the truck, Wakeman just behind her.

From her place in the back of the truck, Mary watched as General Beers approached Allie's parents. Briefly, they spoke, then the general escorted Allie's mother into the back of the Humvee and climbed in after her, leaving the father to ride with Pierce, the Humvee's driver.

The Humvee pulled away, and the truck drew in behind it.

Mary turned toward the soldiers as the truck pulled away. They were silent, as if frozen in dread, and in their dread, the sheer lingering horror that was etched in their faces, she felt something begin to focus in her, a strange revelation.

"Mary?" Wakeman asked, nudging his shoulder against hers. "Can you tell me about it?"

Mary shook her head. "I don't want to talk about it."

"I'm sorry they found the artifact."

"It's not important anymore," Mary said.

"How can you say that," Wakeman asked.

The truck entered a green meadow where a few cows grazed quietly.

"You saw the artifact," Wakeman continued. "It was working overtime. Something is still going to happen."

Mary seemed hardly to hear him. "Yes," she whispered to herself, remembering the way Allie had screened a pasture, and behind it, let time pass and people get away. For a moment, she had stopped the world, stopped time, stopped everything by the simple expedient of throwing up a screen.

One of the soldiers shivered.

Mary's eyes swept over to him. She noted his name,

Walker. "You went in, didn't you?" she asked him. "You went into the craft."

Walker nodded.

Mary leaned forward slightly. "What did you see?"

Walker looked at her like a small child forced to reveal something shameful. "Bugs," he said, his lips trembling. "Cockroaches. They were all over me."

Mary looked at him pointedly. "Have you always been afraid of bugs?" she asked.

Walker nodded hesitantly. "Since I was a kid."

Mary felt it almost physically, an idea so solid, it seemed to add weight to her mind. The bugs were as unreal as the cow she'd seen in Seattle. It was all a . . . screen. "Stop the truck," she said, rising to her feet. "Stop the truck, I want to talk to General Beers."

The driver immediately honked the horn and flashed his lights to get the attention of the general's Humvee ahead. Then he stopped, the Humvee just behind them now coming to a halt behind him.

"General Beers," Mary said as the general leaped from a Humvee behind them and strode over to the truck.

"Where the hell are the mother and father?" Beers demanded.

The soldier glanced up the road, to where the Humvee, the one he had been following, disappeared around a curve in the road.

"They're . . . with . . . you, sir," he stammered.

"What?" General Beers yelped.

"I can explain this to you," Mary said to the general with a thin smile. "But you're not going to like it."

"What are you talking about?" Beers demanded.

"Turn the truck around and I'll show you."

Beers stared at her, still unwilling to obey her. "What-ever you're thinking, you'd better be right," he said.

"Just turn the truck around," Mary said. "And go back to the farmhouse."

"Farmhouse?" the general blurted out. "There is no farmhouse. It was . . ."

"Taken?" Mary interrupted. She shook her head. "Not at all, General. Because everything that happened only happened in our heads."

Moments later they stood before the farmhouse, just as Mary had known they would, all of them staring at it unbelievingly.

"Allie can manifest thought," Mary explained. "That's as simple as I know how to put it. She fooled us, General, pure and simple."

"Then where is she?" Beers asked.

Mary's smile was thin as ice. "This is the part you're not going to like."

As the Humvee sped along, Charlie glanced back to where Lisa sat with General Beers, the two of them talk-ing quietly, in a tone that seemed almost one he might have expected of a father and his daughter. He recalled the strange exchange that had occurred back at the base, the way General Beers had approached them, ordered Pierce to get behind the wheel of the Humvee, Lisa into the backseat, where he joined her, himself up front with Pierce, all of it precisely orchestrated, as if they were playing out a scene that had been written for all time. He'd glanced at Lisa, expecting her to resist getting in the back of the Humvee, and been surprised that she had not offered the slightest resistance to the general's order after he'd said simply, "It's going to be all right," the same words, Charlie remembered now, that Lisa had said to him earlier, and which the general had delivered in exactly the same, utterly soothing tone.

"Sir," Pierce asked suddenly, "where am I going?"

Charlie looked up ahead, to where the woods had been cut away, logs stacked high beside a large Porta Potti. He glanced back at the general, then at Lisa, who seemed utterly within his thrall, and decided that somehow Beers had managed to draw her into a spell it was up to him to break.

He spun around, grabbed Pierce's helmet from the seat beside him and slammed it against his head.

The Humvee veered off the road and crashed into the Porta Potti.

Charlie grabbed Pierce's pistol and aimed it directly between his eyes. "We're going back to find our daughter," he said.

"You don't have to go anywhere."

The voice was Allie's, and Charlie whirled around to find the general now vanished, and in his place, Allie, herself, sitting calmly beside Lisa.

"Allie," Charlie gasped, "what . . ."

She seemed to know his question before he asked it. "They wanted to use me to make a ship come down," she said. "I thought, if I could make them think I'd gone, that I'd been taken, that they'd stop looking for me and everything could just go back to how it was." Her eyes glistened. "But they were going to take you away, and I couldn't let them do that." She shook her head, crying softly. "They're going to find out and they're going to come looking for me again."

"That doesn't mean they're going to find you," Charlie told her.

Lisa drew Allie beneath her arm. "We're not going to let them get you again, Allie," she promised.

Allie looked at her mother softly. "I'm scared," she admitted.

Charlie turned toward Pierce, and saw that he was now in league with them, as aware as they were of the precious cargo they carried. "They'll be coming," he said urgently. "We've got to go." He looked up the road, to where a line of Humvees and soldiers now approached, then turned to Allie. "Can you help us?"

Allie nodded and closed her eyes.

Charlie turned back to the road, expecting the Humvees to disappear or be lifted into the sky, but they remained in place, soldiers still in position all around them. He looked at Allie. "Try again," he said.

Allie closed her eyes more tightly but the Humvees remained unchanged.

"I can't do it," Allie said wearily.

Charlie glanced down the road, his eyes searching desperately for some place to hide before they finally settled on the Porta Potti. There, he thought, as he drew Allie beneath his arm.

Chapter Three

A Humvee came down the road and pulled up to where Mary and General Beers stood mutely, staring at the very farmhouse they'd watched rise from its foundations and soar into the night sky only a few hours before. Then Mary glanced over to where Pierce sat alone. She thought a moment, then approached him.

"You helped Allie, didn't you?" she asked.

Pierce stared straight ahead as if expecting a blow.

"I know you did," Mary told him quietly. "She knew you could be trusted."

Pierce looked at her quizzically.

"When I was with her, she told me you were a good guy," Mary added. She glanced toward where General Beers stood, still talking to the Humvee driver. "I was opposed to this entire mission," she said, lowering her voice conspiratorially. "Taking a little girl, using her for bait. That's sick."

Pierce said nothing.

"If you had to help her, it means she couldn't help herself," Mary said. "Because she's weak." She looked at him pointedly. "How weak is she, Pierce?"

Pierce lowered his eyes . . . and she knew. A smile slithered onto her lips. "Thanks," she said.

She walked back over to Beers, who was still fuming that they'd gotten away, though now she knew they really hadn't.

While Beers berated the soldier, Mary peered about, silently taking in the bustling scene. They were doing all they could to find evidence, but she knew they would find nothing. Soldiers poured over the grounds, and searched the farmhouse, taking radiation readings and looking for any sign of alien presence. She knew what their final reports would be, and that in the end they'd have to deny a truth she felt compelled to state.

"One of your soldiers sees his mother," she said to General Beers. "The person he most wanted to see. Another soldier sees bugs crawling all over him. His childhood fear come to life." She paused and let it all come together in her mind. "What did we all want to see, General? An alien craft taken down by our brilliant technology. What did we fear? That our efforts would fail. That the craft would come and take Allie away. And so Allie gave us all of that. She showed us exactly what we wanted and exactly what we feared."

General Beers continued to survey the activity, as if blocking the very truth Mary was determined to reveal. "We have soldiers at every access," he said. "We'll find them no matter where they are."

Before Mary could protest, Wakeman came rushing up to them. "I checked with Fort Ash. We're getting reports from all over the country. All the implants are falling out."

"Why?" General Beers asked.

"Because they don't need these people anymore," Mary answered confidently. "They have Allie. The product of three generations of selective breeding. Of a genetic experiment of an unparalleled scale. Once they produced her, they sat back and waited for the moment when all that was latent in her became active. When she did what she did here, made us see the craft, all of that. That was her demonstrating. That was when they saw the power they had been waiting to see."

"This extremely powerful little girl," General Beers said darkly. "I don't think I need to point out how important she is to us."

"And I can help you," Mary said.

Wakeman glanced at her apprehensively, and she saw how weak he was, how much like her father, a victim of sentiment.

She returned her attention to the general. "I think she's exhausted most of her power for the moment," she said. "But she'll get it back. And when she does, she'll be unstoppable."

"How do we stop her?" Beers asked emphatically.

"When I showed her the artifact, that thing my grandfather found at Roswell, she saw something that frightened her deeply." She grinned triumphantly. "And I know what it was. Because I saw it too. It's what my grandfather saw years before."

"What?" Beers demanded. "What did she see?"

Mary knew the answer, and the answer was life. What she'd seen, she understood now, was all the minefields that are planted in our paths. In childhood there were only a few. Disease. Accidents. In adolescence more were added. Drugs. Sex. Guns. As time went forward, the field grew more littered, the chances of blowing yourself up steadily increasing until there was no ground to stand on. And so at last you saw not just the journey . . . but its end.

It was that end Allie had seen in the artifact, the whole record of her life and purpose, of everything the "visitors" had done on earth, and finally her own destiny. That was what had frightened her, Mary concluded, that Allie had seen her destiny.

Chapter Four

FORT ASH, GRAND FORKS, SOUTH DAKOTA

The artifact lay inside the container, the markings still, as if the metal itself were sleeping.

"It seems to have stopped thinking for a moment," Wakeman said.

Mary watched the metal, taking in the oddly dormant state into which it had fallen. "My father tried to have it translated," she said. "So did my grandfather."

"I didn't know that," Wakeman told her. He looked oddly hurt that she had kept it from him. "I thought we trusted each other."

"Yes, well," Mary said dryly, then turned to General Beers, who was clearly in no mood for such petty squabbling. "As far as I knew, the artifact never revealed itself to anyone," she told him. "If it did, my father certainly never mentioned it."

"Or your grandfather," Wakeman said huffily.

Mary gave no sign that she heard him. She continued to address herself to the general. "So the question is, how are we going to break its code? The answer is simple. It's the oldest rule in code-breaking. First, you have to know what they're trying to say. If this is their permanent record, then it kicked in because it wanted to record what Allie did. Her fantastic power. So the record of what happened at the farmhouse should be on the artifact."

Wakeman sniffed. "Either that, or a recipe for chicken à la gray."

Again Mary gave no sign that she'd heard him. "I think we can crack the code, General," she said matter-of-factly. "We'll need a team of cryptographers, linguists, mathematicians."

"The Fibonacci code again," Wakeman said. He smiled at Mary. "It's really good, isn't it?"

Mary smiled back, though her eyes didn't. "It's great," she said.

General Beers clearly did not think so. "First, however, we have to find that little girl."

When the danger of discovery seemed to have passed, Charlie, Lisa, and Allie crept out of hiding. Eventually they found an abandoned service station and settled in. Beyond its dusty windows, Charlie could see a dilapidated auto salvage, ancient wrecks piled one on the other, cannibalized for parts, then left to rust.

"We're going to need a car," he said. "Better give me all your money."

Lisa reached into her pocket. "I brought everything I had on this trip," she said as she drew out the folded bills and handed them to Charlie

"I'll do my best," Charlie said.

The man at the salvage yard chomped a short cigar and scratched his chest as Charlie approached.

"I'm looking for a car," Charlie said.

The owner looked at Charlie as if he thought he should have come up with a better line. He nodded toward a battered Datsun. "It runs," he said. "But pretty much on a wing and a prayer."

They haggled briefly, then agreed on a price.

"I'll just do some paperwork and be right out," the man said, and walked into his office. "You can wait out here and enjoy the sights." The sights weren't much, just a desert town so small that the sudden appearance of a police car surprised him. It passed the auto salvage slowly, then made a turn and headed back toward it.

Charlie quickly ducked into a nearby coffee shop.

"Just coffee," he told the waitress, then spun around the stool and looked out the window. The police car had stopped at the auto salvage, and two cops now stood, talking to the owner.

A Durango pulled up outside, and the driver got out and made his way into the cafe. Charlie noticed that he'd left his keys in the ignition. There was only one way to get a car, he realized. Steal it.

He strolled outside and glanced back toward the restaurant. The man had disappeared into the bathroom at the rear of the building. He calculated the thin edge of time, the terrible risk, the desperate nature of the case, and decided that he had no choice.

Allie suddenly tensed, and a strange concentration swam into her eyes.

"What is it?" Lisa asked.

Allie's eyes roamed the interior of the gas station, moving from rusty tools to old tires, and finally to the small window that looked out into the night, where, in the distance, a light began to glow softly out of the surrounding woods.

"Allie?" Lisa asked.

Allie rose, walked to the window and gazed out at the steadily building light. Then she turned suddenly, and her eyes widened in disbelief.

"Hello, Allie," the man said.

He'd come from nowhere, simply materialized out of the light.

Lisa stepped forward. "Get away from my daughter," she warned.

"Don't be frightened, Lisa," the man said. "My name is John. I'm your grandfather."

Allie came out from behind her mother. "I know what you want," she said.

John smiled softly. "We have a lot to talk about, Allie."

"I don't want to talk to you," Allie said. "Go away."

John started to speak, but suddenly a flash of headlights appeared in the window as a truck ground to a halt outside the station, men piling out of it, the barrels of their rifles weaving in the air above their heads.

One of the men stepped forward. They had seen Charlie in town and recognized him from the news reports. "We know you've got the little girl," he yelled. "Come on out."

John looked at Allie and Lisa. "Sit here," he said to Allie. "Let me take care of this." He walked to the door, opened it, and stepped out into the night, his body bathed in the headlights from the truck. "There's no little girl here," he said.

"You're lying," the man said. "Her face is all over the television. Damn near the whole country's looking for her." He grinned. "Figured me and my buddies might get a little reward by bringing you in ourselves."

The other men laughed, but John paid no attention. "There's nothing here for you but trouble," he warned.

The man laughed. "This trouble's supposed to be coming from you?"

John remained silent.

He leveled his rifle, the barrel aimed at John's chest. "Who the hell are you?"

John's gaze bore into the man, and suddenly his eyes went black.

The man stepped back, the rifle falling from his hands. "Stop!" he screamed as he frantically backed away. "Stop! Make him stop!"

The other men stepped forward reflexively, then halted, frozen in terror.

"Shoot him!" the man cried. "Shoot him!"

They fired and John spun to the right as the bullets raked him, geysers of blood leaping like small red flames from his arms and chest as he tumbled to the ground.

The men ceased firing and stood, awestruck by their own violence.

"Go away."

The men looked toward the station, where Allie stood, facing them in the doorway, Lisa just behind her, desperately tugging her back into the safety of the station.

"Go away now!" Allie repeated. She pulled her arm free of Lisa's grasp. "Go away!"

The men didn't move.

Allie closed her eyes.

"Allie, what are you doing?" Lisa cried. She grabbed Allie's arm, but the child now seemed heavy as a planet, dense and immovable, her gaze focused on the truck, bearing down upon it as it began to shake with steadily increasing violence until it suddenly exploded in a huge ball of flame that seemed the form and substance of her ire.

The men dropped their rifles and stood, facing Allie, as if waiting for her command.

"Get out of here," she said very deliberately.

The men turned and headed off into the night, past the oncoming car that slid into the driveway of the station, Charlie behind the wheel.

"What happened?" he shouted as he leaped from the car. He followed the hurried flight of the men. "Who are those . . ."

"They came for Allie," Lisa told him. "But she chased them off."

Charlie looked at the crumpled body that lay face-down on the ground. "Who's that?"

"Allie's great-grandfather," Lisa said. "His name is John."

Charlie looked at her unbelievingly. "They shot him?"

Lisa nodded.

"Good," Charlie said sharply.

Lisa stared at him, astonished. "But he was trying to help."

"Help," Charlie said dismissively. "He's the one responsible for this whole thing." He glared at the fallen body as it turned and he saw John's face for the first time. "What the hell do you want?" he demanded.

"Charlie!" Lisa cried.

"Leave him," Charlie snapped. "Leave him and let's go."

Allie stood in place. "We can't leave him," she said.

"Sweetheart, he's not our friend," Charlie told her. "He's one of them!"

"That doesn't matter," Allie said adamantly. "We can't just leave him here. That's not the right thing to do."

Charlie saw that Allie would not leave without John. He drew in a deep breath. "All right," he said, giving in to her, "all right, we'll take him."

PART TEN

—————

Taken

—————

Chapter One

DOUGLAS, WYOMING

"Hi, thanks for having me on your show, Mr. Jeffreys."

The voice sounded familiar, and Charlie leaned forward and dialed up the volume on the Durango's radio, then glared at John, who sat silently on the passenger side. "What are you looking at?" he snapped.

John's eyes shot away from him and held to the road.

"My name is Dale, and I'm from Seattle, Washington," the caller said.

"Dale," Lisa said. She glanced at Charlie unbelievingly. "It's Dale. From Harriet's group."

Charlie nodded, then glanced into the backseat where Allie lay sleeping in Lisa's arms.

"I'm calling about this little girl," Dale said. "The one the Army is looking for in South Dakota. This little girl, she needs help. She and her parents are out there, all alone against the people that are trying to bring her in."

"Isn't this related to that toxic spill?" Jeffreys asked.

"There was no toxic spill," Dale answered sharply.

"They want to bring this little girl in because she's what these fifty years of all this, of people being taken, has been all about," Dale insisted. "They want to talk to her because she is part alien."

"I guess he thinks he's helping," Lisa said.

Allie moaned softly and Lisa looked at her worriedly.

"She'll be all right," John assured her. "She's just done too much."

"Can you help her?" Lisa asked him.

John said nothing.

"You want to help her, don't you?" Lisa asked. She glanced at Charlie, who seemed to be seething, enraged that he had one of "them" in the front seat of the car.

Dale continued, his voice nearly drowned out by a sudden flurry of static. "I'm not the only one who saw what she could do. There were nine of us. We all saw it. We all saw the things she did."

John continued to stare straight ahead.

Charlie glared at him angrily, whipped to a fury now by his silence. He felt a wave of rage wash over him, jerked the wheel to the right and brought the car to a skidding halt beside the deserted road. "Get out!" he snapped.

Allie suddenly awakened. "Charlie?" she asked softly.

"Get out!" Charlie shouted. He leaped from the car, walked to the passenger side and yanked open the door. "Get out," he repeated furiously.

John nodded, then stepped slowly from the car.

"You're going to talk," Charlie said. He grabbed John and slammed him against the car. "Now! Right now! You're going to tell me what the hell this is all about."

"Charlie," Allie pleaded. "Stop it."

Charlie continued to glare into John's face. "Why are

you here? Why have you been doing this? What the hell do you want?"

John peered at Charlie softly. "We're just trying to understand."

"Understand what?"

"Everything," John answered. He slumped down and collapsed at Charlie's feet. "Everything about you."

Allie rushed from the car and took John in her arms. "Stop hurting him," she cried. "Stop it, please!"

John's eyes drifted up toward Charlie. "We came here to learn about your world," he said. "We came here to learn."

Lisa came around the other side of the car, and knelt beside John, drawing Charlie down with her, so that they formed a half circle around him.

"We're not different from you," John went on. "But there are things in you that we no longer recognize in ourselves." He looked at Lisa and smiled softly. "Right from wrong. That was foreign to us. That what we were doing to you was . . . cruel." His eyes drifted over to Allie. "We lost . . . compassion," he said. "It is a dormant trait in you." He touched her face. "We wanted to awaken it . . . to feel it again . . . like you do. To combine our mind with your . . . heart." His gaze seemed to take all of them in suddenly, as if in a circle of light. "And so, our greatest experiment began." A single finger moved down Allie's face. "It was an unqualified success."

MITCHELL, NEBRASKA

General Beers drew Mary and Wakeman over to the side, away from the men he'd just finished interrogating. The abandoned gas station stood a few feet away, and for a moment they all watched it through the hazy smoke that still rose from the blasted truck.

"They were with somebody," the general said.

"'What do you mean, with somebody?'" Mary asked.

"Another man," the general said. "The other men, the ones who shot him. They say he was in his thirties . . . and that his eyes turned black."

Wakeman nodded. "They were waiting," he said thoughtfully. "They were waiting for her to demonstrate. They see she's got the power. BAM. They're here."

Beers glanced first toward Mary, then back to Wakeman. "You're saying this other guy is an . . . alien?" he asked.

Wakeman smiled. "You're paying attention."

The general stiffened. "You're both in this thing with me," he said hotly. "And right now, I have to go back to Washington and explain what happened out here." He glared at Mary and Wakeman in turn. "Find that girl!" he ordered. "Her and whoever she's with."

"And when we do?" Mary asked.

"Then you'll find me and I'll take it from there," Beers answered. He whirled around and strode away.

Mary walked to her car and got in behind the wheel, then waited until Wakeman joined her.

"Where to?" she asked.

"They're about ten hours ahead of us," he answered. He opened his laptop and Mary hit the ignition. "The big board has been shut down. I didn't want the general to find them. But all of that information is in here now."

"You know where she is?" Mary asked urgently.

Wakeman's eyes filled with a curious vulnerability. "Mary . . . you've been through a lot. First your father, then everything that Allie put you through. I just want you to know I'm here for you."

"I know that," Mary said. She smiled. "You said before that you thought they'd been waiting for her to demonstrate."

"Yeah."

"So what happens now that she has?"

"Pie," Wakeman said.

"What?"

"My rule on any car trip. Pie every day. Let's find a place to get some and I'll tell you my theory of everything."

They headed down the road and found a small coffee shop. Mary brought the car to a halt, and they went inside.

"Okay, tell me," Mary said impatiently.

"What do we know?" Wakeman asked. "They are this whole, this energy. I believe that this energy can manifest in different ways. As the beings we've seen. As their crafts . . . as our thoughts. There's no right or wrong about it."

"No right or wrong?" Mary asked thoughtfully.

"I think they had no concept of cruelty or kindness . . . no way of seeing beyond the oneness of all that energy. It's like the little animal brain we have in all of us. It can be awakened by some . . . experience."

"Experience?"

"Something could have touched one of them," Wakeman went on. "Something small and simple . . . and it awakened this sense of what was missing . . . something gone and half-remembered."

Wakeman looked at her for a moment, as if trying to find the right words. "I think they want something.

Maybe they had it and lost it. Or maybe they never had it, but think they can get it somehow . . . from us." He searched for some glimmer that she understood him. "And whatever it is they want, it's extremely important to them, something they can't do without, and so they're willing to risk everything in order to get it." He looked at her pointedly. "Think of us, Mary. Think of mankind. The species. Not what you want for yourself. But what you would want for the species."

She looked at him pointedly. "To take the next step."

Wakeman smiled. "I love you, Mary."

"I love you, too."

Wakeman's eyes glimmered softly. "We've taken it all the way together, haven't we?"

"I don't know what you mean."

"We're going to be there when it all comes together when it finally all comes together. And we'll know we did our part."

"Our part?"

Wakeman took her hand in his. "They're in the endgame," he said, his tone now filled with a strange finality. "They have to be. By going it on our own . . . by keeping this all from the general, we're helping to keep Allie safe until they can finish their work."

"You're fine with that, aren't you?" Mary asked. "Them 'finishing their work'?"

Wakeman nodded. "I can't wait."

Mary drew her hand from Wakeman's grasp. "So what do you want? Just a front-row seat at the show?"

"They're more highly evolved than we are, Mary," Wakeman said. "And Allie's more highly evolved than they are. It's the way of the Dao. Nature takes its course."

"What if it's our nature to fight back?" Mary asked sharply.

Wakeman looked at her as if she were a small child in need of elementary instruction. "Then we lose. Evolution one oh one."

From a short distance, Charlie and Lisa peered back at the Durango where John sat in the backseat, Allie beside him, nestled in his arm.

"He wants her to go with him," Lisa said. "He came to take her."

"We're not going to let that happen," Charlie said, his voice oddly broken for a moment, before he steeled himself again.

Lisa turned her gaze to Charlie. "There's something more," she said. "A feeling I'm getting." She seemed reluctant to tell him.

"What?" he asked.

"He cares about her, Charlie. He wants to help."

Charlie turned and headed for the Durango. "You ride up front with me," he told John sharply, then noted the odd look he exchanged with Allie, as if to assure her that it was all right.

John did as he was told, Lisa in the backseat with Allie, John on the passenger side up front.

Charlie hit the ignition, and the radio came on, the William Jeffreys show once again blaring out of the speakers.

"Larry King wants to know why our government would cut a deal with a bunch of aliens. Technology, Larry. We need their technology. More of the things they've already given us. Like Velcro."

Charlie's eyes shot over to John. "Is that true?" he asked. "What this guy's saying about Velcro?" His eyes narrowed. "Or were you too busy destroying lives to notice?"

Allie leaned forward. "Don't talk to him like that," she pleaded. "He's hurt. He can't stay human much longer."

"He's not human!" Charlie said desperately, his rage suddenly boiling over.

He pressed down on the accelerator and they drove on for a time in silence, Charlie staring up the deserted road while the William Jeffreys show droned on. Cynthia, another from Penzler's group, called, backing up what Dale had said, and Charlie knew that she was like so many others, another person who seemed to know—or at least sense—that the kooks and crazies, the people who heard voices, saw visions, moved through space and time—had in fact touched, or been touched by, a vague and impossible truth. He knew that some of them were insane, drowning in black pools of madness. But the ones who weren't, the ones who'd actually seen, he knew they had felt an anguish and loneliness that went down to the deep, deep bone. He could feel it in his own bones each time he glanced into the rearview mirror and saw the little girl he had come to love, human and not human at the same time, and yet, beyond all question, his living daughter, the one thing in life he would not let them take.

He looked at Lisa. "Your uncle should have seen the ad we put in the paper by now," he said. "He should call the William Jeffreys talk show tonight."

They drove on in silence for a time, all of them listening as Cynthia continued.

"I saw this same little girl heal a man who'd been shot," Cynthia said. "And Dale, his son was killed in the Gulf War, and Allie . . ."

"Sorry to interrupt," Jeffreys said. "But we've got Tom Clarke, the noted UFOlogist checking in."

Charlie and Lisa exchanged excited glances.

"What do you have to tell us, Tom?" Jeffreys asked.

"I'm afraid I've got nothing for you but a false alarm," Tom said. "I'm calling from the Grayback Dam in Idaho."

"Grayback Dam," Charlie repeated thoughtfully. He looked at Lisa. "I guess we're going to Idaho."

They reached Mount Grayback the next morning. Tom was waiting for them in the wide asphalt lot of the Grayback Dam, where they'd arranged to meet. Allie leaped out of the car almost before it halted and rushed into his arms.

He was in his sixties now, the long years of his struggle weighing down upon him.

"So this is Charlie," Tom said as he brought Allie back down to the ground.

"He's my dad," she said brightly.

Tom smiled. "I know, honey," he said quietly. He offered his hand. "Thanks for taking such good care of the family."

Suddenly John came up to them. "Tom," he said, "it's good to see you."

Tom's face tightened slightly, as if he were a little boy again, facing the stranger who would change his life forever. Then he turned back to Charlie. "We'll go into Mexico through Texas," he said. "A friend of mine from El Paso will meet us at our old place in Lubbock. He'll have all the documents you need to cross the border. Eventually, we'll go to South America. I know people in Buenos Aires who'll pick you up indefinitely." He looked at each of them in turn, but his eyes finally settled on Lisa, the odd look he saw in her face. "What is it?" he asked.

"I don't know exactly," Lisa answered. "It's just a feeling that all of this is going somewhere." She shrugged. "So it's okay, Mexico. It's fine, Uncle Tom."

"All right then, it's settled," Tom said. "Let's go."

Within seconds, they were on the road again, Tom at the wheel at first, then Charlie, then giving it over to Lisa as night fell, John in the passenger seat, Allie beside him, munching a granola bar while Tom and Charlie slept peacefully in the backseat.

Allie offered John a bite from the granola bar. "You eat, don't you?" she asked.

"We eat," John answered.

"So try it," Allie said.

John took a bite of the bar. "It's good," he said with a quick smile.

Allie's eyes were still, green pools. "I don't want to do this," she said.

Lisa felt her fingers tighten around the wheel. Allie was talking to John with a strange sense of equality, one alien to another, each with vast inhuman powers.

"I know," John told her.

"At the gas station, I was going to make those men hurt each other," Allie added. "I could have done that, too."

"But you didn't."

"I almost did."

"Yes."

"But I don't want to hurt people," Allie went on. "So, how can I make this stop? I mean, if I couldn't do any of these things—if I didn't have these powers—then people would leave me alone, wouldn't they?"

"I don't know, Allie," John confessed. "I don't know much about people."

"Is there anything I can do?"

"No, nothing."

"Will the others come for you?"

"It's not important," John said. He looked at her gravely. "Allie, things are going to get hard for you for a while. You'll be afraid, and you'll be alone. You're becoming even more than you already are."

"I'm not coming with you," Allie said determinedly. "I belong here, with my family."

John reached into his pocket. "I brought this for you," he said, opening his hand. The star earring glowed silently in John's palm. "It was your great-grandmother's. She gave it to me when I left. I can't . . . do this much longer."

Allie took the earring from his hand. "I know," she said.

Lisa searched the road ahead, her eyes now focused on the small, roadside gas station that shone out of the night. She pulled into the station, reached for Allie's hand and led her to the bathroom as a second car came to a halt in the gravelly drive.

Inside the bathroom Lisa said, "Give me the earring."

Allie stretched out her hand. The earring rested on her open palm.

Lisa plucked it from Allie's hand. "I'll never let you go, honey," she said. She knelt down, her face very close to Allie's. "Listen," she said, "my dad used to tell me that kids shouldn't ever have to think about anything more complicated than baseball." She smiled softly at her daughter, and ran her fingers through her long hair. "You'll be a little girl again, I promise." She placed the earring John had given her on her necklace, the two now hanging side by side. "There. Together again."

Allie smiled.

"I'll never let you go, honey," Lisa said with a sudden, furious determination, feeling more strongly than she ever had, the deepest of all human bonds. "Never."

The door of the bathroom shot open and Lisa turned to see Mary Crawford facing her, gun in hand.

"That looks lovely," Mary said sarcastically. She stepped forward and pressed the pistol into the small of Lisa's back. "I'm holding a gun on your mother," she said to Allie. "I'm betting that, even if you wanted to do something, I could get a shot into her before you turned the gas station into a flying saucer, or a House of Pies or something."

Lisa looked at Allie. "Don't try to do anything, you understand," she said desperately.

Mary smiled. "Be a good girl," she said to Allie. "Be a good girl and listen to your mom."

Allie looked at Mary angrily.

"Allie, when you were in that farmhouse, you saw something that scared you," Mary said. "I think you know what they want you to do and I don't think you want to do it."

Allie glanced at Lisa, then back at Mary.

"I don't want to hurt anybody." Mary said. "I really don't." Her voice softened into a plea. "You're out of options. You must have figured that out for yourself by now. I have the resources and the technology to help you. You really don't have any other choice. It's them or me. Don't you see, I just want to help you."

"You're lying," Lisa said icily. "You can't help anyone."

Mary looked as if Lisa had spit in her face. The pistol barrel jerked toward the door. "Let's go."

Tom was at the gas pump, removing the nozzle from the tank when they came out of the bathroom, Lisa in front, Mary behind, pressing the pistol at Lisa's back.

Charlie watched them from the kiosk, then turned toward the car that had pulled into the station driveway minutes before. A single man sat behind the wheel, his head turned slightly, watching Lisa and Mary and Allie as they continued forward.

Wakeman! Charlie thought, then stepped out from behind the kiosk. He saw that Wakeman had suddenly noticed him, and that he was now moving frantically behind the wheel.

Instantly, the car's engine fired, and the car lurched forward, throwing arcs of gravel behind the spinning wheels as it made a screeching turn and hurtled toward Mary and the others.

Mary yanked open the car's back door, pushed Lisa and Allie into the backseat, then leaped in behind them.

Lisa glanced out the back window of the car as it spun away. Charlie was still running after them desperately as Tom raced to his car and leaped in behind the wheel. She turned back, and saw it, the terrible change in Allie's face. "No," she whispered, "no, Allie."

But it was too late.

The explosions came one after the other, four of them as each of the tires on Wakeman's car blasted away, so that the car ground to a halt.

Charlie was there in an instant. He jerked open the

door and pulled Mary out onto the road, the pistol falling from her hand and clattering across the roadway.

"Allie, don't do anything else," Lisa cried as Tom pulled up.

"I didn't," Allie said urgently. "I didn't do anything."

Lisa's eyes swept from her daughter to the backseat of Tom's car, where John sat motionlessly, pale and ghostly, as if the last of his human reserves had now been spent.

"That was a little too close," Tom said as Charlie, Lisa, and Allie all rushed into the car.

He stomped the accelerator and the car sped away. "How did they find us?" he asked after a moment.

Charlie looked at Allie in the rearview mirror. "Honey, I want to ask you something."

"Sure," Allie said.

"Those people from the government, when you went with them from Dr. Penzler's, they put something over your head."

"Right," Allie said. "I heard them say it was to block a signal I have in my head."

Charlie looked at Tom. "Lisa would have it too," he said.

Tom nodded.

"If the people who took Allie know enough to block that signal, then they know how to read it. To track it."

"That's how they found us," Lisa said.

Charlie shook his head. "Not much point in getting fake papers and going to Buenos Aires, is there? No matter where we go, they'd find us." He faced John squarely. "You can turn her off, can't you?" he asked.

John said nothing.

"You can do something so they won't be able to read

her signal . . . or mine . . ." Lisa said. "If you can do it,
then do it. You owe us that much."

John shook his head. "No, I'm too weak. But Allie
can."

He looked at Allie. "Find it inside you," he said.

Allie closed her eyes.

"Do you feel it?" John asked.

Allie's eyes remained closed for a moment, then they
opened suddenly.

John peered into them. "She won't register now," he
said. He touched her face softly. "You're on your own,
Allie."

She nodded, and stretched her hand to his, but by the
time she touched it, the hand had faded, simply guttered
out like a candle, five fingers now only four, each with a
double joint. She drew her gaze up his body, human skin
now vanished, all human features resolved into a
smooth, metallic gray.

Chapter Two

The interior of the motel was dingy, but Mary gave no notice of it. She was busy at her laptop. "They're not registering, Chet," she said.

Wakeman lay on the bed, his hand behind his head, feet stretched out before him. "I know," he said.

Mary looked at him, astonished. "You know?"

"Shut off. No signal."

"And you didn't bother to tell me?"

"I was getting there."

"How about their friend in the backseat?" Mary asked.

"Probably shut off too." Wakeman pulled himself up and opened his own laptop. "Look at this," he said, motioning Mary to his side. "The sightings are starting again. Lights in the sky. Centered over Idaho and Nebraska."

Mary stared at the screen. "Then we'd better get ready."

Wakeman shook his head. "You can't do anything, Mary." He seemed to recall the way she'd looked at the gas station, the pistol she'd leveled so firmly at Allie's head. "You would have shot Allie, wouldn't you?"

"I would have stopped her anyway I could," Mary admitted.

"You're not going to let it go, are you?"

"I can't."

He gazed at her sadly, as if she were already lost to him. "Do you know the story of Medusa?"

"If you look at her, you turn to stone," Mary said.

"Unless you know the secret, in which case, you can kill her," Wakeman said.

"Is this going somewhere, Chet?" Mary asked impatiently.

"I used to think we could do something together. New science, maybe, or just get the better of them somehow. But, Mary, we're not ready to be anything but spectators in this. If we try for more, we'll—well—we'll turn to stone."

Mary shook her head firmly. "I'm not giving up, Chet. I'm going to find that little girl, and I'm going to be more than a witness to this."

"But, Mary . . ."

She turned away and watched the screen of her laptop, where scores of new reports were coming in, strange lights appearing everywhere. "Maybe they don't know where she is either," she said.

"That's a thought, isn't it," Wakeman said.

She looked at him. "Will you help me or not?"

Wakeman nodded. "All right, let's think about it then. Suppose they don't know where she is because her signal is turned off."

"But how would they have lost her? She's with one of them."

"That's a very good question," Wakeman admitted. "What are you thinking?"

Mary considered this a moment, then said, "The man who was driving the car back at the station. That was Tom Clarke. Lisa's uncle."

"I thought I recognized him. He's getting a little long in the tooth."

"I had the office upload all my grandfather's files, everything we had on Tom Clarke. You know my grandfather went to Texas once."

"And got the bejesus scared out of him by Jacob Clarke."

"Tom Clarke still owns his mother's farmhouse. The place where my grandfather went to get Jacob."

"You think that's where they've gone?"

"I'm all for taking a look."

"What if they're there?" Wakeman asked. "Then what?"

The look in Mary's eyes gave him the only answer he needed.

When Mary entered the shower, Wakeman picked up the receiver and dialed information. "For Austin, Texas. Tom Clarke." He dialed Tom's number, but got only the answering machine.

By the time he began to leave his message, the bullet had struck, and the phone was dropping from his hand.

Mary stood above his fallen body, her eyes glistening. She knew that no one would ever love her as he had loved her, and the fact that she could put such love aside had now sealed her fate.

She placed the gun on the small table beside the bed, picked the phone off the floor and dialed the number.

"General Beers' office."

"I'd like to speak to General Beers," Mary said. "Tell him Mary Crawford is calling."

Moments later, the general arrived. He glanced at Wakeman's body, then at Mary.

There was no need to conceal anything, and so she told it all in a wild rush, everything that had happened to her, to Wakeman, everything they'd learned and everything they had surmised, down to Wakeman himself, how he'd changed, gone over to the "visitors," so that she'd had no choice but . . .

"Dear God," Beers breathed. "You are one cold and nasty bitch, Mary."

"Will you help me?"

The general peered at her darkly. "When we're through with all this, I'm going to see that you're held accountable for what you've done," he said.

Mary made no protest, and because of that, understood that she was ready to make the ultimate sacrifice. "Do you want to know how we can find Allie?" she asked matter-of-factly.

"Yes," Beers said sharply. "Tell me."

"You've been monitoring the reports from the northwest?" Mary asked. "The lights?"

"So far that's all they've been."

"Dr. Wakeman believed that this is it. They're coming for Allie."

"Why don't they just take her then?"

"Because right at this moment, they don't know where she is."

"But she's with one of them, the one from the gas station."

"Maybe he's the one who shut her off. Maybe he's the one who's protecting her."

"Why would he be doing that?"

"Remorse?" Mary asked.

The general considered this silently for a moment, then said, "Go on."

"I came after Allie in a parking lot," Mary said. "She got away from me in a car with the help of that alien. She's spent, General. And she's also alone. At least until . . . they find her."

"You want to get her before they do," the general said.

"I want to finish what we started," Mary said grimly. "Right now you need someone who understands what you might be dealing with. Right now, you need me with you."

General Beers studied her a moment. "I want you to know that it disgusts me that I have to work with you," he said finally.

Mary smiled thinly. "I can understand that," she said.

LUBBOCK, TEXAS

Tom and Charlie stood outside the farmhouse, staring silently into the surrounding fields. After a time, Lisa came out to join them.

"How's Allie?" Tom asked.

"The same," Lisa answered. "You think they're coming? Mary and the . . ."

Charlie nodded. "It's just a matter of time."

"There's no point in running unless you've got some place to run," Tom added.

Charlie considered this a moment, then said, "Something like this . . . the government can only do what they do because nobody's watching." He smiled. "I have an idea." He looked at Tom. "How far do you have to go to make a phone call?"

Allie lay sleeping in her bed, breathing softly, John watching her silently, his form human again, complete with downy hair on the arms, five fingers on each hand. He touched her softly, and her eyes opened.

"I thought if I looked human again, it might be easier to say good-bye," John told her. His smile was sad and gentle. "I can't stay with you anymore, Allie. If I do, sooner or later, you'll be found."

"How?" Allie asked.

"Because the thing in your head, when it went off, it wasn't just people who lost track of you. But once I'm gone, *no one* will know where you are, and so you'll have a chance to be a little girl again." He touched her hair. "If things get too hard, if you feel that you can't stay here, you can find us again. You can find the part of you that is us. We'll know where you are . . . and we'll come for you. But that will be your choice, Allie. It won't be because we've . . . taken you."

He rose and walked out of the room, and for a time, Allie waited in her bed. Then the urge overtook her, a need, strange but vibrant, to see John again. She leaped from her bed and ran out of the house and along a deserted road until she saw him up ahead, his human form now shed, so that he stood, smooth and gleaming, in the dark night air.

"Can I walk with you a minute?" she asked.

"Just to the edge of the woods."

They walked down the road together, and at last came

to the woods. "This is as far as you can go," John told her.

She saw that his wide, almond-shaped eyes were filled with something new and wondrous . . . emotion.

Then he turned and headed off into the trees, leaving Allie more alone than she had ever been.

They found a diner just inside the town. Tom got out of the car, walked to a nearby phone and dialed the number. "It's about that little girl, Bill," he said when William Jeffreys answered.

"Is this the caller I think it is?" Jeffreys asked. "Tom Clarke from Texas, it says on my screen. Talk to me."

"It's about that little girl," Tom repeated. "The one the Army is looking for. Your listeners have been calling about her."

"We've been getting a lot of calls, yes," Jeffreys said.

"The people who have been calling you are telling the truth," Tom said. "I know this little girl, and I'm hoping your listeners will be able to help me."

A few hours later, after they'd returned to the farm-house, they began to see dust clouds rising from the road, then William Jeffreys' battered old Winnebago as it lumbered forward, others behind him, car after car, the lonely army of the taken rallying in such numbers that the dust cloud of their long journey rose high enough to touch—or so it seemed—the vast, unknowable sky.

Chapter Three

From the doorway of the farmhouse, Charlie and Lisa surveyed the chaotic scene before them. The grounds of Sally Clarke's old home place were now filled with people. In the distance, the military had established a perimeter around the grounds, soldiers everywhere, armed to the teeth, waiting for orders to march in, drive Jeffreys and the people he'd brought with him away, seize Allie and take her with them like a spoil of war.

Tom joined Charlie and Lisa on the porch. "I've got all the papers you need. Passports. Visas. Everything. There's a back road that leads to Highway one seventy-seven. We ran it this morning, and came out on the other side of the perimeter." He nodded toward the crowd. "Our people are armed, too," he said darkly. "If the Army moves in . . ."

"I don't want you to do that."

Charlie glanced down and saw Allie standing just behind him, her eyes concentrated on the milling crowd that covered the grounds of the old farmhouse.

"I want to talk to them," she said.

Lisa swept up behind Allie. "Are you all right?" she asked.

"Everything's ready," Charlie said. "We have to go."

Allie shook her head. "No. Not now. They're scared. They need something." She walked out onto the porch, Charlie, Lisa, and Tom following behind her.

"Hi," she said.

The people turned to face her, their eyes on her expectantly.

"I know you're all scared and you don't have to be scared anymore," Allie told them.

Lisa stepped up and knelt beside her daughter. "Honey, you don't have to do this. You don't have to do anything."

Allie continued to face the crowd. "You have something in your heads," she said. "It lets them know where you are. I can shut them off. When they shut off, they'll fall out. Don't be scared."

The crowd began to inch forward, a thousand eyes locked on Allie.

"They won't come for you anymore," Allie assured them. "They won't be able to find you. No one's going to take you ever again." Her eyes drifted left to right, and with each movement her gaze seemed to reach out to a single, upturned face. "I know it doesn't seem right that they did this to you. But if you saw it from someplace else, you would understand that it was just time for this to happen."

Allie closed her eyes, and the crowd halted its forward motion, as if at her command. Her eyes were very still beneath the closed lids, but a strange energy seemed to come from them, a thousand invisible beams, each directed at a single searching face, probing beneath the lay-ered human skin, past the bone and gristle, to where the alien device was buried, drawing it out once it was found, severing the tiny web of veins that held it, and thus letting it flow out on a warm stream of blood.

The crowd gave a low moan as the first of the devices slipped from a bloody nose and dropped soundlessly to the ground. Then a kind of shuddering release swept over them, as if a heavy chain had been broken, relieving them of their long bondage.

Some cried.

Some laughed.

But in every face was freedom.

The crowd began to move toward the house again, and beyond them, Charlie saw that the Army was moving too. He stepped forward and knelt beside Allie.

Allie remained in place. She looked first at Charlie, then at Lisa, and each saw the end in her eyes.

"You will always be my little girl," Lisa said as much to herself as to Allie.

Charlie bolted forward and cried out to the crowd, "Listen to me. All of you. They're not going to do anything to us here. There are too many of us. Do you want to help?"

The crowd roared back fiercely.

"All of you," Charlie yelled. "Stay in front of the porch. Stay right here in front of Allie. If they want to take her, they'll have to come through us."

The crowd instantly obeyed, forming a semicircle around the porch, then turning away from Allie to face the approaching soldiers.

A loud voice swept over them: "THIS AREA IS UN-DER FEDERAL CONTROL. PLEASE MAKE YOUR-SELVES AVAILABLE FOR IMMEDIATE RELOCATION."

The crowd remained in place, facing the soldiers as they closed in.

The loudspeaker boomed again: "YOUR VEHICLES AND PERSONAL BELONGINGS CAN BE CLAIMED AFTER DEBRIEFING."

The crowd remained resolutely in place.

Lisa turned Allie to her. "Are they going to come for you now?" she asked,

"John left that up to me," Allie answered. She looked lovingly at her mother. "Do you think if we'd just been regular people, Charlie would have come and lived with us and we could have been a family?"

Lisa smiled at Allie gently. "I know that would have happened."

"I don't want to go," Allie said. "I want to stay with you."

"Then stay," Lisa said. "We've got a plan. We can get out of here, right now." She saw that this was not possible, that even as Allie had voiced her hope, she had renounced it.

"It'll be okay," Lisa assured her.

Allie suddenly turned from her, quickly and abruptly, her eyes fixed on the crowd, the military force beyond them. A wave of stones arced out of the crowd and fell upon the soldiers and their vehicles. From beyond the crowd, small explosions sent tear gas canisters hurtling into the night air.

Lisa drew Allie into her arms. "We better get back inside," she said.

Allie stepped out of her embrace. "No," she said.

Suddenly a streak of light shot through the darkness, bold and radiant, as if carried on a comet, and in whose blinding wake the texture of the sky began to change.

The crowd stared upward in silent wonder at the celestial spectacle that raged above them, light flying into light, a play of unearthly radiance against the black field of the night.

Allie's gaze was infinitely still as she turned toward the sea of faces—the stunned and silent soldiers, Mary and General Beers, hushed and awestruck as the light intensified all around them, growing brighter and brighter, as fierce and unknowable as the dawning of a brand-new world.

About the Author

THOMAS H. COOK is the author of fifteen novels, including *The Chatham School Affair*, winner of the Edgar Award for Best Novel; *Instruments of Night*; *Breakheart Hill*; *Mortal Memory*; *Sacrificial Ground* and *Blood Innocents*, both Edgar Award nominees; and two early works about true crimes, *Early Graves* and *Blood Echoes*, which was also nominated for an Edgar Award. He lives in New York City and Cape Cod, where he is at work on his next novel, *Peril*.